THE FAKE DATE

JESS MASTORAKOS

Copyright © 2022 by Jess Mastorakos

All rights reserved.

No part of this book may be reproduced in any form or by any electronic or mechanical means, including information storage and retrieval systems, without written permission from the author, except for the use of brief quotations in a book review.

Cover Models: Real Marine Corps couple, Ryan & Macie

Cover Photography By: Hinesight Imagery

Cover Design By: Amanda Walker

Edited By: Krista Dapkey, KD Publishing

Publisher's note: This is a work of fiction. Names, characters, places, and situations are a product of the author's imagination. Any similarities to real people, places, or things is purely coincidental.

To get a free copy of the novella, Forever with You, visit: http://jessmastorakos.com/forever-with-you

SIGN UP FOR JESS'S SWEET ROMANCE SQUAD

Jess MASTORAKOS
sweet & swoony military romance

Sign up for my newsletter at http://jessmastorakos.com/forever-with-you to get the free ebook version of Forever with You: A San Diego Marines Novella. You'll also get bonus content, sweet romance book recommendations, and never miss a new release!

- instagram.com/author_jessmastorakos
- bookbub.com/authors/jess-mastorakos
- goodreads.com/author_jessmastorakos

1

LYNDI

Adjusting my camera bag over my shoulder, I approached Starlight Manor, ready to capture the big day for a happy couple. Or *two*, actually. The first wedding was a brunch affair—which I didn't even know was a thing—and the second would be a traditional evening event under the stars near the venue's gorgeous private pond.

Starlight Manor was the kind of place that enveloped a wedding in magic, making what was otherwise a lovely event feel like it had been pulled off the pages of a timeless classic.

And it was more than just the setting. It was the talented wedding planner who put it all together. My friend Aria was a magician in Manolos. Taste and class and elegance were so ingrained in her that she couldn't help but layer them over every wedding, right on top of a foundation of small-town charm.

In short, weddings at Starlight were a photographer's dream. My fingers tingled with the urge to take out my camera and zero in on little details in the floral arrangements on the meticulously decorated tables. Or the laugh lines on the faces of the bride's parents as they gazed lovingly at their little girl with the shimmering pond in the background. Maybe even the unshed tears of a lonely guest sitting under the wide oak tree, wondering if she'd ever find a man who would promise to spend forever with her.

I wouldn't include the photos from the last example in the bride's wedding gallery, of course. But moments like that were hard to miss in my line of work, and there was something about the raw emotions sparked by weddings that begged to be photographed. They tugged at me, kneading my own lonely heart to a pulp with their intensity.

As a general rule, deep emotions were confusing for me. On the outside, I liked to keep things light and cheery. I was the one who wore my heart on my sleeve and was always down for a hug. In a way, it was almost like a cover for how I felt on the inside. I always seemed to feel my deeper feelings a little too hard. In a suffocating way, making me want to wrangle them or tuck them away.

So, while I appeared sunny and warm on the outside, internally, things were a lot more tumultuous up in here. It was hard to constantly feel like I was at war with myself when it came to things my older sister seemed to do so easily, like getting along with others or feeling at home in a crowd.

But behind the camera? It was almost freeing the way I could capture emotion with the click of my shutter and then feel at peace knowing someone had acknowledged how simple and pure it was. It brought me comfort in a world where I felt like an outsider. Photography gave me a reason to *be* an outsider that would make sense to everyone else.

As I approached the main house, I grinned at Aria where she stood near the front steps with our town's most-beloved, meddling, busybody of a florist. Ms. Hattie put a hand on Aria's baby bump, bending slightly to talk to him or her.

Aria was due in about five weeks, and even though the baby obviously belonged to her and her husband, Ms. Hattie loved to refer to their child as "our baby." As in, *the whole dang town's* baby. Because in Ms. Hattie's head, we were all one big family, and we all belonged to her.

"Morning ladies," I said in a singsong voice as I approached, giving Aria a one-armed hug against her side.

Ms. Hattie straightened and beamed at me, looking lit up from the inside in her pink Bluffton Blooms polo. "Lyndi, how are you, dear?"

"Great, thanks." I patted my camera bag. "Ready for an awesome weekend."

"Yes, it'll be a busy one," Ms. Hattie agreed. "We haven't had three weddings in one weekend in forever. Not counting Fridays, of course."

Aria put her hands on the top of her bump and sighed heavily. "I know, but we also haven't had a wedding *brunch* before, and I didn't have this little one on the way when they all booked their dates, so I had no reason not to take advantage of a triple-wedding weekend. It sounded so exciting at the time."

I took in her creased brow and the way she worried her lip between her teeth. Aria Paxton was the epitome of a workaholic. She lived in a cottage on the grounds of this very estate, and when she wasn't in her office on the main floor planning events for the B&B her parents owned, she was bustling around the grounds overseeing one.

I didn't know this for sure, but I had a sneaking suspicion Aria even worked while she slept. If anyone could manage that, she could. But now, she was a little over a month away from being a first-time mother, and while I had no idea what that was truly like since I wasn't one, I felt the urge to help ease the transition.

Maybe it would help if she slowed down now. Like doing less over the next five weeks might help make it not so jarring when she had the baby and it had to be a full stop for a while.

Reaching out and taking the tops of her arms in my hands, I turned her to face me. "Hey, there's no shame in a little delegation, remember? We all know you're the world's best wedding planner. You don't need to bust your butt all the way up to your due date, do you?"

Aria chuckled. "I don't know how to relax, Lyn. You know me. If I weren't here working, I'd be crawling up the walls."

"Ha, not in your condition, you wouldn't," Ms. Hattie teased with a wink. "Lyndi's right. Maybe you should pass some things off to the staff and rest during the brunch wedding, then come back later for the evening one."

Ms. Hattie clearly approached the subject from a health standpoint, which hadn't occurred to me. I only knew my friend's drive and wanted her to take her foot off the gas a little in preparation for traffic. But I supposed keeping her from overdoing it so she didn't work herself into an early labor was important too.

Shaking her head, Aria reached up and removed my hands from her arms, giving them a squeeze before dropping them. "You guys, I'm fine. Besides, it's too late to get anyone up to speed on this weekend's events, but if it'll make you feel better, I'll get some help for the rest of them."

Ms. Hattie and I shared a look. Aria's tired eyes said a whole lot more than her words did, but I sighed, relenting. "Fine. Just please let me know if I can help with anything. If I'm not actively taking photos, I'll do whatever I can to lighten your load."

It was the least I could do. When Aria had taken over event coordinating at Starlight, she'd hired me immediately to be their main photographer. My hobby of taking photos of people having fun instead of actually joining them quickly morphed into a lucrative career thanks to the success of her endeavor, and I couldn't be more grateful.

"Thank you," she said, her eyes telling me she meant it. "But listen, I have to get back to it. The wedding party will be here soon, and I need to make sure everything is in order."

This morning's wedding was nontraditional in a few ways. The bride and groom were renewing their vows, so they planned to show up together, already ready for their quick ceremony and the lavish brunch that followed. Which meant I hadn't needed to be here hours early so I could take candid photos in the bridal suite.

And thank goodness for that, considering the doozy of a wedding that would follow this one. There were twelve bridesmaids. *Twelve.* I couldn't imagine having that many women in my life who were so important I'd want them next to me on my wedding day. I liked to keep my circle small, and thankfully, my sister Layla and our two best friends loved me, quirks and all.

"I'll see you later for the next one, Ms. Hattie?" Aria asked her as she turned to head inside.

The older woman nodded. "See you then, mama."

Aria's eyes went wistful as she smiled and turned away.

When she was gone, Ms. Hattie shot me a grimace. "That girl is going to overdo it this weekend. I can feel it."

The corners of my mouth twitched downward. "She'll be okay. I've got her."

"I know you do, sweetheart." Then her eyes searched my face, and a distinctly mischievous glint entered their depths. "I ran into your grandmother at the market yesterday."

"Oh?" I felt my stomach twist and knot, a familiar sense of dread wafting over me.

"Yes. I mentioned my son is coming to town."

Inwardly, I groaned, suspicions confirmed. My grandmother had a knack for making me feel like I was doomed to walk the earth alone for the rest of eternity. As if that same fear didn't already follow me wherever I went.

I knew I was bad at love. I knew my most successful relationships were the ones I had with the men in my romance novels who didn't even exist in real life.

But all of that didn't mean I wanted her to stick her nose into my love life and try to be my fairy *grandmother*. If I never found love, I'd never get my heart broken. And since I already lived my life feeling like my own emotions were harder to wrangle than seemed fair, that was the ideal scenario.

"Great," I said to Ms. Hattie, keeping my voice even and matching her benign expression. "Thanks for that."

Her face softened. "Oh, Lyndi. She just wants to see you happy."

"No, she just wants to see me *married*. There's a huge difference."

Ms. Hattie put her hands on her plump hips and cocked her head. "Well, speaking as a very *happily married* woman, I beg to differ." When I stuck my tongue out at her to take this conversation from pathetic to playful, she dropped her hands with a chuckle. "Brett's coming with me to your sister's wedding."

"You're taking your son and not your husband? Don't happily married women like to attend weddings with their husbands?"

"Well, of course. But then your sister decided to get married three weeks before your cousin plans to. Since I'm invited to both weddings, and Brett will be in town for one of them, my husband decided to sit one out. Let's be honest, there's been quite an uptick in weddings lately."

"Uh-huh," I deadpanned.

If I feared my grandma's matchmaking, Ms. Hattie was about a gazillion times worse. Her meddling was probably the cause of most of the weddings she'd attended recently, including my sister's.

And *wow*, she looked mighty proud of it.

"Anyway," she said with a wave of her hand, "Brett's excited for a night with his mama, and Thatcher can only handle so much socializing."

I knew the feeling. Give me my core circle of friends, my family, and the people in this town like Ms. Hattie who felt like family even though there was no relation, and I was a happy girl. But if I had to be a guest at all the weddings I photographed? I'd lose my mind. In fact, I preferred the company of a good book to almost everyone on the aforementioned list.

Not that I'd ever tell them that. Though, something told me they already knew.

"Well, I guess I'll look forward to Grandma's meddling at Layla's wedding, then. Or shoot, even before. Let me guess, she asked you to ask me if I'd be his date."

"Are you bringing a date?" she asked with a too-innocent expression.

"No, I'm not. But I'm not going to steal *yours*, because then your husband would have to go, and I feel for the guy."

She smirked. "Well played, dear. Save Brett a dance, will you? That'll make your grandmother happy, and I wouldn't hate to see him let loose and have a little fun. He's so serious all the time."

"You got it," I promised half-heartedly.

Ms. Hattie's son Brett was a stud, no doubt about it. But he lived at a Marine base in Okinawa, so obviously there was no chance I'd take a second look at him. I loved my life in Bluffton, South Carolina, and there was no way I'd fall for a Marine stationed overseas and let him whisk me away to join him.

Besides, if *any* Marine could tempt me into leaving

my beloved hometown—and let's be honest, it wouldn't work anyway—it was *Beau Devereux*.

The man with a name that fully embodied his entire appeal. Smooth. Suave. And as swoon worthy as any man I'd ever read about in the pages of my books.

But it didn't matter because Beau didn't look at me like that. I was sure of it. He'd had plenty of opportunities in the year I'd known him to make a move if he did.

Ms. Hattie looked up at the massive white mansion and sighed. "All right, my work here is done, and it's almost go-time. I'm gonna head back to the shop to get things ready for tonight's event. See you in a few hours for round two."

I gave her a wave and started to reply, but then my eyes landed on a familiar cherry-red coupe as it pulled onto the circular drive and my heartbeat stuttered painfully in my chest.

Ms. Hattie slid her gaze over to me conspiratorially. "Oh, look, it's the real reason you won't do more than save a dance for my son."

Without even giving me a chance to deny it, she made a little noise to suggest she was pleased with herself and went on her way.

Frozen in place, I watched as Beau gracefully exited the car and rounded the hood, looking like a full-on snack in a white button-down shirt and crisp khaki slacks. His chocolate belt matched his shoes—as it always did, no matter the color. The man practically *oozed* style.

When he looked up and his hazel eyes met mine, a lump formed in my throat. Oh, how this guy could knot me up from the inside with only a look. He offered me a tentative smile before moving quickly to the passenger door of his car, then he opened it to reveal a beautiful older woman wearing a peach dress with a matching shawl. She slipped her hand in his and allowed him to help her out of the car, then held up a finger to him as she dug her ringing phone out of her purse.

I watched as the woman stepped away to answer it, then my gaze flicked back to Beau. He handed the valet his keys with a nod of thanks, then tucked one hand in a pocket as he loped up the stairs.

Right toward me.

Shaking my head, I managed a smile only half a second later than I probably should have. "Hey, Beau."

"Hey, Lyndi. How are you?"

"Well, thanks." I glanced at the woman still talking on the phone, her shoulders bunched up in a defensive posture as she gestured with her hand while she spoke. "Is that your wedding date for the brunch?"

Not only was Beau an active-duty Marine stationed at nearby Parris Island Recruit Depot, but he also had a side-gig where he traveled up the Eastern Seaboard on weekends to attend weddings as a plus-one-for-hire. He called the business Mr. Fake Date and even had an app developed for women to book his services.

One corner of his glorious mouth lifted. "She's my *client*, yes."

The strong emphasis he'd used on the word *client* caused my brow to quirk involuntarily. "Isn't that what I said?"

"No," he replied with a chuckle. "They hire me as their wedding date, but to me, they're clients. Not dates."

I narrowed my eyes at him. "Seems a little like splitting hairs to me, but you do you, boo."

He laughed breezily, the light sound causing my heart to stutter a little. "Anyway, yes, she's my client. Mother of the bride."

"Interesting."

The woman looked to be in her sixties, and even though I'd been shocked the first time I'd seen Beau at a wedding with a woman of her age, I was used to it now. Beau's clients came in all ages, shapes, sizes, and whatever other classification you could think of.

It seemed like no one—no matter how attractive or delightful or effervescent—was beyond hiring this man to pretend to be her date if there was a good enough reason for it. And standing off on the sidelines while

Beau accompanied these women had shown me they *always* had a good reason.

I wanted more information, my curiosity feeling like fingers scratching inside my brain. But I didn't bother asking. Beau had a rule about maintaining his clients' secrets. He valued privacy and was a master at keeping up the charade in front of the other wedding guests.

I found it to be almost honorable—the way he never outed his dates to other women who daringly flirted with him even though they knew he was there with someone else. *Almost* honorable because his entire purpose for being there was a lie.

But it didn't matter. He didn't need to betray his clients' confidence. I had a thing for puzzles and figuring out the behind-the-scenes drama that caused someone to hire Beau was kind of fun for me.

As a photographer, I was insanely good at reading people. I observed from afar, camera in hand, able to find patterns and stories even without being explicitly told anything.

It was in the way people looked at each other when they thought no one was watching. It was in their body language or the subtext behind their words. I loved capturing moments shared between people that would have otherwise faded into oblivion.

And yes, I knew how stalkerish that sounded, but

hey—at least turning it into a career made it a little less creepy. Right?

"Today should be fun," he said, watching his client over my shoulder. "Are you working both weddings?"

"Are *you*?" I asked, my head pulling back like someone had tied a string to the back of it and tugged.

"Yeah, I like having two appointments in one day. Means I can take a day off tomorrow and actually have some free time for once."

I almost snorted at the way he'd said *appointments*. He took his job very seriously. Well, both jobs. I'd only seen him in action as Mr. Fake Date, not as *Sergeant* Devereux, but I'd overheard him and Zac talking about work and what he did in the Marine Corps.

Judging by the way he talked about it, I could tell it was something that meant a lot to him. The actual job itself—teaching Marine recruits how to use their firearms during boot camp—and also the pride of belonging to the world's sexiest military branch. In my humble, *totally* unbiased opinion, of course.

"Right, well, yes," I said, fiddling with the zipper of my camera bag, "I am working both weddings."

He opened his mouth to respond, but then the mother of the bride let out a loud sigh of frustration as she ascended the steps, looking a little rattled. "Sorry about that. That was my ex-husband. The nerve on that man, I swear."

Without missing a beat, Beau zipped down the remaining steps, then offered her his arm.

She made a little sound like she was charmed, placing her hands in the crook of his elbow with a wide smile. "Thank you."

"My pleasure. Shall we?"

The woman looked at me like she couldn't believe how lucky she was. Like she'd bought a one-dollar scratcher at the gas station and was shocked to find a row of sevens with a thousand-dollar prize attached to it.

Or maybe a million. If Beau were a scratcher, he'd be worth a million. Easy.

"See ya later, Lyndi," he said as they passed me, and I belatedly waved after he'd already turned his back.

For a long moment, I just stood there, watching them disappear through the massive double doors of the manor. Between photographing weddings and being a romance novel addict, I was used to being surrounded by amazing, unattainable men.

That was how I viewed all grooms because clearly, they were amazing enough for someone to want to marry them. And since they were getting *married*, that made them unattainable.

Obviously.

As for the romance novels? The men dreamed up by countless authors who had the perfect imaginary lips and always used them to say the right things at exactly the right moments? Well, duh, they could be the most amazing guys in the world, but they were still fictional. One couldn't find a man more unattainable than that.

And Beau? He was the ultimate book boyfriend come to life. Or rather, a combination of *multiple* book boyfriends. Practically as fictional as the men in my books, he constantly put himself in situations that screamed *fake relationship romance trope*.

And I knew this because we'd spent the last year working the same wedding circuit, and I'd watched him transform himself into whoever his clients wanted him to be. Over and over and over again.

He could be a bad boy whose only purpose was to soften up a woman's parents before they met the actual man she wanted to bring home to them.

He could be the perfect gentlemen, aiming to impress a dad who would only hand over his company to his daughter if she proved she was willing to settle down in addition to having career goals.

Or he could be a potential threat—the guy who would nearly get punched by another man, who for whatever reason needed to see her with *him* in order to realize his own feelings for the woman he loved.

But all of these versions of Beau weren't the real him. And even though six months ago he'd become besties with my sister's fiancé, and I'd thought I'd be able to find out who he was behind the charade, it hadn't happened.

Every time the four of us hung out, I'd watch him over the top of my Kindle from the corner—I'd be present but happier in the background. He'd laugh and smile and entertain, bleeding with the confidence of a man who didn't overanalyze everything or second-guess himself. I actually kind of envied him for that reason. But I never heard him say anything that clued me in to who he was on the inside.

But ... it was for the best. After all, he's leaving for a new duty station in a few months, and as tempting as it was to think about peeling back his layers and discovering who he was beneath his glittering exterior, it wouldn't matter how I felt about what I found out.

I knew I'd never leave Bluffton, and I knew he wouldn't stay.

2

BEAU

The first wedding of the day was officially over, and just as I'd predicted, my client didn't need me to drive her home. She left with her ex-husband, which was the exact outcome she'd been hoping for when she hired me.

Apparently, he'd been so blinded by rage that she'd brought another man to their daughter's wedding that he'd admitted he still loved her and begged for a second chance. And so, hiring me to escort her had been worth every penny. Her words, not mine.

Mission accomplished, I undid the buttons at my wrists and cuffed my sleeves. Then I grabbed a coffee from the bar on the main floor of the B&B and took it out back to relax before round two.

I had a few hours, but it didn't make sense to leave

the venue. It would take me over an hour to get back to the base from here, so it wasn't worth the trip for an hour at home. Besides, tonight's client was in the wedding party and would be arriving with the bride, so I might as well hang here until showtime.

Looking around the sun-drenched pavilion at the back of the main house, I tried to figure out what to do to kill some time. The brunch wedding had been held in the ballroom, but the next one would be out here under a large white tent.

Would it be weird to linger for a few hours even though I wasn't a guest of the B&B? I could go over to my buddy Zac's house and hang out with him and his awesome kid, but his fiancée was a high school teacher who'd been bogged down with finals this week, so I figured they'd want to spend the day together.

I meandered over to a group of wicker tables and chairs, considering pulling up my Kindle app and reading the thriller I was in the middle of. The massive pond and trees dripping with Spanish moss would be the perfect setting to read a book about a woman who'd mysteriously drowned in a lake.

I was fairly sure it was her husband who did it, but the writing was good, and there was still a chance it was the creepy sister who'd moved into their house and started raising her nieces and nephews like they were her own.

My phone buzzed in my pocket, and I smiled when I fished it out and saw my dad's info on the screen. I set my coffee on the table and slid my thumb across the screen, bringing it to my ear with a chuckle. "Hey, Pops. Perfect timing."

"Why's that?" His hoarse voice with its thick Cajun accent came through the line followed by a nasty cough.

The smile fell from my lips, and I looked at my feet, jamming my free hand into my pocket. "Uh, I'm between weddings, so I'm free to talk. And I was bored, so I might as well talk to you, old man."

"Between weddings, huh?"

"Yeah. This morning's was a brunch thing, so now I've got some free time until the next one. Thankfully they're at the same venue. That never happens."

I was used to driving all over the place on the weekends to attend weddings at various venues, churches, or homes. Sometimes I even went to a wedding in one state on Saturday and another one on Sunday, only staying long enough at either one to fulfill the terms of my contract.

It was exhausting. But it was necessary.

"Son, when are you going to stop doing all of this fake date nonsense and find somethin' real?"

I gulped, the hand in my pocket clenching into a fist. Not this again. "Pops, come on. We've talked about this."

"We sure have. And we'll keep talking about it. I don't like this whole thing. It's all a bunch of lies."

"It's not—" I stopped, sucking in a breath of air like it would somehow ease the weight on my chest. It didn't. "It's not about the lies."

"What's it about then?"

I scrubbed my hand over my mouth, not bothering to answer him. He already knew. Money. Plain and simple. The Marine Corps was an amazing organization that I was proud to be a part of, but they didn't pay me nearly enough to manage my old man's medical bills. And since I was the one who'd have to pay them anyway after he was gone because I was all he had left, I didn't have a choice.

So, after a friend of a friend paid me a few hundred bucks to take her to a wedding so her brother wouldn't suspect that she was secretly in love with his best friend, a business idea was born. It'd been full speed ahead ever since.

"What about bartending?" he asked. "I bet you could make a killing working at some fancy martini bar."

"This isn't New York City, Pops. It's South Carolina. There are no other *legal* side gigs that would pay this much. Not any that I'd want to do, anyway."

"Ah, see," he said, pausing to cough again. "That's it right there, isn't it? You *want* to do this. Why not just be honest about it?"

I looked up at the sky, the pale blue a total contrast to the blackened storm clouds hovering around the edges of my mind. "If it'll make you quit asking me to stop doing it, then fine. Yeah. I like what I do. I like helping these women with whatever it is they need me for. And trust me, you don't know all the stories I've heard. These women aren't lying to be cruel. Well, most of them, anyway. They have good intentions."

"You know what they say about good intentions," he croaked.

Man, he sounded terrible. Something deep inside the walls of my chest cracked as I pictured him sitting in his worn-out La-Z-Boy, oxygen tank at his side, tubes in his nose. I swiped the image away. "Listen, let's not talk about this anymore, okay? How are you doing?"

He let out a labored sigh. "Son, that topic isn't gonna be any more fun to talk about. Now, listen up. It's important."

"What?" I asked, standing straighter as the hair on the back of my neck raised. "Is everything okay?"

My pops laughed. Or at least, I was pretty sure that was what it was supposed to be. It morphed into another cough, though, and I squeezed my eyes shut to block out the picture of his pained expression that floated through my brain. He hadn't sounded this bad last time I'd talked to him. How had his condition worsened so quickly?

"I'm dying, Beau. It's not breaking news. So, no, everything isn't okay. But that's why I'm calling. You need to make me a promise while you still can."

I shook my head. "No. Pops, we're not there yet. The doctors said—"

"I don't give a hoot what the docs have to say. You and I both know the end is near. They might have hope that we can beat this thing, but in case we don't, we need to accept the facts. But hey, come on. You know how much I've been missin' your mama. And ... your brother. I'm anxious to see them again."

Nearly choking on the grief that threatened to spill out of me, I doubled over and thankfully found a chair not far behind me. I backed up and plopped into it, running a hand through my hair. "Wow. I can't believe you just said that."

"It's the truth, son." His words cracked, and he paused for a beat. "I'll finally get to be with them again. Doesn't that make you feel at least a little bit better about this crappy hand we've been dealt?"

I wanted to say yes. I wanted to tell him that after spending my entire life watching him move through each day like a man missing his very heart and soul that nothing would make me happier than to see him finally get some peace. But that was the problem—I wouldn't be *seeing* him get that peace. I'd be saying goodbye. And I wasn't ready.

"You there?" he asked, breaking me from my muddled thoughts.

"Yeah."

"You ready to make me a promise?"

I cleared my throat, praying my words wouldn't break. "Not if you're asking me to shut down my app. I can't afford your bills without it."

I hadn't meant to sound so harsh about it, but where did he get off asking me to stop doing a job that actually offered me a little bit of fun in the midst of all the pain and grief that birthed it? Being Mr. Fake Date meant I could be anyone. I could be whoever they needed me to be and the one person I *didn't* have to be —myself.

For a short time, I was able to escape the man who'd lost his brother in a car accident when he was five. The man who'd lost his mom to cancer when he was ten and was now losing his dad to the same thing, though attacking a different organ this time. The man whose entire life was like some sad, sick twist of fate.

It felt like the Fates were cutting golden strings, one

by one, not planning to stop until I was completely alone.

No.

In the Marine Corps, I got to be the devil dog with a ton of awards and badges for expert marksmanship in every weapon they trained us on. As Mr. Fake Date, I got to be a million things. My whole life was like a vacation from reality, and I wasn't about to let him make me promise to hang any of that up.

"Boy, fine. You can keep doing your fake dating business because I know it helps with the bills. But I have a feeling I'm not going to be the one to make you hang up your dancin' shoes in the end."

I leaned forward in my chair, resting an elbow on my knee, and then lowered my forehead to my hand. "What are you talking about?"

"I want you to promise me that in all that dating, you're gonna pick one of them girls and *love* her."

I shot out of my chair, blinking at the pond in front of me but not even seeing it through the blinding shock his words had caused. "*Love* her? What does that even mean?"

"The fact that you have to ask is exactly my point." He coughed for a moment, then wheezed out a sigh. "You're gonna be alone, Beau. I didn't raise you with kid gloves, even when you were a kid, so I'm giving it to you straight, here."

"Okay."

"As excited as I am to go upstairs and spend forever with your mama, I don't like the idea of leaving this world knowing you'll be down here all by your stubborn self. So you need to pick one of these fake dates and make her a real one, and then you need to love her because you can't let me die worried about you. You hear?"

I nodded, my eyes stinging as I stared blankly ahead.

"Beau?" he asked after a minute, obviously not having seen the nod.

"Sorry, yeah. I hear you."

"So, is that a promise?"

My gut rolled, rocks and boulders the size of the house behind me threatened to tear me apart. "Uh, yeah. Sure, Pops."

"You don't sound very convincing."

I let my head fall back and looked at the sky again, this time closing my eyes, unsettled by the calmness of the clear blue. "It's just a lot. It's a lot to ask."

"It shouldn't be. I wouldn't trade the time I had with your mom for anything. As brief as it was. All I want is to know you're going to get the same thing."

"Right, but you're asking me to pick a fake date and

make it real. It's not as easy as you make it sound. I haven't met a single woman I'd want to do that with."

As soon as the words left my lips, I tasted the lie. I actually *had* met one woman I could see myself having something real with. She'd just never been one of my clients.

But no. I'd known Lyndi for a year and had never once gotten the impression that she was into me. How many weddings had she attended in that time, either with a date or without? Several. And not once had she decided to ask me if I'd take her.

Or, okay, not once had she *hired* me to take her. Maybe it was because she hadn't had a reason to pay for a date—because why would she? The woman was a ten on a bad day and a twenty-seven as soon as she smiled. But maybe it was simply because she wasn't into me.

And even if she was ... I wasn't sure I could let her see the real me. The *broken* me. The version of myself that I didn't even let out often enough these days to know what he was like.

It was an odd feeling, now that I thought about it. I spent so much time wearing a mask, my true self was nothing but a stranger.

"Well, Beau, I don't know," my pops said, returning my focus back to him and his brittle, rasping laugh. "Maybe you just haven't met the right one yet. All I'm asking is that when one of your clients comes along that makes you feel something real for her, *love her*, son. Don't let her get away."

My response was some noise of acknowledgment, but it wouldn't qualify as being an actual word. Because I had no words. I had no idea how to express what I felt at that moment verbally. The pain. The grief. The guilt that weighed heavily on my shoulders. The horror of this entire conversation, raining down on me from a completely cloudless sky.

"All right, well, I'm gonna let you go now, son. You take care, you hear?"

I snorted. "Yeah, Pops. You too."

"I love you."

Swallowing back the bile that threatened to rise at the back of my throat, I choked out a meager, "I love you, too," before ending the call with a shaky hand.

Slowly, I put my phone in my pocket and lowered myself back into the wicker chair. Then, I sat with my eyes closed, wishing the ground beneath my feet would open up and swallow me whole.

"Beau?"

I jolted out of the chair again, Lyndi's voice sending a shock of awareness through me. What had she overheard?

"Lyndi, hey." I swiped a hand over my face, trying to

erase the evidence of how I'd spent the last ten minutes. "How's it going? You, uh, you get some good photos of the first wedding?"

Her golden-brown eyes narrowed ever so slightly as she studied me, and my pulse quickened under her assessment. I really hoped I didn't look as messed up as I felt.

"Yeah," she said hesitantly. "Are you okay?"

It took every ounce of strength in my body, but I adopted a casual stance and gave her a wry smile. "Who, me? Of course. Never better."

Please believe me.

"Really? Because you don't look okay."

I swallowed, shifting from one foot to the other. Her eyes told me she could see right through me, but I couldn't open up to her about this. It'd been bad enough having the most honest and jarring conversation of my entire life over the phone, but then relaying it to a third party? Talking about my *feelings*? Talking about my feelings with a *woman*, no less. As ridiculous as it was, that simply wasn't something I knew how to do.

"I'm good," I said after a minute, a real—okay, totally fake, but hopefully convincing—smile stretching over my face. "Just didn't get much sleep last night, and it was a long morning."

She nodded like she still didn't believe me, but then

she sat at the table next to me. Her gaze landed on my forgotten coffee, and she frowned at it for a second before pulling out her Kindle and settling into her chair.

"Color me shocked," I teased, my words coming easily as I took a seat across from her. "I don't think I've ever seen you without either a camera or a book in your hand."

"That's me in a nutshell."

She'd said it with a light tone, but there was something about it that had me holding my breath, waiting for more. Like she was suddenly about to reveal a secret or give me an exclusive glimpse inside to something that was more than what met the eye. More than the little crumbs she'd tossed my way over the last year.

But she didn't. She just lifted her e-reader and tapped on the black-and-white screen.

Taking my phone out, I navigated to the Kindle app and tried to focus on the words. But they kept blurring together, and I found myself having to re-read the same paragraph more than once before I could move on to the next one.

It had a lot to do with my pops. I knew that. But it might also be related to the distracting noises coming from the other side of the table. Lyndi kept making these quiet little grunts. More like *harrumphs,* actually.

Just when I was about to put the phone down and

ask her what was going on, she surprised me by tossing her Kindle into the grass with a flick of her wrist.

"Um ..." I stared at the black rectangle with wide eyes before looking at her, my hand slowly lifting to point at it. "What was that?"

"*That* was my reaction to a crappy ending."

"Okay. And ... it was so bad you *threw* your Kindle?"

She shrugged. "You're saying you've never thrown a book?"

"Uh, no. I've never thrown a book."

With a light chuckle, she got up and retrieved her Kindle, dropping it on the table. "I've been through a lot with this beast. It's indestructible."

The quirk of her lips had me mesmerized for a second, then I shook my head to clear it. "What got you so worked up?"

"I think the author was trying to avoid predictability, or make some kind of statement, but she went too far. There's a pattern to romance ... a formula. She totally messed it up at the end."

My own book completely forgotten, I turned off the screen and slipped my phone into my pocket again. Then I turned toward her and braced my forearms on the table between us. "Hang on, so you're saying you *want* your books to be predictable?"

"No. I'm saying there are ways to stay within the

pattern and still make it interesting. It's like ... she didn't play by the rules. She set me up to think I was reading a romance and then threw in a curveball. Don't get me wrong, I love a good curveball. But not when it breaks genre conventions. It's jarring."

I watched the fire dance in her eyes as she spoke, her passion for the subject as clear as the sky above us. "I read thrillers, not romance, so curveballs are kind of my thing."

"*Good* ones, yeah. But I guarantee you'd hate a book if it threw you a bad one at the end, even if you couldn't put your finger on why it bothered you."

"Maybe I only read good books, then."

She lifted a shoulder, unconcerned. "Maybe so. Either way, I'm on the hunt for a new book."

I cleared my throat, unwilling to be left alone with my thoughts again. Even though I had no intention of allowing myself to be distracted by romantic notions—no matter what my pops made me promise—chatting with Lyndi loosened the vice grip around my heart, and I needed to keep doing it.

"First, you have to tell me what happened. I'm invested now."

Her eyes narrowed into slits as she looked me over. Then she mirrored my pose with her arms on the table and leaned toward me. "They didn't end up together. That's not romance. That's ... *life*."

I cringed, knowing all too well how true that was. Then I quickly slipped on a neutral expression. This wasn't about me and what I'd lost. This was about her and what she clearly deemed as fact, when in my opinion, it didn't have to be true for *her*. "It's not always that way. You're a wedding photographer. You can't tell me happily ever afters don't exist."

She rolled her eyes. "Of course they exist."

"Okay, so why did you say 'that's life,' like they don't?"

Heaving out a sigh, she leaned back in her chair and looked out over the grounds. "I read romance because it's an escape. I love the way everything works out in the end, even when that isn't always the case in real life. I'm not denying that it *can*, I'm just saying it doesn't happen for everyone."

"You're saying you don't think it'll happen for you." I didn't ask it like a question. The answer was scrawled on her face and dripping from her words. It was in the downward set of her mouth and the way her voice had gotten lower toward the end like she was speaking from experience.

Lyndi's breath caught, and her eyes darted to mine. "What makes you say that?"

"Because you read it to escape."

A small crease appeared between her brows and her lips parted, then she closed them and picked up her Kindle again.

I waited while she scrolled through it, hoping she'd put it down and return to the conversation. I had no idea why it mattered to me what she thought about happy endings, but it did.

Maybe it wasn't *really* about her, though. Maybe I just wanted something else to focus on. Something I could fix. Some way I could help with something that *could* be fixed, because nothing in my life seemed to fit that description at the moment.

"Lyndi."

She didn't look up. "Yes?"

"Where did you go?"

"I ... I'm sorry. I'm not good at this." Again, her attention remained on the virtual library in her hands.

"Not good at what?"

Finally, she let the Kindle tip forward and met my gaze. "Talking."

I chuckled. "That's not true. We've talked."

"Sure, but not about anything real."

Her words stung, but at the same time, I knew them to be fact. In all the time I'd known her, we'd kept things utterly surface level. At weddings, we'd joke about the drunk uncle on the dance floor getting yelled at by his elderly mother. When we hung out with Zac and Layla, we'd laugh at Zac's son's antics or we'd socialize as a group rather than directly with each other. And half the time on those nights, she was content reading in the corner instead of actively engaging.

That said, when it came to women and what they were willing to share with me, Lyndi's tendency to keep me at arm's length was *highly* abnormal. My clients always opened up without hesitation. Without prompting. They were literally paying me to be a listening ear or to help them solve some problem they were too ashamed or fearful to admit to anyone in their real life.

But that wasn't the deal with Lyndi. She had no reason to open up to me, so she just ... *didn't*. And if that was because the spark that charged the air between us was all in my head, a one-sided thing that would never go anywhere, fine.

We could keep it that way.

It was much safer.

No matter how much my pops wanted me to find something real, I knew I couldn't do it. Because if I did, and then I lost that person too, I wasn't sure I'd survive.

3

LYNDI

Halfway through the third and final wedding of the weekend, I snapped photos of the bride and groom by the pond. I called out instructions to them on how to place their hands or where to look.

He wore a suit the color of old city sidewalks, and her long, elegant gown flowed down her body like a waterfall, the satin fabric glinting in the afternoon sun. Perfectly timed, a trio of birds flew in just the right spot for me to snag a still of them careening into the trees over the couple's shoulder.

"Beautiful," I said, clicking the shutter a few times before squinting down at the screen of my Nikon, my hand cupped against the black frame to shield the glare. A bead of sweat rose up on my forehead and then trickled down to sink into my eyebrow as I looked through the viewfinder. "One more like this. Perfect. Okay, now put your back against his chest and look up over your shoulder."

Out of the corner of my eye, I saw a man with a similar height and build to Beau, and my breath snagged before I remembered that he wasn't here.

Since he'd worked two weddings yesterday, he'd taken today off. And even though he didn't attend every event I did, I still felt his absence like a phantom limb.

I turned my attention back to the couple, reasonably sure Beau was on my mind thanks to our talk between weddings. Brief as it had been, it was also levied with more depth than any conversation we'd had.

When I'd approached him at that table, I'd thought he was merely resting his eyes. But when he'd shot out of his chair and looked at me like the sound of my voice had been a gunshot, my chest had burned with the need to soothe him.

Which was silly, right? Why would happy-go-lucky, chameleon-in-any-setting, dashingly handsome Beau Devereux need to be soothed by *me*?

He'd seemed completely fine at the brunch wedding. But then from the moment I'd surprised him and for the rest of the day, I could see how troubled he was. He probably thought he was putting on a good show, but it wasn't quite good enough.

There was no doubt in my mind that something haunted him. It ate through his usual charm, and his smiles didn't reach his eyes but instead looked forced in a way they never had before.

And it troubled me too.

It shouldn't. But it did.

Finished with the couple, I thanked them and moved back to the main reception area as they headed toward the bar. Aria sat at a table off to the side, her hands on her round belly, and her red lips puckered into a wrinkled O.

"Hey, are you okay?" I asked, sitting down beside her and placing a hand on her knee.

"Mm-hmm." Aria nodded her head as her eyes slid closed. Then she gave me a shaky smile. "Ms. Hattie might have been right about me overdoing it. My back is killing me."

Aria had complained of back pain several times over the last few weeks, so while this wasn't new information, I tracked her movements and looked for clues that it might be more than that. But I wasn't exactly sure what I was looking for, and as she swallowed the sip of water she'd just taken and her face relaxed a little, I relaxed, too.

"Well, stay off your feet for a little while. The wedding is going well and there shouldn't be much for you to do as long as things don't get crazy. They've already done most of the major dances, and the DJ takes care of all that anyway."

"Yeah, true. I guess I picked a good time to need a rest."

I snorted at her belief that she had any control over this. "Guess so."

"How are you, by the way? Was the whole triple-wedding weekend as rough for you as it was for me?"

"Uh, no." I gestured to her baby bump with a laugh. "But I'm not wearing a medicine ball under my clothes."

Aria managed a giggle, and something inside me loosened. Then her smile grew wider as she peered over at me. "So, how was your reading date with Beau yesterday?"

Her abrupt subject change caused me to blink and sit up straight. "Reading date?"

"Yeah. I hoped you two would get to spend some time together between the weddings, and I got *so* excited when I saw you reading. How was it?"

I waved a hand. "We just sat there and read. It wasn't a big deal."

I left out the part where he'd peppered me with questions I hadn't been prepared to answer. I wasn't used to a man looking at me like I was a puzzle he wanted to solve. Usually, I was the one doing that, then promptly reminding myself to act natural and bubbly so they didn't get freaked out.

Aria blinked. "That's it? You sat at a table—*alone*—with the man you've been crushing on since the day you met him ... and all you did was *read*?"

I squinted at her. "He read too."

Aria groaned and threw her head back, then laughter danced in her eyes when she looked back at me. "You kill me, Lyn. Make a move already. Shelby, Layla, and I have been waiting an eternity for this, and I'm going to go nuts if you don't do it soon."

Rolling my eyes, I sat back in my chair. "Why do *I* have to make the move? Beau's had plenty of chances to ask me out over the last year, but he hasn't. Doesn't that tell you anything?"

"How would you know if he's had plenty of chances to ask you out? You never look up from your Kindle."

I pouted, but I felt the corners of my mouth twitch. "Not fair."

"Totally fair," she insisted. "I love you, girlfriend, but you're so obsessed with the heroes of your romance novels that you keep ignoring the one that's right in front of you."

Oh boy, here we go.

I chuckled, unbothered by the familiar sentiment from my friend. My sister and our other friend Shelby were constantly saying the same stuff. But they didn't get it. The three of them had found their soul mates in ways that belonged in the pages of one of the romance novels they teased me about.

Shelby—Childhood Friends to Lovers.

Aria—Boy Next Door mixed with Brother's Best Friend.

Layla—Second Chance, with a side of the *always* swoon-worthy Single Dad.

There were tropes on tropes on tropes with these three, and it didn't occur to any of them that it wasn't that simple for me.

Before I could even come up with a response, Aria's chest stilled on an inhale like she was holding her breath. She made a strangled noise at the base of her throat, and her brow furrowed in pain.

"Aria? What's wrong?" My pulse quickened, alarm bells ringing at full volume, drowning out the chatter of the wedding guests and the blaring pop music under the tent. I'd seen enough movies featuring a woman in labor to know this kind of behavior from my very pregnant friend could only mean one thing.

Well, I supposed, it could mean more than *one* thing —the one thing being that she was in labor a full five weeks ahead of schedule. But since that would be a bigger deal than something like indigestion or back pain, it took precedence.

"Where's your phone?" I asked, eyes scanning the table in front of her, willing it to appear within reach.

"Over there," she grunted.

I turned in the direction she'd jerked her chin, spotting the antique cabinet in the corner of the reception area. Aria used it as a workstation during events, and inside the wooden doors were her emergency supplies for wedding snafus or minor flesh wounds.

Without delay, I dashed over to it and flung the doors open wide, snatching her phone off the top shelf and unlocking it with the passcode I'd memorized—0808. The date she'd had her first kiss with her now-husband, who was the first person I called as I rushed back to her side.

Will answered on the first ring, alarm in his tone since he likely knew she wouldn't call him in the middle of a wedding. "Aria? You okay?"

"It's Lyndi. I think she's in labor," I said, sitting in front of her and looking her over. My chest felt brittle, like my attempts to remain calm and in control would soon crack under the pressure. "It's too early, right? She's only thirty-five weeks."

"Can you put her on the phone?" His voice was strained yet totally calm.

Knowing Will, he'd say all the right things to get his wife to relax and keep from panicking. They'd known each other since they were kids, lived next door to each other their whole lives.

Will had been there for Aria first as a friend and protector and later as a man out-of-his-mind in love with her. There was nothing he wouldn't do for her and no mountain he wouldn't climb to make sure she knew it.

Those simple facts paired with his measured tone had me passing the phone to Aria with a much steadier hand than when I'd first called him.

She reached out and took it with a wince, pressing it to her ear. "Will?"

The seconds passed like lightning while she spoke to him in short, broken sentences. I couldn't even hear her over the mental to-do list stacking up in my brain. Aria didn't need me to shut down right now. She needed me to handle her event so she could get to the hospital without upsetting her clients.

In a flash, I was out of my seat and giving orders to the few staff members I knew she trusted most. Then I headed for the assistant photographer who came with me for weddings of this size. I told her what was going on and asked her to get all the remaining shots we needed.

Moments later, I was back at her side, feeling confident that Aria's *work* baby was in good hands.

And now we take care of the human baby.

"Okay," she said into the phone, her voice breaking. "I promise. Yeah, I love you, too."

She passed the phone to me, and I saw that it was still connected, so I put it to my ear. "Hey, it's Lyndi. Meet you at the hospital?"

Aria looked up at me with a grateful, teary smile as Will's promise came through the speaker. "Yes. I'll meet you there."

I hung up and slipped the phone into my back pocket, grateful that I'd stashed my purse and keys under the desk we'd passed on the way through the lobby.

"Okay, let's go get you checked out, mama," I said, taking Aria's hand. I helped her stand and draped one of her arms over my shoulders, then slid one of mine behind her back.

"Thanks, Lyn."

I returned her small smile, bumping the side of her head with mine. "Hang in there, A. I've got you."

As soon as we'd arrived at the hospital and gotten Aria checked in, the doctors informed me that she was indeed in labor. I hadn't wanted to leave her side to update Will and her family, but the nurses assured me she had time.

Twenty minutes later, I paced around the small waiting room in the labor and delivery wing so I could meet Will when he came in. He'd been at the shooting range with the guys, but they should arrive any minute.

Yes, I was grateful that Aria was in good hands. But over a month early seemed *too* early. Wasn't it? Babies were supposed to bake for nine months. Ten, actually, since we'd been counting to forty weeks this whole time. Though, I didn't fully understand why *nine months* was the common thing if that was the case.

Not the point, Lyn. Get it together.

I should have told her to take today off. When I'd shown up at the venue this morning, I'd seen the fatigue. I'd seen the shadows under her eyes. But Aria hated that kind of thing and was way too much of a control freak to hand off a wedding to her team with no notice.

Well, except for that one time she did it in the name

of love and a swoony Marine riding in on his new motorcycle, but that was different.

"Come on, Will," I pleaded in a low tone, craning my neck as I waited to catch a glimpse of him through the windows.

This was going to be fine. Yes, I should have told her to take today off. But she and the baby were going to be fine. I just knew it.

"Lyndi," Will called. He pushed his way sideways through the sliding doors of the emergency room before they'd even opened wide enough for his broad shoulders. "Where is she?"

"She's with the doctors," I said as he flung himself against the desk to speak to the woman who sat there.

Just as Will disappeared through the double doors on the left, heavy footsteps drew my gaze back to the door. Will's best friend Paul—who also happened to be Aria's big brother—charged into the lobby, Zac and Beau right behind him.

"Is he with her?" Paul asked me, his breath coming out in jagged bursts.

I nodded. "Yeah, where are Layla and Shelby?"

Zac tipped his chin toward the parking lot outside. "They should be here soon. They were shopping in Beaufort when we called them, and they need to bring Grayson to my sister before they come over."

That was a good call. Zac's young son wasn't a fan of hospitals after having suffered an allergic reaction last winter. Even though I was sure this day would be a happy one for my best friend and her baby, he didn't need to wait around in a hospital on pins and needles like the rest of us.

"And your parents?" I asked Paul.

"They're not in town," he replied, his face pained. "Mom's gonna be so mad she missed this. First grandbaby and all."

I managed a smile, glad he'd defaulted to the simple fact of her missing this big moment and not the scarier angle. The one that had to do with how early it was and how scared Aria looked when the doctor had confirmed she was in labor. *Premature* labor.

Shaking my head, I turned to Beau for the first time. He was watching me intently. *So* intently that for a second, I wondered if he could see into my very soul. Right past my barriers and into the torment that swirled underneath.

"I guess now all we can do is wait?" Paul asked, reaching up to scratch the back of his head.

"Yep." Zac moved to one of the leather chairs and slumped into it, resting his head back against the wall. "You know, it's funny. I missed this whole thing with my kid, and I have to be honest, I'm a little glad." I quirked a brow at him, but he shook his head. "Sorry, wait. No. I'm not. I'd kill to go back and be there for all the stuff I missed. But I just mean this feeling ... the *waiting* ..."

"It sucks," Paul finished for him as he took a seat in the chair next to his friend's.

Zac nodded once. "Yeah. That."

I swallowed hard, my eyes moving to Beau's again. They held a pensive shimmer as he searched my face for something I couldn't find words for. Between Zac's comments about waiting and Beau's watchful stare, it felt a little like the walls were closing in on me.

This was really happening. My best friend—well, after my sister and tied with Shelby—was in *premature labor*. We were sitting here doing all of this waiting five weeks earlier than we were supposed to be.

Her parents weren't here. Her husband wasn't the one who'd brought her in while she was shaking and scared.

I was.

And through all of the pressure, I'd controlled every emotion raging inside of me even though I wished I could disappear into a fictional world and pretend none of this was real. But now that the dust was settling and Aria and Will were with the doctors, I felt disturbing quakes breaking through my control. Like the precursors before a devastating earthquake, the urge to run became too much to take.

"I'll be right back," I said to no one in particular, fleeing through the sliding glass doors without looking back.

4

BEAU

I should sit down. I should take a seat with my friends and show my support for Aria. I'd gotten a lot of business thanks to her connections in the wonderful world of weddings. And now that I'd joined her group of friends, and became close with Zac thanks to additional work ties, they were all starting to feel a lot more like family.

Not that I had a ton to go on, since my family consisted of just my pops, and if he was right and the docs were wrong ... pretty soon I'd have no family at all.

"Shelby just texted me," Paul said, breaking me from my thoughts. "She said they hit traffic on the way back. They still need to drop Grayson off, but they'll be here as soon as they can."

"Good," Zac replied.

It *was* good. Even though there was nothing they could do but sit here and wait for news like the rest of us, I knew they'd rather be here than anywhere else.

Last year, Aria had hired me as Shelby's date when she was still trying to figure out her feelings for Paul, and when they got married a few months later, Layla had been my client. As focused as they were on the weddings or their love lives, one thing was blatantly obvious to me on both occasions: These four women were so different in so many ways, but their friendship —their *bond*—was powerful, and it'd been cool to see.

And that thought had me turning to the floor-to-ceiling windows, searching for their friend who'd dashed out of here without so much as a backward glance.

No, I shouldn't sit.

"Text me if you hear anything," I told the guys. Then I headed for the door, not even waiting for a response.

I stepped into the balmy afternoon air, my head on a swivel, looking for Lyndi. When my eyes landed on her small form facing an alley in the all-black outfit she wore to work, my chest tightened. Warmth spread through me like someone had slid me under an oversize heat lamp and left me there to bake.

Even from this distance, I could tell she was having a hard time. And it hit me as strange to see her like this when I was used to seeing her in her element. When she had her nose in a book, she was the picture of peace. Her face cycled through varying emotions as she read, but even when I figured she must be reading something sad given the downward set of her mouth, she still looked oddly happy.

At weddings, she'd snap away on that big, fancy camera. She'd move through the crowd, capturing photos people would cherish forever, even though they rarely spared her a second glance unless she asked them to pose.

In *those* moments, she reminded me more of a ray of sunshine than anyone wearing all black had any right to. It didn't make sense. Who looked like a ray of sunshine while wearing all black?

Lyndi did. And it killed me.

She wasn't even a bubbly, *sunshine-y* person. She was actually quite reserved. It was more like how the sun stood back, calmly observing things, shining its light without making a big fuss about it. Like it was only there to make life a little bit brighter. It did the world a favor by existing, just like Lyndi.

Or at least, that was what it felt like to me, whenever I was near her.

And even though I knew it was a total contradiction, it *irked* me. Every degree of warmth that Lyndi brought with her whenever she was around made me lose sight of all the reasons I tried so hard not to think about her.

It made me forget that she'd never given me the time of day, so even if I *wanted* to be with her, I didn't stand a chance. "Bad idea," I whispered, considering going inside to sit with my friends.

Playing the waiting game with them seemed a heck of a lot safer than the game I'd be playing out here. Even if it was a hospital, and the torturous smell of cleaning products and fear still lingered in my nose.

Before I had a chance to brave going back inside, Lyndi turned slightly and looked over her shoulder, almost as if she could sense me standing here.

Left without a choice, I approached her cautiously, trying to force down my body's disquieting reaction to her. "How are you doing?"

She let out a choked sound—part laugh, part sigh. "*Me?*"

"Yeah, *you*."

"I'm fine. Just nervous for Aria."

"Aria's in great hands. She's going to be okay."

Lyndi's shoulders lifted toward her ears like she wasn't too sure about that, but then she let them fall, the tense lines on her face relaxing. "You're right. Aria's going to be fine, and so is the baby."

"Exactly."

Silence loomed between us like a heavy mist, even though she really did look more at ease after accepting the truth about her friend. And it was a truth I'd hold onto as hard as I could because if I were a superstitious person, it would be very easy for me to believe that my mere *presence* in this group could cause them to lose someone they loved.

Like I always did.

And if the Fates were too concentrated on weaving all the crappy conditions of life into my destiny that they didn't have time to cut any strings for my friends, I'd gladly stay on their radar if they'd just leave Aria and her baby alone.

Lyndi was watching me carefully, and a tight knot within me begged for release. Just like before, the only thing I could think of to relieve it was to prompt a conversation with her.

"So, let's see. Baby Paxton'll be a week old when your sister's wedding comes around," I said. "Since we know they're gonna be fine, do you think they'll bring the baby?"

My teasing worked, and she rewarded me with a laugh. "Uh, no. I'm new at this honorary auntie gig, but something tells me she won't want to bring her week-old baby to a packed event like a wedding."

"Ah, fair. Are you excited about it, though? Your

always-a-bridesmaid sister is finally tying the knot herself."

"I'm very excited. Zac and Layla are amazing together. And with Grayson, they make the perfect little family. I couldn't be happier for them."

I nodded in agreement, detecting nothing but sincerity in her tone. Even if it was laced with something a little wistful. Something she probably hadn't intended for me to pick up on.

"Same here. And I have to say, going to this wedding as the best man instead of somebody's hired date is gonna be a refreshing change."

Though, if *she* wanted to hire me, I wouldn't say no.

Her head tilted down as she stared at the space between us, then she lifted her chin. Before she could get a word out, she jumped like she'd been poked in the back. I watched as she reached into her back pocket and pulled out her phone with a laugh.

"Sorry, one sec," she said as she gestured with the phone. "Gotta take this."

I flicked my wrist like it was totally fine, turning to pace while I waited for her to finish.

"Beau?"

Pivoting, I quirked a brow at the way she stood there with the phone halfway to her ear. "Yeah?"

"Don't go anywhere, okay?"

Time slowed as I examined her. Her bottom lip quivered slightly before she caught it with her teeth, and there was something urgent and pleading in her eyes that hit me like a scream and a whisper at exactly the same time.

Throat too tight to speak, I simply dipped my chin in acknowledgment. And for the entire five minutes that she was on the phone, I focused on literally anything and everything except the way those four little words made me feel.

The color of the leaves on a nearby cypress tree.

The pregnant woman in a wheelchair being escorted into the maternity wing.

The sound of the birds flitting about on the ground near a discarded Frito-Lay bag.

Anything but, *"Don't go anywhere, okay?"*

Lyndi cleared her throat as she walked up behind me, putting the phone back in her pocket. "Sorry about that."

"No worries. Everything all right?"

"Yeah. Well, no. But it's nothing compared to what Aria's going through, so I should just get over it."

I tucked my hands in the pockets of my jeans and turned toward her. "You're allowed to have feelings, you know."

She snorted—*loudly*—then hid her mouth behind one hand. "Sorry."

"Why is that funny?"

"It's not that it's funny ... it's just that, well, trust me, I have feelings. Probably too many of them."

"Oh yeah?" I moved behind her, circling until I came back to my original position. "Where are they?"

"Hilarious," she deadpanned. "They're in here. Where they belong."

I frowned as she patted her temple. "I don't think that's where feelings live." Then I stepped closer, reaching out and tapping her chest directly over her heart. "I'm pretty sure they're supposed to be in there."

It was barely a second of contact, but when the tip of my finger connected with the soft fabric of her shirt, we sprang apart like repelling magnets.

"Anyway, um, what were we talking about before the feelings thing?" she asked, crossing and uncrossing her arms a few times before finally leaving them wound tightly around her middle.

I wet my lips. "Uh, I think you were about to tell me what you were so upset about."

"Oh, was I?"

"You were."

She considered me for a long moment, then she

dropped her arms and sighed. "It's my grandma. She's very ... *persistent*."

I waited for her to say more, but when she didn't, I arced my hand through the air. "Go on."

"She's trying to set me up with Ms. Hattie's son."

"Oh." It was all I could manage, and it fell out of my mouth like a rock. A lava rock, maybe. One that steamed quietly from the ground at my feet.

"Yeah, I guess he's going to be at my sister's wedding, and she wants me to go with him. But it's a whole thing, and I'm not going to do that," she paused to take a breath, which gave me time to register my own relief. But then she looked up at the sky with a huff. "But I *will* have to dance with him, and she's trying to move him to our table for dinner. I don't think Layla's going to allow it, though. Wedding party only or whatever."

My throat felt dry as I watched her, grateful that if the table were, indeed, only for the wedding party, that'd put me there. Possibly even right next to her.

But then again, why did I suddenly care?

I'd been attracted to Lyndi for a year—I'd be blind not to be—but I'd never been as drawn to her as I was now. I'd never hung on her every word or been jealous of any of the random guys she briefly dated. Let alone one she was being *told* to date even though she didn't want to.

Not until ... *Oh no.*

My pops.

This deep longing in my chest was all *his* fault. That crazy old man and his *make-me-a-promise* dying-wish nonsense had me looking at Lyndi in a whole new light, and I couldn't believe I hadn't realized it sooner.

But what was I supposed to do? Tell her my dad wanted me to fall in love for real and ask her if she wanted to hire me for Layla's wedding so she didn't have to deal with Ms. Hattie's son?

I didn't know the guy but judging by the way she talked about this whole thing, I could tell she wasn't interested in him. Maybe he had a big nose or weird teeth or was a huge jerk to her in the past. Which, by the way, I'd have to have a little talk with him if that turned out to be the case.

Regardless, it was kind of my thing to save women from whatever problem they needed a fake date to fix, so maybe this was my chance. Maybe I could ask Lyndi to hire me, and then maybe—*just* maybe—the way I felt about her wasn't one-sided and she'd be the one I'd find something real with.

"But like I said," Lyndi went on, a visible shudder rocking her body, "none of that is as important as what's happening with Aria. So, I'm just going to suck it up and hang out with him, knowing it won't go anywhere."

"Why won't it go anywhere?" I couldn't help but ask.

"Because he lives in Okinawa."

I shrugged. "You don't like Okinawa?"

"I've never been," she said with a light laugh. "But I'm not going to start dating a guy who would take me out of Bluffton. I love it here."

The level of certainty in her voice caused a current of emptiness to stream through me. It promptly swept away all those bright ideas about asking her to hire me and left a puddle of disappointment in its wake.

There goes that plan.

She stilled, looking up at me as if she'd just thought of something. "Hey, where are you going by the way?"

Since I hadn't made a move to leave, I twisted around to see if she was asking someone else. But no one was there, so I faced her again and put a hand on my chest. "*Me?*"

"Yeah, *you*," she said with a chuckle, parroting my words from earlier. "Aren't you moving in a few months? I don't think I've heard where you're going."

"Ah, yes. That. Um, I'm going to Hawaii."

Not quite as far as Okinawa, but too far for her.

"Hawaii?" she asked. "Wow. Big change. I went there on vacation once."

"Yeah? How was it?"

"It was beautiful. We went fishing and I caught a puffer fish with a Moana fishing pole."

Considering the fact that the Disney movie she referred to was far too recent for this to be a childhood memory, I tilted my head at her. "How old were you?"

"Twenty-four." She grimaced, her cheeks staining like she was surprised she'd even told me about this. "It was four years ago."

I laughed, some of the tightness in my chest dissipating. "And why were you using a Moana fishing pole as an adult?"

"Hey, I love Moana."

"I'm sure it's a great movie."

"It is. But if you *must* know, it was a spur-of-the-moment idea and there were slim pickings at Target. Layla used a Batman one."

Again, a laugh came easily from my lips as I shook my head at her. "Wow. Well, good job with the puffer fish."

"Thanks." She held the smile for a second longer, then looked away restlessly. "How long do you think it'll be until we know anything?"

I turned and peered at the hospital entrance like I expected there to be some kind of Countdown to Baby Paxton sign on the window. Then, I shrugged, scratching my neck. "I'm not sure. I have exactly *zero* experience with any of this. If you believe the movies, it should have already happened, right?"

"Right. Though, if this were a movie, that baby would have been born on the dance floor at the wedding."

"With the bride playing doctor," I added, enjoying the new turn of this conversation and the length of it too.

I didn't know if it was because she was so wigged out about Aria that she needed the distraction, but I didn't think I'd had this long of a conversation with her in the year that I'd known her, and it was ... amazing.

"Of course. And *miraculously* there wouldn't be a single blemish on her perfect white dress afterward."

I wrinkled my nose. "Oh, absolutely not. Not if we're talking about a rom-com. Horror movie, though? Maybe the dress wouldn't even be white anymore."

"Oh my word, hush," she exclaimed, throwing her head back to laugh. "That is *not* a good image."

"Sorry. But you have to admit, it would make for great photos."

Her eyes twinkled as she peered at me. "What do you know about rom-coms, anyway?"

I shrugged. "I've seen a few. Before I realized I could make more money by booking weddings only, I used to do everyday stuff, too. Movies, dinner, holidays with the family."

"What? Why would someone need to hire you to take them out to dinner? New restaurant in town and they wanted to try it but didn't want to go alone?"

"Actually, yeah, one time. But usually, it was a double-date situation. Same with the movies. Always rom-coms."

"I bet you *loved* that."

I pursed my lips. "You know what? I actually don't mind rom-coms."

"Really?"

"Yeah, I practically live through them every weekend with my clients, so I'm pretty well-versed in the patterns. I guess it's like what you said yesterday about the formula of romance novels. They fit the same pattern, right?"

"Pretty much. So, I guess that means you're acknowledging that you're trapped inside a *Groundhog Day*-style fake relationship movie?"

Laughing, I moved over to a nearby bench and took a seat. "Yeah, I guess I am."

"Doesn't that get old?"

"What?"

She made her way over and sat next to me. "The fake relationship thing."

"Oh. Well, no, because there are other little differences that make it interesting."

What I *didn't* add was that it didn't matter if it got old, it was lucrative, and I had hundreds of thousands of dollars in medical debt on my shoulders. This light conversation was as addictive as drugs probably were, and I wasn't about to cut myself off by discussing that.

"What kinds of things?"

"The different reasons they hire me."

"Ah," she drawled with a nod, "the secondary tropes."

"The what?"

"There're always secondary tropes. So like, when you did the fake relationship thing with Shelby, the secondary trope was that she was secretly in love with her best friend. It's referred to as friends-to-lovers."

Understanding, I nodded. "Got it. So yesterday, when the mother of the bride wanted to get back together with her ex-husband ...?"

"Second chance," she supplied.

"And the one in the evening, when the bride's cousin was in love with the best man?"

She frowned. "I think I need more info. Who was the best man to her?"

Normally, I didn't like talking about my clients and their motivations for hiring me, but this was too much fun. I didn't have to give away too many details, but I couldn't help but play along with her.

"I think they all grew up together."

"Childhood best friends," she said with a nod. "Were either of them parents?"

"He was."

Lyndi let out a long sigh. "Ah, single dad, too. I love that one. There's just something swoony about a single dad, doing his best for his kid while also following his heart. Gets me every time."

I tried not to take offense that she loved a *swoony single dad* since I wasn't one. Then I bumped her shoulder with mine. "Crushing on your sister's fiancé?"

A giggle escaped through her shocked expression, and she reached out and swatted my knee. The simple touch caused sparks to shoot up my thigh. "Um, ew, no. Zac is great, but he's *not* my type."

"What is your type?" I asked before I could stop myself. "Besides single dads, of course."

And besides guys who plan to stay in Bluffton for the rest of their lives.

She gave me a sidelong glance, but her lips curved up into a small smile. "Um, let's see. I love it when a guy has major reasons why he can't date the heroine, but they're snowed in with each other in a cabin, so he can't escape her. And then those major reasons become *minor* the more they get to know each other."

Confused, I angled my head. Was that a type? Or a book description?

"I also love a workaholic doctor falling for a free spirit. The way he fights his attraction because he has a duty to save lives and doesn't have time for romance? Kills me."

Again, what in the world made her think that answered my question?

"Oh," she said, holding up a finger, "and even though enemies-to-lovers isn't my favorite trope because sometimes it gets a little ridiculous, I love it when he can't stand the heroine but then he's forced to marry her. So it's mostly the marriage of convenience thing, but the sparks are fun when you throw in the enemies part."

When I didn't say anything for a minute, she dipped her head and caught my eyes. Her lips parted and her cheeks flamed red, the absolute picture of embarrassment.

"What?" I asked, chuckling at her almost-comical expression.

"*You*, what?" she retorted, narrowing her eyes at me. "I feel like I just dumped all this word-vomit in your lap, and now you don't know how to tell me to go away."

A full-bodied laugh burst out of me as I leaned back

on the bench. "I'm not going to tell you to go away, Lyndi."

Unfortunately.

She blinked at me, waiting for more.

I shrugged. "I guess I'm just surprised by your answer to my question about your type."

"Why? I love those tropes."

Moving slowly so as not to spook her, I shifted on the bench and rested my arm along the back of it so I could face her more directly. "Lyndi, I asked you what your type was, and you rattled off a list of fictional scenarios. None of that has anything to do with *your* type of man. The ones that are out here. In the wild."

Intense astonishment touched her sun-kissed face, but before she could reply, someone called her name.

We both turned to see who it was, and Lyndi bolted from the bench the second her eyes landed on her sister and Shelby coming up from the parking lot. I watched them disappear through the hospital doors, sitting forward once more and bringing my elbows to my knees.

Well, okay, then. Good talk.

5

LYNDI

"Have you heard anything?" Layla asked Zac and Paul as soon as we made it through the sliding doors.

Zac took her hand and shook his head. "Not yet, but—"

The doors behind us burst open, cutting off whatever Zac had been about to say. Will strode through with his arms in the air, fists clenched, a triumphant smile on his face. "It's a boy!"

Cheers rang out around us, not only from our group of friends but from the other people in the waiting room and the women behind the desk.

"It's a boy," he said again, softer now, as he let his hands fall to his sides. "And he's fine. They're both great, actually."

We took turns hugging and congratulating Will, but then after he finished with each of us, his face took on an ashen quality. With a sharp intake of breath, he pitched forward and put his hands on his knees.

I glanced up at my sister, who was peering over at him with the corners of her mouth turned down.

Sensing the need to do something—though I wasn't sure *what*—I started to step forward. But then Paul beat me to it and went to Will's side, placing one hand on his brother-in-law's upper back, making small circles over his shoulder blade.

Will's face was angled toward his knees, but even though I couldn't see the tears, I knew he was crying. Silent sobs racked his body, making his biceps shake under his weight as he held himself up.

No one spoke. No one tried to remind him that his sweet little family was okay. He knew it. But apparently, the man just needed a second to collect himself. In a safe space. Surrounded by his people.

My chest burned as I stood there watching him, wishing more than anything that I knew what to do or say. I couldn't imagine how scary it was for Will to hear that his wife was in labor five weeks early, and he'd probably been a total wreck throughout the entire delivery.

A wreck who would never let himself *be* a wreck on

the outside. Because he didn't love anyone or anything as much as he loved Aria, and I knew he'd never let her see him fall apart when she needed him the most.

But now, it was over.

And in the comfort of this otherwise cold and monochromatic lobby, he could fall apart for as long as he needed to.

But then he straightened, wiping his reddened face with both hands. "Sorry about that."

"Hey, man," Zac said, patting his shoulder, "don't apologize. We got you."

My heart cracked at the truth of his sentiment. It was the same thing I'd said to Aria before I'd brought her here, and a lump formed in my throat just thinking about it.

Will's head bobbed back and forth as he looked around the lobby with a furrowed brow. "Where's Beau? Did he leave?"

My eyes widened. "*Shoot*. He's outside. I'll go get him."

"Oh, no you won't," Will surprised me by saying. "I'll go tell him myself."

"Are you sure? If you want to go be with Aria—" I started, but he shook his head.

"I would, but we had to send the little guy off to the NICU for some tests, and Aria wants her girls." He chuckled and hooked a thumb over his shoulder toward the labor and delivery rooms. "I should have sent you in there right away, but I got a little ... *you know*. Anyway, hurry it up. She'll kill me if I don't send you three in there within the next thirty seconds or so."

I considered asking him again if the baby was okay, but I held back. He said he was, so he was.

And knowing Aria, she was probably steaming over the fact that she couldn't come out here and see us on her own two feet. If there was one thing she hated, it was not being able to do something herself.

"Struggling with delegation already?" Shelby asked him with a shake of her head. "It's gonna be a long maternity leave."

"Ah, I don't know," Will mused, his eyes shining when he looked over at us. "Wait till you see the way she looks at the little dude. He might turn out to be the one thing that gets her to slow her roll."

I patted his shoulder as we passed him on the way to the doors. "Don't feel too bad, Will. He's probably just a lot cuter than you."

Will grunted something that sounded like an agreement and headed outside with the guys while us girls took off for the wide double doors. I led Layla and Shelby to Aria's room as they chatted excitedly behind me, chest tight with the potent emotional overwhelm that threatened to burst forth.

I felt bad for getting distracted by Will and forgetting that Beau was outside. Actually, I felt a little bad for leaving him sitting out there in the first place. But he'd had me so rattled I couldn't think straight.

Between the electric shock he'd given me when he'd touched a finger to my heart and the way he'd asked about *my type* before calling me out on the romance-hero thing, I'd been a bit of a mess. And then when Layla called my name, I couldn't get out of there fast enough.

It was fine, though, because now Will would get to tell his friend about his baby boy, and one of them would probably bust out some blue cigars and they'd stand around acting manly for a while.

Wait, could you even smoke cigars near a hospital these days? Did these guys even *like* cigars?

Personally, I found them to be a little repugnant. But that was what they'd be doing out there if this were a romance novel—a thought that only served to remind me of *Beau*, now, thanks to his probing questions.

Hey, maybe they'll have cute blue bubblegum cigars in the gift shop if not. I should check.

Shaking my head to clear the tangent, I led my chattering friends to Aria's door, knocking quietly.

"Come in," I heard her say in a low tone.

When we stepped inside, tears blurred my vision. Aria sat upright in the bed with extra pillows surrounding her. She wore a floral robe, and her hair and makeup were nearly as perfect as they had been when I'd brought her here from the wedding.

"Oh, of course," Shelby said in a jovial whisper. "I knew I'd walk in here and find you looking impossibly perfect right after giving birth."

Aria chuckled. "Hush."

"Seriously, you look gorgeous," Layla agreed, moving to our friend's side and hugging her gently. "How do you feel? Congratulations, mama."

"Thank you. I feel okay." She hugged Shelby and me before we stepped back and framed her bed in a triangle of support, then she looked down at her hands. "I hope they don't take too long with the baby in the NICU. They said since he's a little over thirty-five weeks he won't have to stay in the NICU if he passes some tests. Little guy just barely made the cutoff for their policies for releasing preemies, but it's all these other scores that matter more than his gestational age right now."

"Well," I said, my voice thick with emotion, "you've always been great at tests. So, if he's anything like you, I'm sure he'll pass with flying colors."

Aria choked out a giggle and shook her head. "Yeah,

well, he looks *exactly* like Will, so we'll see how much of me he actually has in him."

"Do you have any photos? I'm so excited to see him." Shelby put her hands in front of her chest like she was praying. When Aria nodded and reached for her phone, she let out a little squeal and grabbed for it with greedy hands. "Ah, he's so beautiful."

I stepped closer and looked over Shelby's shoulder at the image on the screen. Will must have taken it shortly after he'd been born. Aria looked tired, but still so pretty, her tiny—oh my goodness, *so* tiny—baby boy nestled in her arms.

The three of us stared at the photos in awed silence as Shelby scrolled through them, and as I studied the little baby who'd just victoriously made his early debut, I felt like my heart was about to break into a million pieces.

Well, *that*, and my hands itched to reach through the phone and grab him out of Aria's arms so I could squeeze the heck out of him.

I blinked up at Aria. "Did you know there's a thing called cute aggression?"

A laugh stuttered out of her. "What?"

"Cute aggression. It's when you see something so cute it makes you want to squeeze it." I punctuated my statement by lifting my hands in front of my face and squeezing the air between them, making them pulse slightly. "It's a thing. It's like an animal instinct or something." My friends laughed, but my sister widened her eyes at me like I'd lost my mind. "What?" I asked with a laugh, dropping my hands. "I saw it on TikTok."

Again, more laughter, but then Aria took the phone Shelby held out to her and cuddled it against her chest. "Okay, weirdo. But don't squeeze my baby. He's too delicate."

"How *is* he doing, other than the tests and stuff?" Shelby asked, sitting on the edge of Aria's bed. "Did the doctors say anything else?"

"It all happened so fast, but they're really happy with how developed he is for a preemie. We got to hold him for a while before they took him. I think they might let him stay in here with me until I'm discharged, and then hopefully we can go home together in a few days. Fingers crossed, anyway."

"Hold up," Layla said, waving her hands, "what's his name? You still haven't told us."

"Oh. Um, well … that's because we haven't named him yet," she admitted.

We all stared at her with wide eyes, then Layla shook her head. "You're kidding, right?"

"Nope. You guys, I was 99.9 percent sure he was a girl." Aria looked at us as if that explained everything, but when she was only met with more staring, she let her head fall back against the pillows. "Will kept wanting to talk about boy names just in case, but I insisted we wouldn't need one."

Silence stretched over us like a heavy blanket, and then all at once, the four of us started laughing hysterically. Aria's laughter turned a little weepy at the end though, and since I already felt like I was at the end of my own emotional control, I was desperate to keep it light.

Poking at a flower on her robe, I grinned down at her. "Seriously, I know I brought you in here wearing a maternity dress from Nordstrom. Where did you get this robe?"

"Oh, this? I may have been carrying it and a few other little things in my bag just in case this whole thing took me by surprise." She nodded at the behemoth of a Louis Vuitton purse that sat on the end of the couch along the wall.

"Like anything could take *you* by surprise," Layla teased.

"I've also got my toiletries, special socks, and Baby Paxton's coming-home outfit. Though, I think I might need a new one because my mom said I was a big baby, and Will's a giant, so I bought a bigger size just in case. The poor thing's going to be swimming in it."

"Don't worry, we'll go get you something for the baby and whatever else you need," Shelby promised her. "And speaking of things you need, is there anything we can get for you now? Are you thirsty or hungry or anything?"

Aria bit her lip and looked down. "Actually, I just had to see you guys because ... well, because I love you. But right now, I think I might just need Will."

Understanding appeared on both Shelby and Layla's faces, each of them having a man they loved just as much as Aria loved hers. On my end, I suddenly felt like an outsider in a place that I used to think of as my *shelter* from the outside.

It was stupid, I knew. And logically, I didn't begrudge my friends their happiness. I'd told Beau the truth when I'd said I couldn't be happier for my sister, and I felt the same way for Aria and Shelby.

But none of that changed the deeply rooted hollow feeling in the pit of my stomach as I stood here with them now. Like I'd lost what was once a totally safe place for me to be myself and not worry about how different I felt from my peers.

Because nothing could fix the thing that made me different in this case. I wasn't like them in the ways that would make me the kind of woman who got a romance novel-worthy happily ever after.

It was why I was more content falling for the men in my books. They didn't have to love—or even *know* —the real me. They just had to be their perfect swoon-worthy selves, and then they could be shelved again before something I said or did could ruin anything.

"You know what?" I asked, backing toward the door. "You two stay here, I'm gonna grab Will. That way Aria doesn't have to be alone while she waits for him to put out his cigar."

Aria grimaced. "Cigar?"

"Nothing, no. Never mind," I said, shaking my head. "I'll send him in. I love you, congrats again."

"Love you, too," I heard her say as I slipped out of the room in record speed.

Then I zipped through the long hallways of the maternity ward with blinders on, not stopping until I made it through the exit and into the fading light outside.

I turned to the bench where Beau had been, and sure enough, the guys were there with him—and no, they weren't smoking anything. Just standing around and chatting, grins on all their equally handsome faces.

Well, *almost* equally handsome.

The fleeting image of Beau and I paired up so we could round out this group of couples stabbed through me like a knife. It was sharp and painful since I knew it would never happen.

But instead of dwelling on that, I worked a practiced, smiling mask onto my face as I approached them and tapped Will on the arm. "Aria wants you. Layla and Shelby are waiting with her until you get in there."

"Can we come with you?" Paul asked. "I just want to tell my sister congrats, but I won't stay long."

"And I'll wait outside if she wants," Zac offered.

"Nah, man, both of you come," Will said with a flick of his wrist. "I'm sure she'd love to see you for a sec."

The three of them started toward the hospital entrance, but then as the other guys kept walking, Zac looked over his shoulder and stopped when he saw Beau wasn't with them. "You coming?"

I turned my gaze on Beau, finding him staring intently at me. He didn't take his eyes from mine as he answered his friend. "No, you guys go. I'm taking Lyndi home."

"You are?" Zac and I asked in unison.

"Yeah," he said, finally looking at Zac. "She's not feeling well."

"Okay, we'll keep you updated, Lyn," Zac said. "Hope you feel better."

"Thanks," I replied, totally stunned.

When he was gone, I peeked over at Beau. "You don't have to take me home. I drove here and—"

"I came with them, so my car's not here. I'll take you home in yours, then I'll walk to mine at Zac's place."

"But I'm fine—"

Something in his eyes cut off the rest of my words, and a chill rose on my spine. It was strange, and I almost didn't believe it, but it looked like he was ... *concerned* for me. Like the perfect mask I knew I still wore had holes that he could see right through.

Before I could stop myself, I launched into his arms, hugging him tightly around the waist. I closed my eyes, pressing my cheek to his hard chest—okay, his *solid-like-a-freaking-brick-wall* chest. But it was oddly comforting, despite what you'd think based on that description.

He only hesitated for a moment before he wrapped his arms around my back, and then, like Paul had done for Will, he made small soothing circles with his palms.

The pulsing ache that had thrummed beneath my skin ever since the moment Aria had scared the crap out of me by going into labor during a wedding seemed to lessen with each passing second that he held me. This unexpected hug was a balm, calming and peaceful, and exactly what I needed.

And I couldn't be sure, but there was a bit of a hitch to his breath, a slight increase in the speed of his heartbeat beneath my ear, that made me think maybe he'd needed it, too. Maybe whatever was up with him yesterday—*wow, only yesterday?*—was still troubling him today.

It occurred to me then that Beau had only spent about four seconds within the walls of the hospital. He'd stood in one spot just inside the lobby doors, and for the rest of our time here, he'd never gone back in. Did that have anything to do with it?

Stop it, Lyndi.

I squeezed my eyes shut, trying to block out my overactive imagination. Not every hot guy had a tortured soul or a backstory that would make you white-knuckle your Kindle until he got his hard-earned HEA.

Finally—regretfully—I stepped back and gave him a grateful smile. "Thanks, Beau. I needed that."

One corner of his mouth twitched up, and then he jammed his hands into his pockets. "Anytime. Now, let's get you home."

6

BEAU

I squinted toward the targets, the bright sun making it admittedly hard to see. "Okay, now line up your sights. Good. All right, recruit, let's see what you got."

I stood back and analyzed the young future-Marine's posture as he held his gun, his shoulders not shaking in the slightest.

When he finished, I stepped up and patted him on the back. "Nice work. Now, reload and get ready to go again. I'm gonna hydrate."

"Yes, sir," he replied.

I walked over to my canteen, took a huge pull, then wiped my sleeve across my mouth. A drill instructor I didn't recognize came up and nodded at me. "Hey, did you say they weren't supposed to advance to table two unless they had perfect scores on table one?"

"Yeah, that's the word of the day."

He snorted. "Great. I don't see any of these guys hitting a perfect score for a while."

"Guess we should prepare for a long day then," I replied, more than a little bummed that I'd likely miss karaoke night.

Mickey's Pub in Bluffton hosted it every Thursday night, and even though it was home to some of the worst singing I'd ever heard, it was a good time when paired with the right company. Paul, Shelby, Chase, Zac, Layla ... and *Lyndi*, of course. Though I told myself she wasn't the reason I was excited to go. It was the others. It had to be.

Aria and Will were the only ones from our group who'd be skipping it, as they'd be home with their baby boy—who finally got a name right before they left the hospital. Oliver James Paxton. He was half a week old now, even though he wasn't technically due for another four. But they were doing well, thankfully.

The new DI quirked a brow as he looked me over. "Big plans or something?"

"Nah." I shook my head, laughing to myself. "I'm Beau, by the way. Beau Devereux."

He took the hand I held out to him and gave it a firm shake. "Logan Grant. This is my first cycle."

"Right on. Welcome to the jungle. Where'd you come from?"

Grant sighed heavily. "Hawaii."

"No kidding? K-Bay?"

"You been stationed there before?" he asked, crossing his arms over his chest.

"No, but I've got orders there in a few months."

I tried to look happy about it, too. Because I should be. I mean, getting orders to Hawaii was like a golden ticket for a guy like me. The number of weddings held there would surely knock this area out of the water, which was why I had to travel as part of the deal so I could have enough bookings. But having them all on the same little island? Gold.

Not only that, but it was Hawaii. I'd never surfed before, but I'd make the effort to learn while stationed there. Add in the general beauty of the place and the laid-back lifestyle that was sure to come with it, and I should be in like Flynn.

But instead, just the thought of moving that far away had my stomach clenching. Leaving my pops in his condition after being gone so long already ... not being a weekend's trip away ... it gutted me. And thinking of him only brought one more reason to mind.

Lyndi. But I brushed her and her gorgeous eyes and shy smile right out the way it came in.

Grant let his head fall back and sighed. "Man, I'd kill to go back. I was there for four years and loved it."

"I hear it's pretty great," I offered, reminding myself as much as I was telling him. "Bet it's been a rough transition from there to here."

"Worse for my wife than for me, honestly. She's having a hard time."

"Oh yeah? She's not a fan of mosquitos and mold?"

He chuckled. "We had plenty of both in Hawaii. But her sister is pretty much her only family, and she's still stationed there."

"She's a Marine?"

"Yeah, and married to one, too. A buddy of mine. We had a super tight group, lots of support for my girls ... and now she's got no one. Not even me most of the time because I'm stuck in the squad bay until I move up the ladder."

Drill instructors had their own mountains to climb, separate from the main one of rising in the ranks in the overall Marine Corps. At the beginning of drill instructor duty—you were an enforcer, what they called a kill hat.

A kill hat's whole purpose in life was to destroy and obliterate recruits if they messed up. Which they did, and often. Most kill hats talked like they'd smoked a pack a day their whole lives because screaming for eighteen hours a day did a number on their vocal cords. But beyond that, they also spent the most time with the recruits, and that meant the least amount of time at home with their families, if they had one.

When a kill hat moved up in the food chain, he'd become a J-hat. They were like the teachers, rather than the ones doling out punishment. Usually a lot nicer, too, if a Marine DI *could* be nice.

And finally, after spending time as a J-hat, they became seniors. Everything got a lot more chill for those guys, as they took on more of a father-figure role and spent the least amount of time with the recruits themselves.

Grant had a long road ahead of him until he made it to that last round, and by the sound of things, so did his wife. It was moments like these I was grateful to work at the range and not be an actual drill instructor. Not that I had a wife to worry about, but more because my gig was about teaching recruits how to use their weapons, not completely creating a new crop of Marines every single cycle.

Okay, yeah. There was some pressure attached to making sure these kids could shoot. Still, it was nothing like what the DIs went through. But they were incredibly important to the Marine Corps. They were the first introduction recruits had to what it meant to be a

Marine, so they were impressive, immaculate, and intimidating as all get-out.

I didn't know if I'd ever draw the short stick and get told to do three years as one, but if I did, at least I'd have firsthand experience after working alongside them while here at Parris Island. Whether or not that was a good thing, I wasn't sure.

It occurred to me that Grant had said *girls*, as in plural, and I cocked my head at him. "Wait, did you say *girls*? Does that mean you have a daughter?"

"Yeah, we have a three-year-old and another one on the way," Grant said, unable to keep the wide smile off his face. "What about you? You got a wife and kids?"

Even though it'd been about a decade since I'd gotten yelled at by a kill hat, it still freaked me out when they smiled. I had to remind myself that most of them were just normal dudes when they weren't playing their part, and I could definitely relate to that.

"Nope. It's just me. Living the dream."

Hopefully he didn't detect the massive amount of sarcasm that sat below the surface of my words. It wouldn't have been there a couple weeks ago, but thanks to my pops and the surprisingly sentimental heart I didn't know he had, I'd become a little less happy with my life as a single, unattached Marine.

"Hang on," Grant said, his entire expression

morphing into one of fury before I could even wrap my head around the change.

I watched as he tipped the brim of his giant Smokey Bear cover into a more menacing position, then stomped over to one of his recruits with clenched fists. He screamed into the side of the guy's face, spit flying from his mouth and disappearing on the recruit's sweaty skin.

Unfazed by this—as it was pretty much a regular occurrence working at the recruit depot, I took another sip of water then returned to the recruit I'd been working with before. I liked that I got to be the guy they dealt with who didn't have to lose their mind on them. Unless, of course, they did something unsafe with their weapons. In that case, I'd been known to blow my lid, too.

A couple hours later, another opportunity for a break rolled around, and I sat down on a bench next to Grant. We had to stay just out of sight from the recruits as they hydrated before starting another round of practice fire because they couldn't see their hardcore DI taking a break. It might ruin the illusion that he was an invincible robot whose only need in life was to slay them if they messed up during training.

"Anyway, so no wife and kids," Grant said, picking

up where we left off, "and you're headed to Hawaii after this."

"Yep."

"Man, I don't even remember what I used to do with all my free time before I met Tess. She already had Sadie, so once we got serious, we got serious fast. It's been dad life 24-7 since then. Until now, obviously."

"I don't have much free time, actually. The days are long here, and I've got a side gig that keeps me pretty busy."

"Oh, yeah? What do you do?"

"It's called Mr. Fake Date. Women use an app to book me to be their fake date to a wedding."

He leaned to the side so he could see me fully, one hand propped on his knee. "For real?"

"Yep."

"So you get paid to go to weddings?"

"Sure do."

"That's cool. And maybe a little crazy. I don't think I'd want to do that much socializing with a girl's family. Sounds stressful to always be sized-up like that."

"Eh, it's not really like that, though. It's not really *me* they're judging, it's kind of like ... the character I'm playing."

He made an impressed noise and nodded. "Yeah,

okay. I can see that. But why can't they go to the wedding alone? What's with the need to pay someone?"

I bit back a sigh. It was always one of the first questions people asked when I told them about my job as Mr. Fake Date. By now, I had a practiced speech ready to go, listing all the potential reasons someone might hire me rather than finding their own date or going alone.

When I finished, he rubbed a hand along his perfectly shaved jaw. "Huh. You learn something new every day."

"Hey, you know what they say about the best ideas. They're the ones that seem so simple yet nobody's thought of them. It's a great way to make some extra money, and I'm filling a void in the market."

"The dating market or the gigolo market?" he joked, laughing at my feigned scowl. "So what happens if you fall for one of these dates? You gonna quit doing it?"

My face scrunched into an actual frown. "What?"

"I don't know. Seems to me like it would be a great way to vet a woman."

"How do you figure?"

"It's like you're getting a lot of the weird stuff out of the way in advance," he explained in that gravelly voice of his. "Weddings can bring out the best and worst in people, so at least you'd be able to see how she handles it. Almost like you're taking her—and her *family*—for a test drive before committing."

I laughed heartily, shaking my head. "Bro."

"Seriously. If they're all nuts and you want nothing to do with them, no harm, no foul. Then again, I guess if I would have met my in-laws before I fell for Tess, I might not have gone there. So maybe ignore everything I'm saying."

I smirked, taking a drink from my canteen. "I'll do that. Besides, this is a business. It's not about catching feelings. That's probably the worst thing I could do."

I swallowed hard then, hating how *yet again* Lyndi's face popped into my mind.

"Yeah, I mean, if this side gig is something you think you wanna do forever, sure. But if you catch feelings and you're already technically dating, why not make it a thing and hang up the side gig if it works out?"

I glowered at the dirt under my boots. Now he sounded like my old man. And it was a far cry from the normal reactions I got from fellow Marines when they found out about my business. Sure, there were the gigolo jokes. But this was the first time anyone had ever suggested that it was a good way to enter into a relationship after *test-driving* a woman and her family.

"I don't know," I said, pushing air through my pursed

lips. "It's not really something I've ever thought about. Hanging it up, that is."

I didn't add the *until recently* that flitted through my mind.

"Yeah, well, like I said. Probably better to ignore everything I'm saying. Anyway, gotta get back out there and stomp some maggots."

I laughed as I watched him go, marveling at the way the casual set of his shoulders went rigid as he turned the corner. Though, really, what I did when I arrived at a wedding wasn't much different. Minus the screaming, of course.

Thanks to Grant and the other DIs scaring the pants off the recruits during table one, my day wound up being a lot shorter than I thought it would be. I made it to karaoke only an hour late, and the sounds of people laughing, glasses clinking, and terrible singing filled my ears the second I walked into Mickey's Pub.

I nodded at Mickey as he waved at me, then my eyes traveled around the bar, scanning the faces in the crowd for my friends. When I spotted them seated around a large table, I was glad to find Chase Mitchell seated with them. That way it wasn't Paul and Shelby with Zac and

Layla, leaving Lyndi and I to automatically feel like the fifth and sixth wheels.

We definitely weren't the third *couple* and having Chase there as a buffer would allow me to remember that.

So far this week, I'd done a decent job not thinking about Lyndi and the way my pops had spurred these new feelings I had no right to have. Except for today, of course, but that was probably just because I knew I'd see her tonight.

I didn't think about the hug she'd surprised me with as we stood outside the hospital.

I didn't think about the way she seemed to feel like she was made to sit beside me as I drove her home, along for the ride wherever I went.

And I definitely didn't think about the timid yet completely breathtaking smile she'd given me when she thanked me for seeing her home. It'd made my stomach flip in a totally new and uncomfortable way, and I'd barely managed to choke out a reply before she hurried into her bungalow.

But now, meeting her eyes as I took a seat at the table had it all flooding right back. She looked at me with that same mix of shyness and gratitude, and it had me searching for words as if I weren't a master at saying the right thing as Mr. Fake Date.

"We just ordered a bucket of beers," Paul told me, saving me from having to address her without looking like a bumbling fool.

"Great," I replied. "How's everybody doing?"

They all answered with the usual mix of pleasantries, Layla adding that Aria and Oliver were doing well, too. She handed me her phone to show me a photo of the little guy, and I took it with a wide grin.

He was tiny, no doubt. But also looked so peaceful and happy in his mother's arms that you'd have no idea he'd had such a scary birthday if you weren't there.

"He's adorable," I said, smiling stiffly and handing it back.

Since when did I use words like adorable? *I blame Lyndi.*

"He really is," Layla agreed as she put her phone away. "I think Aria's finally convinced she didn't put herself into labor with all that work. The doctors told her she didn't do anything wrong because she'd been working that hard her whole pregnancy, but she felt really guilty at first."

Paul shook his head. "Wait, she did? Man, now I feel like a jerk."

"Why?" I asked.

"Because I may have teased my little sis about that

very thing if she didn't chill out," he replied, his lips tugging up on one side.

"I'm pretty sure we all did that," Shelby told him as she rubbed his back. "But seriously, the doctors said she was fit and healthy, so being on her feet so much wouldn't have been enough to cause it. Sometimes babies are just ready. It was scary at the time, but everyone's okay now."

I looked at Lyndi then, instantly spotting the shadow of fear I knew I'd find there. I waited until she met my gaze, then gave her a small, encouraging smile. As freaked out as I'd been to be at the hospital that day for my own reasons, I'd hated to see how worried Lyndi was for her friend. I wanted to remind her that everything was fine, just like I'd told her it would be.

Her eyes brightened slightly, the residual fear slipping away. Then she replied with a more relaxed smile of her own, and it made me sit up taller, glad to have helped.

"How was your day, Beau?" Shelby asked, pulling me out of the silent conversation with her friend.

I ran my hand over the back of my neck. "It was long but could have been worse. I met a new DI. He's a good kill hat already, despite being such a nice dude when he's not in front of the recruits."

Zac chuckled. "Those are my favorite DIs. The ones

who are chill in real life, but then they're so good at being scary, it's almost scary."

"Oh, that was definitely him," I said with a laugh. "He was cool. We talked a bit between sets, and he told me he just came from the base in Hawaii."

Chase perked up at this. "Wait, who is it? Maybe I know him."

"What, just because you're from Hawaii, you think you know everyone who's ever lived there?" Paul joked, then turned to me. "But hey, I might actually know him. I was stationed there, too."

"Ha, wouldn't be surprised," Chase replied with a laugh. "If there's one thing I've learned since becoming a Marine, it's that the only thing smaller than Oahu is the Marine Corps."

"Aren't there several islands in that chain that are smaller than Oahu?" Layla teased him, ducking when he picked up Shelby's straw wrapper and chucked it at her.

"His name is Logan Grant," I told them, causing Paul's mouth to fall open. "No way. You really know him?"

"Yes, and I totally forgot he was coming out here. My buddy from recruiting duty told me to invite them to hang with us once in a while since they didn't know anyone out here."

"Told you, small world," Chase said, holding up a finger and tapping it to his brow line.

I turned to Chase, eyes wide. "Okay, yeah, the Marine Corps is definitely smaller than Oahu."

"It gets worse," he snickered. "The guy he's talking about, Wilson, was my recruiter. And he's married to Grant's sister-in-law."

"Yeah, he mentioned something about his sister-in-law being a Marine and also married to one. You don't know Grant, though?" I asked, all the connections making my head spin.

Chase shook his head. "Nah, I might have met him since Wilson's friends were always hanging around while I was there, but I don't remember."

"Well, you'll meet him soon enough," Paul said. "Grant's gotta stay at the depot a lot since he's still a kill hat, but I need to start inviting his wife around so she can be friends with Shelby."

Shelby rolled her eyes with a laugh. "I don't mind being her friend since I'm sure it's hard being away from her family, but don't make her feel obligated, Paul."

"No one who knows you would feel obligated to be your friend," he said, looking at her with so much love in his eyes that it made me a little queasy. "I would know, I was your friend for *years*. Too long, in fact."

She made a little enamored noise and they started to

kiss, so I looked away, desperate for something—anything—else to focus on. But then my eyes found Lyndi's again. Okay, not that either.

"I'm gonna go hit the head," I said, hopping up. I didn't really have to go to the bathroom, but apparently Chase being there wasn't making me feel any better about hanging around these couples in my disturbingly *mopey* state.

Again, I sent a half-hearted angry thought toward my old man. But it wasn't his fault he was dying and wanted to see me happy. It was probably mine for not being strong enough to risk a shot at happiness in the first place. Not that I wanted to start now, no matter what I'd promised him.

I went into the bathroom and tried to get my head on straight—or else I should leave, because this wouldn't turn out to be a very fun night if I didn't. When I came out and ran into Lyndi in the hallway—literally smacked right into her—the feel of her soft arms under my hands as I kept her from falling brought me right back to thoughts I didn't want to have.

Thoughts about not letting go of her arms but bringing her close and touching my lips to hers. Thoughts about what that would feel like if I did.

7

LYNDI

"What, are you following me?" Beau asked after a second, his smooth voice a total contrast to the flustered look in his eyes as he stared down at me.

"No." I looked at one of his hands as he still held the tops of my arms, quirking a brow at him. "Mind letting go?"

He opened his hands and I stumbled back, not realizing he'd been holding me up at an angle until my heels hit the floor.

Beau winced as I steadied myself. "Sorry."

"It's fine."

"So, if you weren't following me, what are you doing back here?"

I scanned the long, dark hallway. Then I pointed to

the sign depicting an outline of a girl in a triangular dress. "Bathroom."

"Right, right." He scratched the side of his head. "I'll ... uh, see you back at the table, then."

Something in my face must have interested him though, because he started to step away, then stopped, stepping backwards until he was in front of me again.

"What?" I asked with a laugh.

"What was that face? You don't want to go back to the table?"

Man, had Beau always been this freaking observant? Giving in, I sighed. "I just needed a minute."

"Everything okay?"

The notable difference between the noise level here and the one inside the main room of the bar was not only soothing the loudness *inside* my mind, but it also allowed me to clearly hear the concern in his tone.

Why was he suddenly so concerned about my well-being? First taking me home from the hospital when he could tell I was having a rough time, and now *this*?

"Layla and Shelby are talking to a teacher from their school," I said, hoping it was enough.

Sadly, it only seemed to pique his interest even more. "And you don't like her?"

"I don't really know her."

"Then what's the problem?"

"I don't really know her," I said again, chuckling at his confused expression. Apparently, he didn't get it. "I'm not good with people."

At this, Beau stood straighter and crossed his arms over his broad chest. He looked at me with almost humor swimming in his dark eyes, but his lips were set in a determined frown, like he was low-key disappointed in me.

"There you go again," he said, finally.

"What?"

He shrugged, eyes holding mine. "Saying you're not good at something you *are* good at. Not good at talking, not good with people. These things simply aren't true."

"Beau, come on." I brought my arms up and crossed them, holding myself together while also trying to appear tough. "You barely know me. How could you possibly know those things aren't true?"

"I know enough. And I've seen you. I've seen you talk with your friends—as long as you don't have a book on you, of course."

"I always have a book on me," I mumbled under my breath, not looking at him.

He dipped his head so he could catch my gaze. "Tell me you didn't bring a book to karaoke night."

"I didn't bring a book to karaoke night," I said in a flat tone.

"Very convincing. Now, tell me the truth."

With a sigh, I lifted the wrist that held the strap of my clutch and brought it between us, unzipping it to reveal my Kindle tucked safely inside along with my ID, a couple cards, and some cash. It only had room for the essentials, after all.

Beau's eyes crinkled gorgeously around the edges as he let out a low laugh, then he shook his head and looked at the ceiling. "You didn't bring a *book* to karaoke night, you stuffed a library in your wallet."

"Yeah, well, if you were as observant as you think you are, you wouldn't be so surprised," I said with a lifted chin.

This only made him laugh again, though. "This is my shocked face. Anyway, like I was saying, I've seen you talk to people. And the more I talk to you, the less convinced I am that you're bad at it. And I've seen you be good with people, too. So why do you keep saying this stuff?"

Good question. It wasn't usually something I led with. But for whatever reason, I felt comfortable enough with Beau to admit it.

"Maybe you don't know what you're seeing." *Or*

maybe it doesn't feel all that good to me. Maybe it feels like I can't say anything without overthinking it first, and by the time I figure out the right thing to say, the conversation had already moved on.

Or maybe it felt like after talking a lot I had to go hide somewhere quiet, because talking and laughing drained me in a way it didn't drain my sister. She seemed to be energized by interaction. She sought it out after a long day so she could refuel. But me? I sought out solitude most of the time. Unless you counted the cast of characters in whatever book I was reading.

Beau stepped forward, his jaw clenching slightly as he peered down at me through his thick lashes. "Lyndi, you're not listening to me. When I say I've seen you, I'm saying I *see* you. You have a habit of not giving yourself enough credit."

I gulped, my mind growing loud again despite the quiet around us. It wasn't noise that wreaked havoc on me now. It was the combination of his nearness, the scent of his cologne—spicy yet somehow sweet—and the way he looked down at me in a way that made me feel like he really *could* see me.

"Okay, well, I guess I didn't realize you paid this much attention," I said, working to keep my voice even.

He stepped back, leaning against the brick wall on

one side of the hallway. "Neither did I, I guess. But maybe it's because of my job."

"As a Marine?"

"Um, yeah. I'm pretty sharp on the range. Gotta keep an eye out for squirrely recruits holding loaded guns for the first time. But I meant my other job."

"As Mr. Fake Date?"

He pursed his lips. "Yeah. I don't know. I have to be pretty good at reading the room."

"Why?"

"Because it's up to me to play my part. I figure out how I'm supposed to act based on what my clients want from me, so I guess I've gotten pretty good at reading people so I know if I'm hitting the mark."

Slowly, I faced him with my back against the opposite wall. "Sounds a little manipulative."

"Fair. But it's the job."

I considered this for a moment. Beau could really see me because he got paid to see his clients. He got paid to see their wants and needs, and then attend to them. So the fact that he seemed so attentive with me was probably a reflex. He'd practically said it himself. No use letting my tummy get all fluttery over a guy who probably just saw me as another puzzle to solve.

Though, one question remained, and I considered

not asking it. But as we'd already established, I had a thing for puzzles, too. "When you're not acting a certain way, who are you?"

One corner of his mouth quirked up automatically, and it felt like an eternity before he answered. "I don't know."

A loud crash sounded from the bar area, making me jump. The resulting laughter and cheering told me someone had fallen off the karaoke stage and had me ready to squirm out of my skin.

Okay, we get it, someone's clumsy. Shut up about it, already.

When I met Beau's eyes again, he was no longer leaning against the wall, but standing straight with one hand in the air between us. He let it fall and studied me for a second, then jerked his head toward the patio door. "Hey, do you wanna sit outside for a while? It's ... quieter."

Wow. Yeah, he saw me, all right. He saw more than most. But unless it was all part of his act, he also seemed to care more than most, too. And I really *could* use a break from all the noise—despite the turmoil Beau himself caused.

Though, for better or worse, I was starting to think I kinda liked *this* particular kind of turmoil. I nodded once. "Sure."

"That is, of course, unless you really did need to use the restroom."

"No, I didn't."

He smiled a little, then led me to the patio door, opening it and holding it wide while I passed through. The cool evening air immediately relieved some of the pressure in my head and chest, and I closed my eyes to take a deep, cleansing breath.

There were only a couple people out here, but they were huddled together at the far end of the patio. Twinkle lights zigzagged over our heads, and a country song played softly in the background. *This* was much more my speed.

But was it his?

"You sure you don't want to be in there doing karaoke with everyone?" I asked as we took a seat at one of the wrought iron tables.

Beau let out a breezy laugh. "Uh, no. Zac and Layla have like five songs on the list by now, and I swear I can't handle hearing him do another terrible rendition of 'Don't Go Breaking My Heart' tonight."

"I love watching people sing. I'd never do it myself, but it's fun watching other people. For a while, anyway."

A bittersweet smile touched his lips as he stared out at the dark parking lot beyond the short patio wall. "My dad's a big karaoke fan."

"Oh, yeah?"

"Yeah, that's actually how he and my mom met."

I blinked. "Wait, really?"

"You ever seen *Top Gun*?"

"Yes," I said with an eyeroll. Who hadn't?

"You know how good ol' Maverick has everyone sing 'You've Lost That Lovin' Feelin'? Well, Pops was in the navy back in the day, and not even kidding, he and his buddies re-created that scene so he could hit on my mom."

Jaw dropping, I gaped at him. "Stop it."

"I swear."

"How did it go? Did he crash and burn?"

Beau's eyes sparkled with laughter as he held out his hands. "I'm here, aren't I?"

A laugh tore out of me before I had time to stifle it. "That's *amazing*. Your dad sounds hilarious."

"Oh, yeah. He's a real comedian."

"Where do they live? Your parents?"

He picked an invisible piece of lint off his jeans, then ran his large hand over his thigh. "Uh, my dad lives in New Orleans."

"And your mom?" I asked it so quickly I hadn't had time to read his expression first. When he didn't answer and looked toward the parking lot again, my heart cracked. "I'm so sorry. Is that why you didn't want to spend much time in the hospital?"

His gaze returned to me with a surprised twitch of his mouth. "Noticed that, huh?"

"I guess I'm pretty observant, too. Must be because of my job," I said, stealing his words from earlier.

"Yeah, I'm not a big fan of hospitals. In my experience, people go in, but they don't always come out."

I didn't know what to say, but I had to say something, so I racked my brain for whatever would be the most normal response. "I'm really sorry about your mom, Beau."

He squinted into the night again. "Thank you."

Sadness as deep as the ocean welled up in my chest, feeling way too big for the moment. Desperate to return the mood to the lightness it held before, I sat straighter in my chair and pasted a smile on my face. "The *Top Gun* thing is epic though. Perfect grand gesture."

"Grand gesture?"

"Yeah, you'll find them in every romance novel. Right after the black moment."

He relaxed, leaning forward too. "Okay, I'll bite. Break that all down for me."

"The black moment is the inevitable breakup, and the grand gesture is the big thing the hero—*or heroine*—

does after they realize they love the other person and can't live without them."

"Well, in my parents' case, the *Top Gun* thing was how they met. Is there a fancy name for that?"

"Meet-cute," I supplied with a smile.

"Huh. I assume two people have to meet in some sort of cute way or they're not meant to be, then. Right?"

"Well, in books, if it's just a random, boring thing, it's kind of a clue to the reader that the other person isn't significant. Otherwise, their meeting would have made an impact on them. So, I guess it doesn't have to be *cute* as long as it's ..." I trailed off, realizing he was staring at me with his lips pulled into a thin smile. "Wait, why are you looking at me like that?"

"Like what? I'm just listening."

"No, you're not. You're thinking something."

"I'm not allowed to think something?" Whether or not he'd meant it as a rhetorical question, I didn't know. But when I didn't answer, he sighed. "Fine. I was thinking that I love how passionate you are when you talk about books and how they work. You should have some kind of book review channel on YouTube or something."

I snorted. "Um, no. I'm not good at being in front of the camera. That's Layla's area. I'm better behind it."

Beau dipped his chin and gave me a pointed look.

"Do I really need to tell you not to talk like that? We already went over this."

"Well," I started, then paused to clear my throat as the playful dominance in his tone made my belly flip, "since you have no way of knowing what I'm like in front of the camera because I rarely allow it to happen, you won't win this time."

He held his hands up, leaning back in his chair. "Valid point. I'll hold out."

"For what?"

"For Layla's wedding this weekend."

I frowned. "What?"

"You're the maid of honor, Lyndi. You'll be in front of the camera plenty. And when the wedding video that cost Zac—and I quote, 'almost as much as Grayson's school supplies'—comes back, I'll prove it to you."

Again, more reactions deep in my belly. I had to hand it to him, the guy had a way with words that would make any romance reader call him her newest book boyfriend. It was working like a charm on me, that was for sure. Too bad it was likely all part of his ever-important act.

But since that was probably all it was, I didn't have a problem telling him I was onto him. "You know, for a guy who doesn't date for *real*, you sure say all the swoony things my book boyfriends say."

"Book boyfriends, huh?"

"Yep."

The chuckle he'd tossed out a second ago faded into the night air, and he leaned forward again, genuine curiosity on his smooth features. "What if I told you that you were playing a losing game with all that?"

"With what?"

"The book boyfriend thing. No man can actually be like the fictional guys you're comparing them to. They have problems, they say the wrong thing, and they mess stuff up. The perfect guy is a fantasy. And I would know, because I may not date for *real*, but I get paid to *be* the fantasy."

All the fluttering from before melted into a hard stone, and I swallowed, shaking my head. Okay, enough torture for one evening.

Yeah, sure, I fell in love with the unattainable men within the pages of my books, but sitting here, letting Beau make me swoon only to remind me it wasn't real, was nowhere *near* the same thing.

"Well, I guess we'd better get in there," I said, standing. "I just remembered I ordered some food right before I left, so I bet it's there by now."

Beau nodded, then got up and wordlessly led me back into the pub. And he didn't say anything else as we walked back to the table to rejoin our friends, so by the time we were seated, all the sparks between us had faded away.

"Where were you guys?" Layla asked me as I slid back further into my seat.

"Out back, talking."

"About what?"

I shrugged. "Not much. Just the wedding and stuff."

"Oh, shoot. That reminds me." She turned to Beau and tapped the table in front of her. "Beau, do you already have a date lined up for my wedding?"

"A date or a client?"

"Is there a difference?" she asked with a chuckle.

"Yes," I heard myself saying, shocking the heck out of him. And myself. And my sister, too, judging by her expression.

Beau chuckled. "Yes. There's a difference. But I haven't lined up either one. Why do you ask?"

"I have a cousin who might want to hire you. I gave her your info, I hope that's okay."

My throat felt like sandpaper as I swallowed, and I looked down at my hands. There was no way I wanted to watch as my sister arranged a fake date for Beau. Maybe I shouldn't have been so convincing last time I told her I wasn't interested in him.

Though, that was dumb. I *shouldn't* be interested in him. Not only was he leaving soon, but he was also doing a number on my emotions lately. That wasn't something I should want, right?

No, I should be running in the other direction.

And yet when he cleared his throat and gave her a noncommittal, "Uh, yeah. Sure. I'll keep an eye out," every cell in my body hoped whichever cousin it was would lose his number.

8

BEAU

The day of Zac and Layla's wedding, I kept checking my phone in case Layla's cousin decided to request my services under the *day-of* category. It had a huge surcharge, so even though normally I would have been excited and hope she'd do it, not today.

Today, I needed my notifications to be completely silent. I couldn't afford to turn down a job with such a high payout, but I really didn't want to have a client for this particular wedding.

I finally let myself breathe when it was showtime and there still hadn't been a new request. No way would she wait until *minutes* before the ceremony to book her fake date. Hours, sure. It happened. But not minutes.

"You ready?" Paul asked Zac, slapping him on the

shoulder hard enough to make the gold medals of his uniform clink together.

"I've been ready for a long time," Zac replied.

The rest of us groaned at his cheesiness, and I jerked my chin toward the door. "Let's get this show on the road, then."

We filed out of the groomsmen's dressing suite at Starlight Manor, and as we made our way to our positions in front of the guests, I couldn't help but stare at the table where I'd sat when I talked to my dad last weekend.

The pain from that day came crashing back in a rush, causing all the air to leave my lungs in a quiet burst. It'd been too much. *He'd* been too much. How could a father really get on the phone with his son, from hundreds of miles away, and say stuff like that?

It killed me that I'd been stationed so far from home for the last ten years. Maybe things would have been different if I'd stayed. When I joined the Marines, I'd been eighteen and eager to see the world. Eager to run from the fact that I'd lost my mom not long after losing my brother, and I wanted to skip out of the town where everybody knew it. They'd looked at me with such sadness in their eyes, and I was just ... over it.

Pops had given me his blessing with a smile and a simple "Don't be a stranger," and then sent me on my way. But once he'd gotten sick last year, I wished more than anything he would have kept me out of the military. Maybe I'd have ended up at the same factory he'd worked at, and I would have had a completely different life.

Maybe not better but different. Closer with him. Less feelings of guilt, maybe?

"Hello, Mr. Devereux," Ms. Hattie said as she ambled up to her place as the wedding's officiant. Which made sense since she'd had a hand in the matchmaking of this couple. *Add another notch to your belt, Ms. Hattie.*

"Hi, Ms. Hattie. How are you?"

"I'm well, thank you. You look dashing this afternoon."

I rubbed a hand over the gold buttons down the center of my dress blues. "Thank you, ma'am."

She turned her Cheshire cat smile toward Paul and greeted him, too, then winked at the groom. It was a bummer Will had to miss this, but he'd opted to stay with Aria and little Oliver since they'd just brought him home from the hospital a week ago.

"Who are you escorting this evening?" Ms. Hattie asked me with a wink.

"No one. I'm off duty tonight."

"Oh, how fun. Well, enjoy yourself. My son is a Marine, too, you know. Maybe you can all spend some time with him tonight since he doesn't have any friends here."

Ah, the infamous target of Lyndi's grandma's matchmaking. Great. I bet Ms. Hattie was in cahoots with her, and that meant Lyndi was in for it. I'd never seen Ms. Hattie strike out when she zeroed in on two people she knew were meant to be together.

"Who's your son?" I asked, looking into the crowd of guests in the white chairs before us.

I spotted him right before Ms. Hattie whispered that he was wearing a navy-blue suit. Yep, he sure was. And it was a pretty freaking great suit, unfortunately.

Not only that, but the dude didn't have a big nose, like I'd imagined when I'd talked to Lyndi about him. In fact, he had a great nose. In a totally objective way, the guy was handsome.

And that really sucked for me, since I'd hoped he wouldn't be. Then again, I still had hope that the guy was a jerk. If so, he could be as handsome as a movie star, but I'd never let him get anywhere near Lyndi. And if he didn't back off, then I could *break* his pretty nose.

"Yeah, we'll hang with him," Paul said when I remained silent, nodding at the guy. "He's in town from Oki, right?"

While Paul chatted with Ms. Hattie, I kept sizing him up. He looked like he could tell his meddling mother was up here trying to make him some friends, and I laughed a little to myself, relaxing a bit. It wasn't his fault his mom was a bulldozer. Maybe he didn't even *want* to be with Lyndi.

Though, I wasn't sure what his reason would be for not being interested.

But still.

And hey, at least I wasn't the only fully grown man on the planet whose parent tried to force into a relationship. And my pops might have my head a total mess right now, but it could always be worse. He wasn't nearly as bad as Ms. Hattie.

The music that signaled the start of the ceremony broke me from my thoughts, and I looked up to find Shelby coming down the aisle in a red dress with a bouquet of red roses.

I flicked my eyes to Ms. Hattie, seeing a gleam in her eye as she looked at them. Yep. The only thing Ms. Hattie loved more than meddling in people's love lives was floral arrangements.

When I turned back toward the guests, my breath caught in my throat. Lyndi. There was Lyndi, walking toward me in the very same dress Shelby had on. But on her ... wow. I couldn't even think. I couldn't feel my dang toes.

She was the most beautiful thing I'd ever seen,

which was crazy, because I'd seen her in bridesmaid's dresses before. This wasn't new. But this was the first time I'd been standing up here next to the groom, and at this angle, it just felt … different.

Some sappy part of me couldn't help but imagine her walking down that aisle for a *different* reason. In a *different* dress.

But then I caught sight of Ms. Hattie sticking out a finger to point Lyndi out to her son, and the resulting smile on his face made my stomach turn. *Oh, brother.* So much for him not being interested in her.

Lyndi had been looking down at her flowers with a slight blush coloring her cheeks, but as she neared the aisle, her eyes found mine. Heat spread through me like a wildfire, and I gulped, tugging at the suddenly way-too-tight collar of my blues.

She slipped over to her place on the other side of the aisle, and the spell was broken. And then I spent the entire ceremony doing my best not to look at her. The trees, the ground, shoot—the back of Zac's head. I tried to look anywhere but at her.

I failed miserably, of course.

And judging from the way her eyes dashed away from me every time, she was having the same problem.

When the ceremony was over and the bridal party was huddled off on the side of the house to take photos, I meandered over to Lyndi and leaned over, speaking low in her ear. "Uh-oh. Looks like I get to see you in front of the camera sooner than I thought."

"Hush."

I chuckled. "Don't be so nervous. You look amazing."

My eyes slid over her petite form in that apple-red dress, and when I looked up to meet her eyes again, I found them slightly narrowed. But then her lips twitched into a small smile that made my pulse jump. "Thanks."

"You're welcome."

"Okay, she wants to do the bridesmaids first," Layla said, gliding up to us in her pristine white dress. "You ready, Lyn?"

"As I'll ever be," she replied, tossing me one more glare as she went, like she was daring me to encourage her again.

I'd pump her up all day if I needed to. The woman deserved it. Besides, it was kind of part of my charm as Mr. Fake Date. Compliments were my specialty, and Lyndi looking the way she did in that dress made it easier than most.

In fact, the more time I spent with her, the more I wanted to compliment her. She seemed completely oblivious to her own appeal. Not in an annoying or self-deprecating way, but in a way that suggested she genuinely had a hard time seeing that the things that made her feel so strange were the same things I found so alluring.

It wasn't simply that she was beautiful. She was, but that wasn't it. It was the little things. Like how she set alarms on her watch so she'd remember all the different things she wanted to photograph during a wedding.

It suggested an attention to detail that was incredibly attractive to me for some reason, but it also showed that she had a tendency to get lost in the moment if she didn't have reminders, and I liked that, too. I'd be down to get lost in the moment with her sometime.

I also enjoyed how she could get so lost in a book that you'd need a forklift to bring her out of it. Bombs could be going off around her and if she was in the zone, she wouldn't look up. It was cute. It made me laugh. Even before I realized how much I liked what I was looking at.

But now, as I stood here watching her pose for photos with her girls with that shy smile and wariness in her eyes, I wanted nothing more than to walk right up to her and remind her to relax.

And that was when it hit me. I was in big trouble. I never looked at women the way I was looking at her now. I paid attention to the little things out of obligation, not out of yearning.

This woman didn't simply light me up, she made me burn. I burned *for* her, but I also burned because I couldn't have her. And somehow at the exact same time, I burned because I couldn't stay away, either.

Layla leaned over to Lyndi and whispered something in her ear, then turned back to the camera and smiled widely. Just in time for the shot, a blinding smile broke out over Lyndi's face.

Whatever Layla told her was surely in an effort to create that smile. Over the last year, I'd noticed Layla always brought out this level of comfort in Lyndi that no one else could, and it was fun to watch. Lyndi would be quietly socializing, looking like she'd rather be anywhere else—like she'd settled for sitting in a chair with her nose in a book, offering witty remarks but not much else—then her sister would show up, and a relaxed, confident, energetic side would emerge. I was glad to see that if I couldn't go up there and help her in some way—since, obviously, why would I?—at least she had her sister to do it.

After we finished taking photos, the bridal party was released to join what was left of the cocktail hour so Layla and Zac could get their photos taken alone. I walked in the grass beside Lyndi as we headed for the large white tent.

"It's weird not to be the one taking their photos," she said, sighing as she watched her sister and Zac walk over to the pond.

"I'm surprised you didn't tell Layla you wanted to do it instead."

"I tried. She wasn't having it. She said I'd taken a million special photos of her over the years, and today she wanted me to have fun."

I shook my head with an exaggerated scowl. "The nerve."

"I know, right. You really *do* see me."

Meeting her eyes then, I swallowed. "I think I do, yeah."

"Oh, there you are, Lyndi," Ms. Hattie said, breaking the moment as she walked up with her son on her arm. "You remember Brett, right?"

"I do, yes. It's good to see you."

I lifted a brow as he smiled at her, pointing between them. "You two know each other already?"

"Small town," Lyndi said with a shrug.

"We practically grew up together," Brett explained.

Oh, peachy.

"Hey, man. I'm Brett," he said to me, sticking out his hand.

I shook it firmly—yes, *that* firmly—and gave him a tight smile. "Beau. Nice to meet you. Your mom said you're a Marine, too?"

"Guilty as charged. Gotta love moms. They always lead with the Marine thing, you know?"

His comment was simple and there was nothing wrong with it, but I couldn't help but think of my own mom. The truth was, she hadn't lived long enough to see me as a Marine. But if she had, she'd probably have been the same way. I brushed off the uneasiness as quickly as it had come, but then when I looked down to find Lyndi staring at me with a massive amount of concern in her eyes, a lump formed in my throat.

Shaking my head, I turned back to Brett. "Right. So, where are you stationed?"

I already knew the answer, but it was the natural question when Marines ran into each other in social settings. I didn't want to highlight the fact that we were standing in the middle of Ms. Hattie's matchmaking attempt by letting him know we'd been talking about him.

"Okinawa. I'm here for a month since I don't get to come back that often."

"Oh, wow. That's great," Lyndi said.

Ms. Hattie reached out and tapped her arm. "Hey,

Lyndi, Brett will still be in town for your cousin Clara's wedding. Do you have a date yet for that?"

"Actually, she does," I said before I even knew I'd opened my mouth. Then, to make matters worse, I draped an arm around Lyndi's shoulders and squeezed her tightly against my side.

Ms. Hattie gasped, looking between us with wide eyes. "No way. Lyndi, did you hire him?"

Brett frowned. "Wait, *hire?* Am I missing something?"

"Beau has a business where women pay him to be their dates," Ms. Hattie explained.

"To weddings," Lyndi blurted. "Just as their wedding dates. Strictly weddings."

"Right," Ms. Hattie said. "So, did you hire him, Lyndi?"

"I—"

"No, she didn't hire me. We're going together *off the books*," I said, internally groaning at the way my mouth kept spitting stuff out before I could stop it.

"Off the books? As in, you two are a couple now?"

I patted Lyndi's arm as I answered Ms. Hattie. "Yep. We're a couple. Isn't that right, sweetheart?"

"Right," Lyndi said, managing a smile.

Ms. Hattie's eyes narrowed slightly as she looked between us. "Uh-huh. Well, isn't that *lovely?* Sorry,

Brett. I suppose I was wrong about Lyndi being single."

"Suppose so," Brett said, looking annoyingly disappointed about it. "Shame."

"Excuse us. Nice to meet you, Bruce."

"Brett," Ms. Hattie corrected me, but her words landed on my back as I'd already spun Lyndi around and guided her to a safe space to chat.

As soon as we made it inside the main house, I steered Lyndi off to the side and out of sight. I had a feeling I had some explaining to do, and I didn't want an audience.

"Beau, what the heck was that?" She pulled her hand out of mine, using it to swat me on the arm.

"Ow," I said as I paced away from her, hand on my forehead. "I don't know."

"You don't *know?* You just told the biggest gossip in this entire town that we were dating."

"Yeah, I did."

"Why?"

I stopped pacing and looked over at her, hoping my face looked as apologetic as I intended it to. "Would you believe me if I said it seemed like a good idea at the time?"

"Uh, whether I believe you or not, it wasn't a good idea."

"Why not? You said it yourself, you don't want to be with someone who's leaving Bluffton."

"Okay, but how—"

"So, now you don't have to deal with Ms. Hattie and your grandmother trying to set you up with him."

She thought about it for a second, then she shook her head. "I get that, but now I'm going to have to deal with them constantly asking me about my *boyfriend*, and we're just pretending."

"Will you, though? Because in my experience, people don't care after the couple is paired up. They move on to the next single person."

"What? That's crazy …" She trailed off, then her eyes lit up. "Oh my gosh, it's like in books."

I couldn't help the laugh that escaped me. "Of course it is."

"Stop it, I'm serious. It's like how you read a series and each book features a different couple. Yeah, sure, there's like an epilogue that shows they're happy in the future, but sometimes readers are ready to move on to the next couple. If they see the other couples in the background, cool, but they aren't the focus anymore."

I shrugged. "Exactly. So, we'll play our parts. We'll exist in the background, and then we'll fade away when I leave. You can blame the breakup on me leaving and you wanting to stay, actually. So it's good timing."

"Or, we can say we're still together even after you leave, just in a long-distance relationship. That way they'll keep thinking I'm taken and won't try to set me up again as soon as you leave."

"Fine with me. Whatever you need to tell them."

She nodded. "Good. Plus, I don't love the way that first option makes me look."

At this, I angled my head and looked down at her with a smirk.

"What? I'm just saying. I wouldn't like it if the heroine broke up with the guy she loved because his job relocated him and she didn't want to go with. Especially if he were in the military. It seems unsupportive."

"Right ..."

"What? Why are you making that face?"

I relaxed my expression and chuckled. "Because you wouldn't like it in a *heroine*, but you'll do it in your own life."

"Beau, come on. Fiction *imitates* real life, but it's not real. This isn't the same thing."

I took a step toward her. "Oh, yeah? How is it not?"

"Well, for one thing, we're not in love."

She had me there. "True."

"And for another, even if this were a work of fiction, I'm not the heroine."

"You're not the heroine because we're not in love? Or

because I'm not the hero?" I asked, taking another step. "Does that mean you would leave town if it was for the right guy?"

"No, ugh." She backed away, shaking out her arms. "Trust me, if there was a right guy …"

She'd spoken so low I couldn't be sure I'd heard her correctly. Surely, she hadn't said what I thought she said. Right?

I moved into her line of sight, my heart racing. "Sorry, what was that?"

"Nothing. What I'm saying is, I'm not the heroine in this story with *you* or *any* story."

"Then what are you?"

"I'm the … sister. Friend. *Cousin*, for crying out loud."

I straightened, pulling my lips together in a hard line so I wouldn't lose it on her. Did she really believe that?

She let out a breathy laugh and paced away again. "I'm the girlfriend who gets referenced in those tiny paragraphs from the hero's POV that are supposed to highlight his dating history in a way that doesn't make the reader believe he's still hung up on his ex, while simultaneously showing that the spark or connection between him and the heroine is the real deal in comparison. You know what I mean?"

I blinked. "Uh, no."

"Ah, you know. It'll be like … 'His mind was in overdrive as he kissed her deeply, marveling at the way she fit against him like no one had before. He'd had girlfriends. Plenty of girlfriends. But no one had ever made him feel like this.'"

She stopped speaking, the silence echoing in my ears. "Wow."

"Yeah, don't judge me. I'm a reader, not a writer."

"So," I started, my feet carrying me to her again without conscious thought, "you're saying you think that if your life were a romance novel, you'd be the aforementioned *plenty of girls*?"

"Hands down."

"You're wrong."

Her mouth opened and closed a couple of times as she looked up at me. "What makes you so sure?"

"You're not anyone's two-sentence love life recap, Lyndi. You're the whole point of the book."

I hadn't realized how close we'd gotten until I felt her quiet gasp against my mouth. It woke me up, though, and before I committed the ultimate mistake and made everything so much worse, I leaned back.

"Someone's book, anyway," I said as I backed away from her. "Excuse me, I need to use the restroom."

9

LYNDI

"I thought about the fake dating thing," I said as I dropped into the chair beside Beau.

We hadn't really spoken since that talk inside the house. We'd just gone through the motions of the reception, all while seated next to each other at the wedding-party table. Which, by the way, had lost a bit of its luster considering the fact that I'd made things so awkward between us with all of my 'I'm not the heroine' talk.

"Oh yeah?" he asked, looking slightly guarded.

"Yeah. And I want to know what's in it for you."

He frowned. "What do you mean?"

"I mean, there has to be something in it for both of us. You can't just do me a favor and pretend to be my boyfriend so my family will stop trying to set me up. It won't work. In fake relationship books, they both have to get something out of it."

"I thought you said this wasn't like one of your books."

"Okay, fine. Maybe I don't want to think of you doing me this annoying favor when it's basically your job. So, if you don't have a reason, then I need to insist on paying you for it. What's your app called?"

I pulled my phone out of my clutch and navigated to the app store. Like I didn't know what his app was called. Like I hadn't downloaded it and then deleted it multiple times over the last year.

I hadn't planned to use it to actually book his services or anything, but my curiosity had gotten the better of me on multiple occasions, and I'd filled out the interest form once or twice before deleting everything.

Before my app store could even load, Beau reached out and put his warm hand over mine, lowering the phone. "I'm not taking your money."

"You have to," I insisted, pulling away and looking at the phone again. "Because if you're not getting anything out of this, then I'm a freeloader. Rules are rules. I'll hire you, sign a contract, deliver the payment, and follow your guidelines to the letter. *Ah-ha*. Mr. Fake Date. Found it."

"Lyndi."

I looked up, surprised by the edge in his tone. "What?"

"I already told Ms. Hattie it was unofficial, so you can't *make it* official."

"Not good enough."

Seeing that I wasn't going to give in, he let his head fall back. "Fine. My pops made me make him a promise, and I'm hoping that if I can tell him about us, it'll count."

"What was the promise?"

He closed his eyes. "*Lyndi*."

Taking a risk, I reached over and put my hand on his knee. The soft royal blue of his dress uniform did nothing to prevent a shock from going up my arm at the contact. "Beau?"

He sighed heavily, running a hand through his hair. "He wanted me to promise I'd find something real and stop doing the fake dating thing."

Hope stirred in my chest, but I did everything I could not to show it. "And you think you could find that with me?"

"No," he said quickly, something a little like panic flashed in his eyes before he looked at the dance floor and rolled his broad shoulders. Then, when he looked back at me, he was all business. "Like you said, you don't want to be with someone who's leaving. I'm leaving,

Lyndi, and I don't want to be with anyone *at all*. So, as much as I think we'll have fun pretending, I don't plan to make it real."

And just like that, the bottle rockets in my chest were doused with water.

"Okay," I all but whispered. More words tumbled around in my brain, begging for release, but I held them back. What else could I say without sounding totally pathetic?

Shifting in his seat, he gestured to the phone in my hand. "Is that good enough? Can we move forward without you trying to pay me now?"

"Yeah," I said, something like doubt sliding over me. How was I supposed to fake date the guy I'd been totally crushing on for a year without messing it up by falling for him? Then I got an idea. "But wait, one more thing."

"What?"

"We still need to sign a contract."

He balked. "We do?"

"*Yes*, Beau. I like structure. I like rules. I imagine you do, too, or you wouldn't be a Marine and you wouldn't have these insanely detailed contracts for your clients. I want the contract so I know what to expect, but I promise I won't try to pay you."

He considered me for a moment, then shrugged. "Fine."

"Great. Let's do it."

"Now? What, you want me to pull it up on my phone?"

I rolled my eyes. "*Duh*, that's where the contract lives, right? You operate your business out of an app."

"We're at your sister's wedding."

"Are you kidding? Look at her. She's having the time of her life and all eyes are on her. This is the perfect time. Anyone would just think we were sitting here hanging out because we're a couple and that's what couples do."

Oh, how I wish we were really a couple. Especially after seeing him in those dang dress blues. I'd attended how many of the same weddings as Beau in the last year? Tons. But this was the first time I'd seen him in the iconic uniform, and when I'd first laid eyes on him as I was coming down the aisle, I'd almost tripped on my dress. Talk about *swoon*.

But no. Beau was right. There was no sense in thinking about it. He was leaving. He didn't want a relationship. All signs pointed to a big, fat finish line on us, as soon as we were done playing pretend.

I waited while he got out his phone, then watched as he clicked around on it. This would be good. There were all kinds of rules in Beau's contracts that would prevent me from getting too close to him.

"Give me a minute to draw one up that fits the ... circumstances," he said, not looking up from the screen.

"You got it," I replied.

While I waited, I looked around the beautifully decorated reception. Layla and Zac's wedding was small in comparison to most of the weddings Starlight had recently hosted. And not just the bridal party, since we were down by two with Aria and Will being absent. There were relatively few guests, too. It was likely because his family was pretty small, so many of these guests were from our family.

Oh, man. Our family. Hopefully we'd be able to make this whole thing work for two weddings. Beau didn't usually attend multiple events with the same clients. I'd heard him say once it was hard to remember stuff because he did so many of these things, and he didn't want to get caught in a lie.

The idea of lying caused the hair on the back of my neck to stand up. Lying. That was what we'd be doing. And a whole lot of it, too, if we were going to keep this up for an extended period of time. It felt ... *wrong*.

"Okay, look it over," Beau said. "But this may not be the best time to talk about the details."

I looked back at him and was immediately sucked into the hazel eyes that stared back at me. My heart rate picked up at merely the sight of this man, never mind what the prospect of getting to feel his strong arms around me as we pretended to be a couple would do. When he'd put his arm over my shoulder earlier, I'd thought I was going to spontaneously combust.

Then our fingers brushed when I took the phone from him, and suddenly I wasn't all too concerned with the fact that I'd have to lie to my family for the foreseeable future. Because even fake dating Beau for a while was better than never dating him at all, right?

"Um, excuse me," Layla said, stomping over to us, "did I seriously just find out through the grapevine that you two are dating, and that it's *not* a business arrangement?"

I looked over at Beau and he winked, turning my insides to mush.

Let the games begin.

⚭

An hour later, Beau took off to skip rocks and drink beer with his fellow Marines by the pond. But not before he'd insisted we wait on the contract for a time when we could have a little more privacy.

We'd also introduced him to my grandmother and parents, who'd given me several not-so-stealthy nods of approval while chatting with him. And my mom had even pulled me aside afterward to let me know how proud of me she was for finally telling Beau I liked him.

Of course she'd known about my crush. It'd been a long year, and doing some harmless gossiping about his swooniness with my sister and mom hadn't seemed like a big deal at the time. But now it kind of felt like one since I had not, in fact, told Beau I liked him. If anything, I was very much pretending I didn't, while simultaneously pretending I did. My mind was spinning from the effort.

And all of that would have been bad enough, but he'd also insisted on not one but *two* slow dances in the name of keeping up appearances. I was still reeling from what it felt like to be held by him as we danced to two of my favorite love songs when Layla and Shelby came up and pulled me aside.

"I was just about to sneak off for a little break," I told them. "Wanna take a walk?"

"Gladly," Layla said with a laugh. "Clara's over there holding court talking about all the cute stuff she's going to have at her wedding. I feel like I'm on an episode of that old show where the brides attended each other's weddings and ranked them on a bunch of different categories."

"Ooh, *Four Weddings*," Shelby said. "I loved that show."

I nodded as we walked out from under the tent and over to the tables where Beau and I had talked that day. "That and *Say Yes to the Dress*. Man, I wish Aria was here, speaking of those wedding shows."

"I guarantee shows like that were a big reason she got interested in weddings," Layla agreed. Then she grabbed Shelby's arm. "Wait, would it be weird to go over there and say hi to her?"

The three of us turned to look at the small, white cottage that sat tucked into the trees on the corner of the property. Aria had lived there for years since it provided easy access to the venue for work, and Will had moved in after they'd gotten married.

The cottage was dark except for a small light in the living room, but I knew she'd probably done that on purpose so her house didn't attract attention or show up too obviously in the background of wedding photos. Just when I was about to look back at Layla, movement caught my eye from one of the windows. *That little sneak was spying on the wedding.*

"Doesn't hurt to ask," I said with a shrug, laughing to myself. "Anyone have their phones on them? We should make sure we won't disturb Oliver."

We all looked down at our gowns with no pockets, then back up at each other with a laugh.

Layla wagged her brows. "Let's just sneak over there

and tap on the window. Not loud enough to wake the baby or anything."

Decision made, we linked arms and made our way down the cobblestone path that led to Aria's cottage. When we reached it, Shelby slipped up the steps and tapped on the front window before dashing back to us.

A moment later, Will opened the door, brow furrowed in confusion until his gaze landed on us. A huge smile split his face, and he shook his head, calling softly over his shoulder, "You win."

"Of course, I win," Aria said as she appeared at the door and grinned down at us. "I bet him you'd come over and say hi, but he thought you'd worry about disturbing us."

"Ha, like we care," Layla shot back with a smirk. Then she wrinkled her nose. "We didn't disturb the baby though, did we?"

"Nope, he's fast asleep." Aria stood on her toes and pressed a kiss to her husband's cheek, then slipped out the door and waved us onto the porch. When we were all seated on her adorable vintage furniture, she clapped her hands together in front of her chest. "How's it all going?"

"Oh, it's a disaster," Layla said.

"Yeah, total mess without you," Shelby added.

I shook my head at them and squeezed her leg from

my seat next to her. "It's amazing, A. You should be really proud of the staff for doing such a great job without you."

Aria's eyes got a little misty, and she waved her hand in front of her face. "Ah, sorry. Hormones."

We laughed, none of us knowing firsthand what that was like, but it made sense.

"So, you don't have anything interesting to tell me?" she prompted, looking between us like she was almost disappointed to hear how smoothly the event was going.

Layla gave me a pointed look. "Lyndi? Anything *interesting* to tell her?"

I bit my lip. So far, since we were at the wedding and there could have been people listening, I hadn't wanted to tell Layla and Shelby that my relationship with Beau was just a sham.

But I should, right? I mean, we couldn't exactly lie to our people just because we were lying to my entire extended family and, well, his dad.

What would a romance heroine do? I thought back to all the fake dating books I'd read, trying to remember how many of them had told their besties and how many had kept it totally under wraps. And despite the fact that I *wasn't* heroine material myself, that clarified it a lot.

"I'm pretending to date Beau," I said in a rush, wincing at Layla's shocked face. "I know, I know, I told you it was real. But it's not. But I mean, technically, it's not a Mr. Fake Date kinda thing, so it's unofficial. But it's fake either way."

When I was done rambling, Layla adjusted the top of her wedding gown like she was suddenly finding it hard to breathe. Then she shook her head. "No."

"No?" I asked, blinking at her like she couldn't have just said that.

"No. You're not doing this."

I looked at Aria and Shelby, but they only seemed to be on Layla's wavelength, which I still hadn't wrapped my head around.

"What do you mean, I'm not doing this? Why not?"

"Because you've been in love with that man for a year now, and I'm not going to let you fake date him. You're going to get *hurt*, Lyn."

I waved a hand, but it felt like I was trying to push it through quicksand instead of air. "First of all, I haven't been *in love* with him. I've been crushing on him in that same way we crushed on Justin Timberlake back in the day."

Layla snorted. "You crushed on Justin. I was more of a Nick Lachey girl."

"Anyway," Shelby said with a chuckle, "it doesn't matter what you'd call it. You definitely have feelings for Beau that aren't fake, and we all know it. You have to admit it's risky to have him turn all that charm on you only to end it when the charade's over."

"How long are you going to fake date him?" Aria asked. "If it's not a Mr. Fake Date thing, does that mean it's more than just this one wedding?"

I shifted in my seat. "Well, it'll be two weddings, I guess. And a nonexistent long-distance relationship after he leaves so Grandma will leave me alone about finding someone. And also ... a little faking it for his dad because he made him a promise that he'd date someone for real instead of just pretending all the time."

My friends and sister did not react well to that, Layla worst of all. "See? This is exactly what I'm worried about. He's going to introduce you to his family and make you feel like you're the one, but it's all going to be for show. Can you really not see how that's going to mess with your head?"

"Also," Aria piped in, "without the Mr. Fake Date side of it, there'll be no contract. And no contract means some of the stuff he usually avoids so it doesn't get awkward won't be there. Like the kissing clause."

My lips tingled at the very thought of needing to kiss Beau for appearances and not having a little thing like a kissing clause in our way. Which was actually kind of mind-blowing considering the fact that as a general rule—I wasn't a fan of kissing. But kissing Beau?

For some reason it didn't seem like it'd be much of a hardship.

But then I remembered the contract and shook my head. "No, we're still having a contract. At my insistence, actually, so yeah. I do see how this could be a problem if I let it become one. But I won't. Because we'll have our rules, and no one will be dumb enough to break them."

Layla sighed and pushed up from her chair. "I assume there's no talking you out of this?"

"No, it's already in the works. Beau sat with Grandma for ten minutes talking to her about what it's like to work on the shooting range at the depot, and she's completely obsessed with him."

Who wouldn't be?

"Fine. But you'd better keep me updated so I can try to sabotage it if I think you're going to get hurt. I wouldn't be your big sister if I didn't try, anyway," Layla said, heading for the steps. "All right, I should probably get back to my wedding before my husband worries he has a runaway bride on his hands."

"If you were a runaway bride, wouldn't you be a little late with the running away part?" I asked.

"Yeah, well, romance tropes are your deal, not mine," she teased. "Aria, I love you, I wish you were able to be there, but give that sweet baby boy kisses from Auntie Layla."

"I will," Aria said with a laugh. "And I'll tell him Auntie Layla will never let him forget that his arrival caused me to skip her wedding."

"Good," she replied.

Shelby and I stood too and hugged Aria before heading back to the wedding with our runaway bride. It'd been a brief visit, but a good one. Because the four of us wouldn't be us if we didn't come together during major life events.

And though Layla's wedding was the main focus tonight, I couldn't help feeling like there was something else pretty major about this arrangement with Beau. Whether or not that was a good thing, we'd soon find out.

10

BEAU

"Hey, Pops," I said into the phone, rubbing my temple. "How are you?"

"I'm hangin' in there. How are you?"

I looked around the crowded coffee shop, nerves swirling in my gut. "I'm good. And I'm actually glad you called."

"Oh, yeah?"

"Yeah. I wanted to let you know I'm seeing someone." It wasn't exactly a lie. I'd be seeing Lyndi in about five minutes, when she showed up to go over this ridiculous contract with me.

Pops coughed into the phone, then a scratching sound shot into my ear before the cough became muffled, like he'd put his hand over the phone. "You're kiddin' me, right?"

"Nope."

"Well, I have to say, I didn't see you following through on this one, son. Not that you're not a man of your word or anythin'. It's just ... well, never mind. Tell me about her. What's her name?"

"Lyndi. She's a photographer."

"Huh. So, she's an artsy type?"

I wrinkled my nose, then shook my head. "Eh, I don't know about that. She's not like a free-spirited hippie artist or anything."

"Well, what's she like, then?"

Words to describe Lyndi flashed through my mind, one after the other. She's beautiful. Kind. Complex. She's shy but still manages to be friendly and warm. She's oddly into karaoke night even though she needs to sneak away from the chaos halfway through. And she has this weird habit of sneaking into my mind when I least expect her to.

But of course, I didn't need to go into all that with him.

Finally, I shrugged and adjusted my grip on the phone. "She's great. She photographs people, not landscapes. Mostly weddings, actually. That's how we met."

Again, all true. As long as I stuck to the facts, maybe this wouldn't be so hard after all.

"Well," he started, pausing to cough again. "That means she isn't a client of yours, then?"

Another easy one. Perfect. "No. She's not a client. We have friends in common, and I've known her for about a year now."

"And she makes you happy?"

"Yes," I answered without even having to think about it. Then I pushed down this nagging thought at the back of my mind that it shouldn't have been quite that natural of a thought.

"Good. That's all I care about."

Satisfied that I'd done enough to make good on the old man's promise, I made an attempt at chitchat for a minute now that the hard part was over. But it was short-lived. My dad had never been much of a phone guy, even before he was so low on energy. So, we wrapped it up, said our goodbyes, and I promised to call him soon.

As I slipped my phone back into my pocket, I looked up to find Ms. Hattie walking toward me like she'd won a prize. "Hello, Beau."

I nodded, bracing myself for whatever shenanigans she had in mind today. "Ma'am."

"Coffee for one today?"

"No, Lyndi's on her way."

She beamed. "Ah, wonderful. I have to admit, when

you told me about the two of you at the wedding last night, I was quite pleased."

"You were?" I blinked at her, trying to figure out if the wide smile on her face was actually sarcastic rather than genuine.

"Of course, dear. Why wouldn't I be?"

I shifted in the booth, not sure if I should be blunt or play it off. Eh, whatever. She was the one with the near-constant matchmaking schemes, so she probably wasn't unused to being called out. "Uh, I don't know, maybe because you were trying to hook her up with your son?"

"Oh, please," she said with a hearty laugh. "Brett was just acting as a catalyst."

"A catalyst?"

"Yep. You see, Beau, I've had my eye on the two of you for a while now. You two were my real targets, and I couldn't be more pleased to have successfully pushed you together."

All I could do was stare. She'd placed a hand on the table between us and leaned down, speaking softly with that gleam back in her eyes. This woman was really something else.

"Wow. I don't even know what to say right now."

"They never do, honey."

"Does Brett know about this?" I asked.

Just then, he came up behind her with a to-go cup of

coffee in each hand, giving one to his mother. "Know about what?"

Ms. Hattie accepted the cup with a smile. "About my plan to get Beau and Lyndi together."

"Oh, that," he said, blowing out a long breath. "Yeah, sorry, man. My mom's no joke, but I'm used to her."

"Again, speechless."

He nodded, sliding his gaze to his mother with a smirk. "She does have that effect on people."

The bell above the door chimed, drawing my attention. I flicked my gaze there out of reflex more than anything, but when my eyes landed on Lyndi, I couldn't look away.

She wore a soft purple tee and jeans—so casual, so ordinary ... and yet not at all. Her brown hair was woven into a thick braid over her chest, sunglasses hiding the light brown eyes that had always fascinated me. They were so light they could almost pass for hazel like mine, but without the green flecks.

"Lyndi, good morning," Ms. Hattie said as she and Brett stepped aside to give her room to slide into the booth.

She gave them each a small smile as she removed her glasses. "Good morning, Ms. Hattie. Hi, Brett."

"Hi," I said, intending to ask her how she was, but then Ms. Hattie sent me a stern look. I held my hands out in front of me to let her know I wasn't going to bring up her little plan at the moment. It would probably only make Lyndi uncomfortable anyway. "How are you?"

"I'm okay," she replied, a light blush coloring her cheeks.

"Lyndi, I'm glad I ran into you," Ms. Hattie said, stealing her attention. "My niece—you remember Nikki, right?"

"I think so, yes."

"Well, she called today to let me know she and her daughter are planning to come home for a visit from California. She recently got engaged, and I'd love to hire you to take their engagement photos if you have the availability."

Lyndi brightened, her entire posture changing from apprehension to excitement. "Oh, wow, I'd love to. Thank you for thinking of me. When are they coming?"

"After I leave, thankfully," Brett grumbled.

I quirked a brow. "Not a fan of your cousin?"

He snorted, taking a swig from his coffee. "I'm not a fan of her fiancé. The dude's a huge tool."

"Now, now, Brett," Ms. Hattie scolded him. "Take it easy. We hardly know him."

"I don't have to know him. It's just a gut thing. I hate all the stuff he posts online like she's his property or something. It's weird."

Ms. Hattie harrumphed and turned back to Lyndi. "I'll send you the dates so you can see what would work best for you."

"Sounds great, thanks."

They started to step away, then Ms. Hattie stopped abruptly, nearly causing her son to run into the back of her. "Oh, Beau, what does this mean for your business?"

I watched her finger as she pointed between Lyndi and me, then looked up at her with a frown. "What?"

"You know, you and Lyndi being together. That means you're shutting down your app, right?"

Ice ran down the back of my neck. I couldn't do that. There was no way. Was Lyndi expecting me to shut down my app? "I ... um."

Before I could come up with a logical response, Lyndi straightened. "No, he's not."

"No?" Ms. Hattie asked, one hand on her hip. "And why not?"

I looked to Lyndi, also eager to hear her answer.

She cleared her throat. "Well, I trust Beau. He doesn't need to shut his business down just because we're dating. It's totally professional between him and his clients."

There was a long pause while Ms. Hattie studied her, then she sighed. "How very big of you, sweetheart. But this is a small town. If Beau shows up to weddings at

Starlight with another woman on his arm, people will talk."

"He's not planning to accept jobs in Bluffton anymore," Lyndi answered with a shrug. *Where had that come from?* "He travels a lot for these weddings, so he'll just make sure to stick to out-of-town ones."

"Uh-huh. Well, it seems like you two have it all figured out, then," Ms. Hattie said, tossing a look toward her son that told me she wasn't convinced.

Panicking, I reached across the table and took Lyndi's hands in mine. Though the simple contact made my entire body light up, I didn't pull away. "We sure do."

"Yep," she added. But her eyes landed on the table like a dropped quarter, her hands going stiff in mine.

Ms. Hattie gave us one last suspicious look, then nodded once. "All right, we'll leave you to it. Have a nice day, lovebirds."

When I was sure she was gone this time, I turned back to Lyndi and let out the breath I'd been holding. "Thanks for that."

"What?"

"Covering for me with the business."

She pulled her hands out from under mine and fidgeted with her braid. "Well, I could tell you wouldn't want to shut it down."

Of course, I didn't want to shut it down. How else

would I be able to afford my dad's medical bills? What was I supposed to do, start flipping burgers or something? It wasn't like I had many marketable skills outside of teaching someone how to shoot an M16. But I had my charm. *That* I could sell.

"Is that something you'd want me to do?" I asked, hoping the answer would be no.

"If we were really together? Probably, not gonna lie. But since we're not, I don't see any reason to ruin all your hard work for nothing."

Relief swept over me. "Thanks. I really appreciate it."

She watched me a little too intently, almost as if she were trying to decide if she wanted to dig deeper into this subject.

Please don't.

Finally, she must have decided against it because she linked her hands in front of her and squared up with me, like she was ready for business. "So, did you finish drafting up the contract?"

"Do you want to grab a coffee first?" I asked.

"No, thanks. I've already had a couple cups this morning."

I looked her over. "That doesn't make you jittery?"

"Um, no. It doesn't. Anyway, what's the first thing we should discuss?"

Taking my laptop out of its case on the seat next to

me, I opened it and pulled up the file of the contract I'd drafted. "So, the first item we should discuss—who's in on the arrangement?"

"Um … that's an item on the contract?"

"Well, usually what I do is have a page with specific items that we want to make sure to agree upon ahead of time and also a checklist of things we should simply discuss so we're on the same page. This is from that list."

She nodded slowly, leaning back against the booth. "Oh, got it."

"It helps me to know who I need to be extra careful with and who's in on it. But I have to let you know, the more people who know about the arrangement, the less secure it is. You ever heard that saying about two people being able to keep a secret if one of them is dead?"

She chuckled. "Dark analogy, but yes."

"It's like that. The fewer people we tell it's fake, the better."

"Well … can Layla, Aria, and Shelby count as one person since I'd never be able to tell just one of them and not the others?"

I peered at her over the top of my screen. "We could. Or you could just keep it from all of them. Might make it easier." When she didn't answer, just bit her full bottom lip between her teeth, I snorted. "It's too late, isn't it?"

"Just a little. I told them last night during the wedding."

Several things made sense at that moment, and I shook my head. "Ah, no wonder."

"What?"

"After we told Layla we were a thing *for real*, she was super friendly to me. Then later that night I kept getting a death glare. I thought it might be her way of telling me not to break her little sister's heart or something, but now I get it. She's not pleased that we're doing this?"

Lyndi swallowed hard and fidgeted with her braid again, sliding her fingers between the strands below the black hair tie. "No. She thinks ... well, she thinks I shouldn't put myself in this position."

"What *position* is that, exactly?"

Her eyes bulged. "Um, all the faking, I guess. The lying. Anyway, can we get back to the other items on your list?"

"*Sure*," I said, dragging out the word. "Next up, we should talk about the events we expect to attend together."

"Okay, great. Well, the big one is my cousin Clara's wedding."

"Right, and when is that again?"

"May 4."

"Are they *Star Wars* fans?" I wondered if this would

be another themed wedding with Storm Troopers and light sabers. That wedding had been a trip and a half.

She cocked her head in confusion. "What?"

"May the fourth be with you," I said, slowly, but it didn't help so I just laughed. "Never mind. It's a *Star Wars* thing."

"Right. And you know it's not here in town, right?"

"Yeah, Zac mentioned it. How many days of leave would I need to take?"

"We're heading over there Friday night and coming back Sunday after the wedding. Layla didn't want to get a sub, and Zac didn't want to take more leave since he's taking a week for his honeymoon. Plus, Grayson's still in school, so he doesn't want to miss all the end-of-the-year fun."

I grinned. "Ah, to be in first grade again."

"Right?"

"Okay, so I won't even need to take leave, then. Moving on." I turned back to the screen, found my place and typed what she'd just told me in the appropriate spaces. "Normally, I only have to worry about one event, but since these circumstances are different, we'll likely need to have more appearances together. So, let's figure those out."

She balked. "What kinds of appearances?"

"Public outings together, family dinners, stuff like

that. You want your family to believe we're really a couple, right?"

"Yes," she said, more than a little hesitation in her tone.

"Okay, so if there's nothing planned at the moment, we can handle those as they come up, then."

"What about your dad?"

I stilled. "What about him?"

"Well, how are we supposed to convince him we're in a real relationship if we're not in the same state as him?"

"Oh. That's already taken care of. I talked to him this morning and told him I was seeing you, and he's happy for me. So, that box is checked."

She narrowed her eyes at me, looking a little unsure. "You think it's really that easy?"

"Should be. He's not like a meddling grandmother—or florist—who will care about the details. He just wants to know I'm making an effort."

"Which you aren't."

My mouth worked soundlessly; no coherent words able to find their way from my muddled brain into the open. Of course I wasn't making an effort. What good would that do? Liking Lyndi might be as easy as drinking sweet tea on an August day, but falling in love with her only to lose her? No. I wouldn't—*couldn't*—do that.

"It's fine. That's none of my business," she said, walls back up. "What's next?"

Looking back at the editable PDF, I almost smiled, my own issues forgotten. *Oh, this will be a fun one.* "Why don't you tell me about your past relationships?"

11

LYNDI

"Uh, past relationships?" I repeated, a cold sweat forming on my palms.

Why in the world would that be relevant to him?

He shrugged, one corner of his mouth twitching up, almost like he was enjoying this. "Yeah. Your past relationships."

"What about them? And why does it matter?"

"Well, it helps to know why it didn't work out for guys in the past. Also helps because it clues me in on what I'm up against, as far as your family's perceptions."

"Why?"

He lowered the lid of the laptop slightly, staring directly into my eyes. "Lyndi, this whole thing may be fake, but I aim to please."

Did he mean for that to sound so ... inviting?

"Okay ... well," I started, reaching into my bag to pull out a retractable pen. I needed something to do with my hands short of sitting on them. "I don't really have a lot of relationship experience. I've gone on plenty of dates only to end things before they really start, I guess."

He looked genuinely surprised, his mouth opening slightly like he hadn't expected that. "Really? Why's that?"

"Well, I don't know, none of them were what I was looking for. Or maybe *I* wasn't what *they* were looking for. It's obvious right away, for the most part."

He raised his screen again and sat back. "Interesting. So, what kinds of things should I make sure *not* to do, so I'm not a bad match for you?"

"Are you going to write it down? On the thingy, I mean?" I tapped my pen on the edge of the laptop.

"Well, that depends. Is it a long list?"

Fuming at the way his eyes seemed to hold laughter when he'd asked it, I straightened my shoulders. "Not that long. For starters, don't chew with your mouth open."

"I have impeccable table manners, thank you very much. Professional wedding date, remember?"

"Right. Okay, don't be annoyed with how much time I spend reading."

His head tilted like a dog hearing a whistle. "Why would I be?"

"I don't know, but apparently it's a thing."

"What else?"

I thought about it for a second, then held up a finger. "Don't take me to see scary movies."

Beau grinned. "Ah, that old move?" When my brow furrowed, he continued, "You know, like, 'If I take her to a scary movie, she'll hold onto me, and I can comfort her.' That move."

"Yes, only it turned into the girl-runs-out-of-the-theatre-because-she's-spinning-out move."

He pursed his lips with a short nod. "Noted. Rom-coms only. Anything else?"

Well, sure. I could tell him about how one guy didn't like that I didn't like to listen to music in the car. It distracted me.

Another guy wasn't a fan of my preference to order my drinks in their original bottle or can at restaurants, since hello, the cups they used were probably disgusting.

And then there was the guy who didn't think it mattered that he used the wrong homophone while texting me. It mattered. A lot. Learn the difference between *you're* and *your* and *they're, their,* and *there,* dude!

But no, I didn't really want to get into all of that with Beau, lest he feel the same way. Something told me it was best not to shatter the illusion I'd been carrying that he was the perfect guy. Plus, a poor reaction from *him* would be nothing but embarrassing for *me*.

But then I did think of something else worth mentioning, as hard as it was to be honest about. "Last thing—when you meet my family, don't tease me."

His face jerked back, and then he shook his head in short, rapid bursts as if to clear it. "What?"

"You know, like … point out my little quirks and pretend they're cute and try to use them to relate with my family. It's annoying."

His jaw dropped. "Someone *did* that?"

My fingers tingled, so I clicked the pen a few times before answering. "Yeah. I dated this one guy for a few months over the holidays and made the mistake of inviting him to our Christmas dinner."

"What kinds of things did he point out?"

I shrugged. "You know, the usual. The reading obsession, the number of reminders I have on my phone, the system I use to organize my bookshelf … how *sensitive* I can be."

"None of those things sound like anything to tease you about," he said, the quiet kindness in his eyes making my chest hurt.

"He managed."

Beau held up a hand. "Hang on, I'm not touching the sensitive comment with a ten-foot pole, but how do you organize your bookshelves?"

I managed a laugh and clicked my pen. "Um ... well, I guess most people either don't have a system, or they just do it like a library ... alphabetically by author and then by title. But my system is a little more ... intense."

"I gotta know."

I glared at him. "Why? Is that in the checklist, too?"

"No. But you have me curious now, and it's gonna drive me nuts."

After only a moment's hesitation, I gave in with a sigh. "Fine. I have a separate bookcase for my TBRs, which is organized by sub-genre and trope, so I can easily find something I'm in the mood for."

"Okay ..."

"Then once I've read one of those, I either move it to my bookcase for keepers, or I pack it in a box to trade in. The keepers are organized alphabetically by the author, grouped in series, with the series in chronological order. If it's an author who writes multiple series in the same world, of course."

"Of course. How big are these shelves?"

I bit my lip. "Pretty big."

He let out a breathy laugh, then jerked a shoulder.

"Okay, I mean, it's intense but it's not *that* bad. I'm sure any fellow bookaholic has their own system. The fact that you have an entire *bookcase* of books you haven't read yet is a little surprising, but—"

"Hey, I can't help it. I buy more books than I have time to read!"

"I'm not judging, I promise." His laughter was infectious, so I giggled a little, but then he sobered and held my gaze. "Also, the fact that any guy would think it was a good idea to tease you about any of that in front of your family just blows my mind. Don't worry, that's not something I'd even think to do."

I felt a blush creep up my neck, so I looked down at the pen before he could see it on my cheeks. "Thanks."

"Okay, so I think I have a pretty good handle on how *not* to be your fake boyfriend. But is there anything you want to tell me about how you *do* want me to act?"

"Uh … I don't know. Like, what characteristics I'd want my boyfriend to have?"

"Yeah."

Wow. How ridiculous was it that this was a normal part of his process? He sounded like an actor trying to get to know the character he was supposed to play in a movie.

No, that's exactly what he's doing. And the sooner you remember that, the better.

"I don't really know," I replied. "Book boyfriend qualities come to mind, but it feels a little too much like I'm crafting you out of Play-Doh."

A wide smile stretched across his too-handsome face. "That's part of the fun, trust me. I can be whoever you want me to be."

It was probably supposed to be a silly little comment that I shouldn't think too hard about, but something about it made my stomach turn.

"Maybe just do the opposite of the *don'ts* and we'll be good," I said.

"Fair enough. All right, I think we can move on to the actual contract now."

"Sounds great."

"First thing's first," he said, clicking around on his screen. "We need to get our stories straight, and I have it outlined in the contract as an area not to be embellished upon. Embellishment leads to getting our stories mixed up, and we both need to be really clear on the details."

"How very thorough of you."

"Oh, *thorough* is my middle name." He wagged his brows, and my stomach turned for a very different reason.

Shaking it off, I focused on the task at hand. "Great. So, how did we meet?"

"Well, I already told my dad that you're a wedding

photographer and that's how we met. I didn't give him details though, since we hadn't discussed all of this yet. Any ideas?"

I thought about it, realizing this felt a little like we were crafting the meet-cute for a couple in one of my books. Only not, because the best meet-cutes just happen. You can't fake them.

"Well," I started, my eyes wandering toward the window that looked out over Main Street, "we should probably stick close to the truth, right?"

"Closer the better."

"Okay, so we met at Bobby and Cassidy's wedding. You were there with Shelby, which is fine to tell people because they already know about your business. And you told me to hire you if I ever needed a fake date."

He swallowed hard, the movement causing his Adam's apple to bob. "Uh, yeah. I did. And yet, I noticed you didn't."

"Well, I haven't needed a fake date until now."

And also, I never planned to, because deep down I knew this would be tortuous.

"Good point. Okay, so that's how we met." He typed it out, then looked back up. "Anything else you want to add or should we just keep it simple?"

"Simple is great."

"Perfect." He looked down at the screen again, then

gave me a smile that could only be described as *devilish*. "Next, and *ridiculously* important, are the ground rules for PDA."

"PDA?" I asked, realizing quickly what that meant, and then wincing at the way my chest tightened in response. "Oh, right, the infamous *kissing clause*."

He laughed. "Yes. But it's more than just kissing. We'll get to that in a minute."

"Can't wait," I mumbled.

"So, the usual. Hand holding, arms around each other, hugging, all fine. But as you know, with my usual contracts, kissing has a surcharge."

"Because it's gross?"

Beau's face contorted into one of utter shock, like he was a cartoon version of himself, and his eyes were about to bug out of his head. "Uh, no. What did you just say?"

"Nothing," I squeaked.

He leaned forward, closing the laptop all the way this time. "Lyndi Robinson, did you just ask if I charged extra for kissing because it's *gross?*"

I shook my head. "Definitely not. That would be weird." *Dang it, Lyndi. What is* wrong *with you?*

"It would be," he agreed, nodding slowly.

"Exactly. So, can we forget I said that?"

"*Definitely not*," he quoted me.

I threw myself back against the seat and let my head hit the soft leather of the booth's top. Then I looked back at him with my brave face on. "Okay, listen. I told you. Things fizzle out pretty quickly one way or the other when I start seeing a guy. Usually, we don't even make it to kissing."

Again, more slow nodding. "And when you *do*, you think it's *gross*."

Flailing my hands in front of me, I let out an exasperated noise. "Ugh, it's the mechanics of the whole thing. It's never as romantic in real life as it is in books."

"It definitely can be." He didn't say it, but his eyes told me what he was thinking.

It definitely can be ... with me.

Shaking my head to clear that frighteningly appealing image, I stood my ground. "Well, I disagree. So, no need to put anything in your contract about us kissing. There won't be a need."

"We could put certain parameters around it, though. Like, if certain things happen, and we have to kiss, we will."

The snort shot out of me before I could stop it. "Sorry, but *when* has that ever happened in real life, though? When does a kiss *need* to happen?"

"Could be anything. We're supposed to be a couple, so if the situation calls for a kiss, we'll kiss. But if not, we won't." When I didn't respond, he leaned closer again. "Are you going to get all wigged out if I have to kiss you, Lyndi? Because if our first kiss has an audience and you push me away so you can avoid throwing up, that's gonna be a problem."

I pictured the scene playing out in my mind and barely contained the laughter it caused to well up in my chest. "I really hope not." Though, of course, the idea of kissing *Beau* didn't sound gross to me. At all.

"If you were a client, I wouldn't even suggest this, but—"

I held up a hand, eyes wide. "Beau Devereux, if you were about to suggest …" I trailed off, looking around to make sure no one was listening, then I leaned close and kept my voice low. "If you're about to suggest that we do a practice kiss before the wedding, I might actually kill you."

"What? Are you serious? Can you blame me?"

"For that level of cheese? I absolutely can. The practice kiss is like the number-one trope under the fake relationship umbrella, and buddy, it's not happening."

Full-blown laughter poured out of him, causing him to throw back his head and put one hand on his flat stomach while the other covered his eyes. When he collected himself, he looked down at me with way too much of a sparkle in his gaze.

"Okay, you win. No practice kissing. And as much as I'd love to show you that you're wrong about it being gross, I'm also a little relieved."

I caught my jaw before it dropped, simply blinking at him instead. "You are?"

"Yeah. Kissing has a surcharge, remember? I'm not going to kiss you any more than I have to."

When he opened his laptop like the conversation was over, I snaked out my hand and closed it again with a soft snap. "Hold on. If it's not because *you* also think it's gross—which, yeah, yeah, we've established is weird—then why do you charge extra for kissing? What do you have against it?"

He licked his lips, causing me to avert my eyes. But then I looked back at him because I was way too curious about this to not try to read his reaction to it.

"Because kissing can lead to ... feelings."

There was something about the wariness in his tone that made me want to probe him for more details about why he avoided feelings like the plague, but I stopped myself, deciding to crack a joke, instead. That was my thing—joking instead of feeling—after all, so who was I to judge?

"I mean, it *could* lead to feelings ... unless she thinks it's gross."

His lips turned up into a slow, crooked smile. "She wouldn't think that."

Gulping, I felt my skin flush under his gaze. *This guy is trouble.*

"What makes you so sure?" I asked, unconsciously tipping toward him like he was a magnet, and I was a puny paper clip with no choice but to obey.

"I already told you," he said, meeting me halfway so there was barely six inches between our lips. "I *aim* to please."

Someone dropped a dish behind me, and I sat back with a start as it shattered. Looking over my shoulder, I saw the source of the interruption and shot laser beams of gratitude to the clumsy barista who'd dropped it.

Turning back to Beau, I tapped on the top of his laptop. "Okay, Romeo, put down that it's *only* allowed if necessary; but I'm fairly certain that will never happen."

"Fine," he said with a triumphant little smile.

I bristled. "Are we done here?"

"Almost. But the rest is fairly boring. It'll go fast."

I nodded in agreement, but if I'd learned anything over the course of this conversation, it was that nothing with Beau Devereux could *ever* be boring.

On Wednesday, I sat in my empty bungalow that used to house both me and my best friend of a sister, but wouldn't for long, reading in my favorite spot on our gray sectional. I had my favorite pink blanket on my lap, my favorite tea in my favorite mug, and a faux-fireplace flickering away on our flat-screen—on mute, of course. Because that crackle is not my jam.

When my phone buzzed on the coffee table, I was shocked when I looked over to see that Layla was Face-Timing me from her honeymoon.

Terrified that something horrible had happened while she and Zac were in the Bahamas, I slid the button across the screen with a shaky thumb. "Layla, are you okay?"

She frowned at me through the screen. "Uh, yeah. I'm fine, why?"

"Um," I said, putting a hand on my heart to slow the rapid beating, "maybe because you're FaceTiming me from your honeymoon?"

"Lyn, look, we're fine. I'll show you."

She panned the camera to show me that she was sitting in her favorite bikini in a lounge chair, Zac in a chair of his own at her side. There were two empty cocktail glasses on the table between them—complete with discarded umbrellas on toothpicks.

Then she moved the phone again, and the sunny

weather and turquoise water from the pool squashed the fear that a sudden out-of-season hurricane was ravaging their resort.

I calmed down. "Okay, then why are you calling?"

"I just missed you and wanted to see how you're doing. It's weird not traveling with you." She looked over when Zac said something like, *hey, what about me* in the background. "I'm just kidding, Zac. I love that it's just the two of us."

"Uh-huh," I heard him reply dryly.

Putting my face close to the phone so she could read my lips, I said, "I'm fine. Go enjoy your time with Zac."

I started to hang up on her, but she waved her hand. "Not so fast, how are you and Beau doing?"

Flaring my eyes at her, I pointed to the right to remind her that I didn't want her husband to know it was all for show. She rolled her eyes and huffed at me, but I glared at her and zipped my lips to show her I wouldn't talk until he wasn't within hearing distance.

"Hey, babe," Layla said to Zac, "would you mind grabbing us a couple of refills?"

I waited, wondering if he'd do it, then sighed in relief when I heard him tell her it'd be his *pleasure*.

"Thank you, love you!" she called after him, then centered her face in the screen again. "Okay, he's gone. Now, spill."

"Spill what? There's nothing to spill."

She groaned. "Have you guys talked about the contract yet?"

"Yes, we met for coffee and signed it Sunday morning. Well, he had coffee, anyway."

"Good. That helps, at least. But I hope you made sure to put the no-kissing rule in there."

I wrinkled my nose at her. "It's in there, but more like ... if it needs to happen, fine, but if not, also fine."

"*Needs* to happen? What is this, a rom-com?"

"That's what I said. But yeah, apparently, there really are situations that might warrant a kiss. I don't know. He's the professional."

She guffawed. "Professional *heartbreaker* if you ask me."

Feeling oddly defensive of my fake boyfriend, I narrowed my eyes at my sister. "Um, excuse me, but you've been very Team Beau this entire time. Why are you suddenly so against him?"

"Because he's playing with my little sister's heart, that's why," she snapped, softening slightly when I rolled my eyes. "Lyn, if you guys had gotten together in a normal way, it'd be different. But this? This is like, 'Hey, let's do all the fun stuff without the real feelings, because I'm Mr. Fake Date and I don't do real feelings.'"

I cackled at her impression of him. "He doesn't talk like that."

"Fine, insert his tone of voice, and it's all still true. I'm not a fan."

"What if I'd hired him for a wedding like you've been encouraging me to do ever since we first met him? Would you still feel this way?"

She shook her head without pause. "*Nope.* Because then you'd be the one making the move, and he'd be the one helpless against your amazingness, and he'd probably wind up telling you he wants it to be real after having such a good time with you. But him instigating this, and then telling you he doesn't want anything real to come from it is sketch, in my humble opinion."

Suddenly, I really regretted telling her anything about this. Maybe Beau was right. Maybe I should have just kept this whole thing to myself and not told her or our friends. Not only would it have minimized the risk of it getting out to the family I was trying to convince, but it would have also saved me this hassle I never saw coming.

"Okay, well, thank you for your concern. But I have it handled. He's helping me avoid the matchmaking, and I'm helping *him* in a similar way. So don't worry about me. Just enjoy your honeymoon."

She studied me as intently as her dark sunglasses

would allow, then sighed. "I will. It may be weird not having you here, but Zac's amazing, and I'll be sad to come home in a few days. Well, we've both missed Grayson, of course. But Jo says he's doing great. Trevor has been a big help, too."

"Does she know to call me if she needs a break or anything?" I knew Zac's sister and her fiancé had it handled, but I still needed to do my auntie duty and offer.

"Definitely. Thank you. Okay, Zac's back with fresh drinks, so that's my cue. Love you, mean it."

"Love you, most."

I disconnected the call and put my phone back down on the table. Man, this house was quiet without her in it. She was always humming something or making noise in the front room where she kept her art supplies. Or she was cooking, or had Zac and Grayson over, or had some trashy TV show on while I read. It wasn't the same without her.

And now that she and Zac were married, she'd be moving out of here and into the apartment he lived in above Ms. Hattie's flower shop. It had plenty of room and Grayson had only just gotten settled there after they came here from California, and they hadn't wanted to uproot him. So on my end, that would mean more silence. Less Layla. And when she moved away with him when he got new orders, it would be even worse.

Shaking my head, I settled back under my blanket and picked up my Kindle. Nope. I didn't like the tightness in my chest that all of that brought on, and the best thing to do when I felt it was distract myself with some good ol' fashioned fiction. It was way easier to deal with made-up emotional turmoil than reality. And lately? I'd had *plenty* of that.

12

BEAU

Taking my tray of food over to one of the long tables of the chow hall, I sat down alone and put my camouflage cover next to my tray. Good thing Zac would be back from his honeymoon tomorrow.

It'd been a long week of solo lunch breaks without him to talk about nothing with, and since there was a lot more than *nothing* going on with me at the moment, I'd be glad to have him back come Monday.

"How's it going, man?" Grant asked as he dropped his tray across from mine.

"Whoa, who let you in here like a normal person?"

He grinned. "I'm not on chow duty right now, but I was supposed to be."

"Nice. Gotta love surprise time off. You didn't want to go home for lunch, though? See the fam?"

"Tess and Sadie are at some petting zoo across the bridge, and I didn't want to ruin their time by telling her I was free. So, here I am."

I cocked a brow. "'Ruin their time'? How would that ruin their time?"

He ran a hand over his extreme high and tight—drill instructors always had that or a shaved head—and heaved out a beast of a sigh. "Man, I feel like she *intentionally* tries to keep her schedule clear on the off chance something like this will happen and I'll be able to come home for lunch. I don't like it, so I encouraged her to take Sadie to do something fun. If she found out I had some free time, and she wasn't home to hang out? Ah, I don't even want to think about it."

I swallowed, feeling bad for the guy. But then again, if he'd remained blissfully unattached like I had, he wouldn't have to worry about all that.

"That sounds rough. I'm sorry."

"It's all good, she'll adjust. I just hope it's not so hard for her by the time the baby comes. I'm trying to hit J-hat before then so I'll have more time off."

"I hope you make it," I offered with a small smile.

"Thanks. Have you done a B billet yet?"

Every Marine had to do a B billet at some point after they made sergeant, and it was usually one of three duties: drill instructor, embassy guard, or recruiter.

That last one had always been the one I'd had my eye on because I figured I'd kill it. But I likely wouldn't have a choice. Being a DI seemed hard but manageable, and the idea of spending three years in three different countries guarding an embassy actually sounded pretty cool. But so far, I hadn't been told I was needed for any of the three. It was only a matter of time, though.

"Nah, not yet," I replied. "But I'm thinking I'd make a good recruiter. I've got good people skills."

He smirked and pointed at me with his fork. "I bet you'd have to with your little side gig."

"Exactly."

"Being a drill instructor is insane. I swear, I think the hardest thing is the yelling."

I frowned as I swallowed a bite of my burrito. "Yeah? What, like you feel bad for doing it?"

"No. I mean, yeah, kind of, in the beginning. But I got over that pretty quickly because otherwise I wouldn't be a good enforcer. Gotta remember it's just mind games, and they'll be all right in the end. We all were."

"True."

I thought back to my time in boot camp with a shudder. Kill hats were total psychos, and it still blew my mind that Grant was able to be such a chill guy with me one minute and such a hard-core screaming machine the next.

"But yeah," he went on, wincing as he touched his throat, "the thing about the yelling is ... I had no idea how *bad* it would hurt. The first yell of the day? I dread it. I wake up every morning, and I'm not even mad about going to work itself, it's that the second I make that first yell, I know it's gonna feel like someone's digging a knife around in my throat."

I cringed. "Ugh, dude. That sounds terrible."

"It is *not* fun. I'm starting to wonder if I'm ever gonna have a normal voice again, and this is only my first cycle," he said, the same scratchy voice every DI had illustrating his point.

"I'm sure you will. I've known plenty of former DIs, and they talk normally now. I bet you'll get used to it."

"Right, yeah. Same."

Before I could blink, an idea flew into my mind. If I got orders to be a drill instructor, I might not have to leave. I could be stationed at Parris Island for another three years instead of moving to Hawaii.

And even though it was Lyndi's face that popped into my head first, I swiped it away for a more logical reason. My pops. It would mean I'd be only a short trip away from him if he was right about his prognosis and he didn't have much time left. It wasn't like I'd get to see him all the time, especially not while I was a kill hat myself, but it'd be better than being across the Pacific in Hawaii.

I took a drink of my Coke and nodded at him. "Hey, so uh, what else can you tell me about drill instructor duty? You know, just in case I wind up getting *volun-told* to do it."

"Uh, well, be prepared for very little sleep. And when you *do* sleep, don't be surprised if you find yourself sleep-IT'ing someone in your closet."

My burrito was halfway to my lips, but I lowered it. "Hang on, back up. What?" Of course DIs would sleep-IT instead of sleepwalk.

IT stood for Incentive Training—as in, "here's a little *incentive* not to do whatever you just did again." It could be push-ups, bends and thrusts, side straddle hops, sit-ups, leg lifts, you name it. They'd call you out in front of the other recruits and make you keep going until they'd made their point, and after the first time I'd gotten IT'd in boot camp, I'd spent the rest of the time not doing anything that would prompt them to do it again.

Grant laughed. "No joke? The other night I woke up to Tess pulling on my arms, yelling that it wasn't real. But in my head? I totally saw it, clear as day. I wasn't at home in my walk-in closet, I was on the drill field telling some recruit to do push-ups for dropping his rifle."

"Seriously?"

"Seriously. When I snapped out of it and realized what was going on, you have no idea how happy I was that it wasn't Tess I was yelling at. She would *not* have enjoyed that. At all."

Since I'd seen this guy lose his mind on a few recruits, I totally understood why she wouldn't. In fact, it sounded like it'd be pretty terrifying for her.

"Did your daughter wake up?" I asked.

He smiled. "Nope. Kid sleeps like a rock, thankfully. And she has one of those white-noise machines, you know? Best twenty bucks I ever spent, and I didn't even know it would come in handy for *that* reason."

"That's wild."

Okay, maybe I didn't want to be a drill instructor after all. The worst thing that could happen on recruiting duty is that I'd have a dream I had to do pull-ups during a high school lunch hour in the nude. That would be terrifying, sure, but it definitely wouldn't qualify as being a walking-nightmare like what Grant had described.

I felt my phone buzz in my pocket, so I put down my burrito and fished it out. Seeing that it was my dad, I rose from the table and held up a finger to Grant. "Hang on, man, it's my dad."

"Cool," he replied through a mouthful of food.

When I stepped away, I quickly answered the call. "Hey, Pops. Everything okay?"

"Sure is. Just wanted to ask you somethin.'"

Relief mixed with curiosity flowed through me. "Okay, shoot."

"You think you can get them to give you some time off so you can come out and see your old man?"

I blinked, looking around the room, though I wasn't sure what for. "Uh, I don't know, when? And *why?*"

"No reason. Except I wanna meet this girlfriend of yours."

My stomach dropped right into my boots, and I stifled a groan. "Ah, hmm."

"What? You can travel every weekend to take your fake dates to weddings but you can't spare some leave to see your dying father?"

I curled my lip at his wording. "Ouch, tell me how you really feel."

"Sorry, but the truth hurts," he teased, coughing. "Son, you haven't taken leave since who knows when. I'm sure you've got plenty to burn. Why don't you take a couple weeks off and come see me next weekend."

"Pops ... I'm a professional wedding date. My weekends are always booked solid."

"Is it booked next weekend?"

I frowned. Actually, it wasn't. I'd only had one

wedding on the calendar for next weekend, and the couple had called it off. And it was a shame, too, because my client had booked one of my more expensive packages.

"No, it's not. But Lyndi works weekends, too. I'm not sure it'll work for her."

"Yeah, well, that's why I said to take a couple weeks. Weekend doesn't work? Come during the week. You know I'm not going anywhere Monday to Friday these days. Get some R&R for yourself and fit it in when you can."

I hummed in response, thinking it over.

"Come on, Beau," he went on, his tone very near pleading. "It's been a while. I'd love to see you."

I closed my eyes as he coughed again, guilt moving to the forefront of my mind. Why had I even entertained the idea of becoming a drill instructor to stay in Parris Island if I wasn't going to make the effort to see him?

Oh, right, because you're a selfish jerk and the reason you thought of it started with Lyndi and shifted to Pops. Some son.

"All right, yeah. I think I can swing a trip out there. And you're right, it would be cool to burn some leave before I rack up too many days and I'm forced into it."

"Yeah? Great. I'm looking forward to it. And hey, there's a festival next weekend. You can take your girl."

"Oh, great," I said. "I'm sure she'd love that."

Actually, now that I thought about it, I was fairly certain she wouldn't love it. I imagined Lyndi's reaction if I pulled up in front of a hot, sticky, loud, chaotic festival in the middle of New Orleans.

Unless they had karaoke or I framed it like an opportunity for her to play paparazzi and take photos of the other attendees, I highly doubted she'd want to hang out there. But we could worry about that if she even agreed to go on the trip itself.

"Thank you, Beau," he said, his voice oddly misty. "Talk soon."

"Bye."

I hung up and went back over to the table, sitting down but not bothering to reach for my burrito. I didn't think I could stomach it if I tried, despite how famished I'd been when I walked in here.

"What's up?" Grant asked, looking me over.

"Oh, just my pops. He wants me to come out and visit."

"Cool, where does he live?"

"New Orleans."

His face lit up. "Right on. Is that where you're from?"

"Yep."

"When are you going?"

I sighed. "Next weekend, apparently. If I can get the

leave approved and if my—well, yeah just the leave. If not, I'll figure something else out. He seemed pretty insistent on it."

"Well, good for you, man. I wouldn't go visit my dad if he was on his death bed, so that's cool you guys have a good relationship."

A sharp pain slid through my chest, but it wasn't Grant's fault. He didn't know my pops was sick, so of course he wouldn't know not to say something like that.

But yeah. It was a good reminder. I needed to go visit my old man, and despite him making utterly tasteless jokes about dying, I still had hope that he wasn't. But just in case I was wrong, I needed to do what I could to spend time with him *while* I could.

Realizing I should probably check with Lyndi to make sure she was okay with the idea before I changed my leave dates, I pulled out my phone and sent her a text.

Me: Hey, do you have any plans next weekend? Any weddings or anything?

The dots appeared to show me she was responding immediately. Maybe she'd been scrolling TikTok when the message came in.

Lyndi: Actually, no. I had one, but it got called off. Cold feet, I think.

Interesting. I'd bet my last dollar I would have seen

her there if they hadn't called it off. What were the odds they were different weddings? The question now was, how was I supposed to ask her to come on a weekend trip with me? Would she freak out and turn me down? What would I say to my pops if she did?

Me: Bummer for them, but uh, I was hoping if you were free you'd do me a favor. As per our arrangement, of course.

Lyndi: What kind of favor?

Me: Will you come to New Orleans with me to see my dad? He wants to "meet my girl."

The seconds crawled by without a response from her, and even though I attempted to chitchat with Grant while I waited, my eyes kept drifting to my phone.

Finally, the screen lit up, and I snatched the phone off the table to see what she'd said.

Lyndi: For how long?

Me: Friday to Sunday, I guess. It's a ten-hour drive, and I'll need to get special permission to go that far, but I don't want to stay longer than necessary.

She hadn't given me a no, but I hadn't gotten a yes yet, either. Again, I waited with way too much nervousness while she took her sweet time replying.

Lyndi: Well, I guess it's only fair. You're coming to a wedding out of town with me.

My heart rate shot through the roof as I read and re-read the words on the screen.

Me: So, is that a yes?

Lyndi: It's a very hesitant yes. I'm not the best travel companion, but I'll deal with it. For you.

Lyndi: I mean, as per our arrangement.

I let out a chuckle at the way she'd sent that second text almost immediately, and I pictured her cringe when she did it. When Grant looked at me funny, I just waved him off and went back to the phone.

Me: Thanks. We'll have fun. I promise.

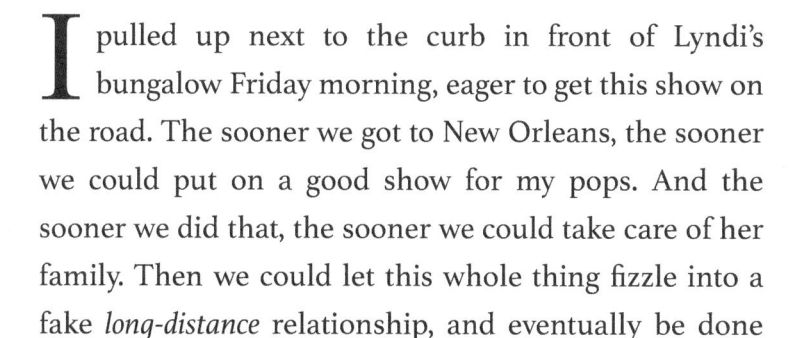

I pulled up next to the curb in front of Lyndi's bungalow Friday morning, eager to get this show on the road. The sooner we got to New Orleans, the sooner we could put on a good show for my pops. And the sooner we did that, the sooner we could take care of her family. Then we could let this whole thing fizzle into a fake *long-distance* relationship, and eventually be done with it altogether.

Halfway to the front door, I paused, jamming my hands in my pockets. This was insane. Why hadn't I just let Ms. Hattie attempt to set Lyndi up with her son? Why had I played right into her hand by interjecting? I could have let that relationship go nowhere fast, and Lyndi and I would still be hovering around each other's worlds, neither one of us intending to step in for our own reasons.

But now? Now I was picking her up to take her to my childhood home for the weekend. To meet my pops and let her see a side of me I didn't show anyone. Why was this a better idea?

Almost like she knew I was here, Lyndi opened the door and poked her head out. "Morning."

I forced my feet to move toward her as she heaved a carry-on sized suitcase onto the porch. "Morning. I got this."

Her lips flattened into a tight line as I picked up the bag. "Thanks."

"Be honest, how many books are in here?"

"Only a couple," she said with a laugh. "But don't ask me to tell you how many are on my Kindle, because I'm pretty sure you don't wanna know."

"You're probably right." We headed toward the car, and I popped the trunk, placing her bag inside before closing it with a thud. "You ready for this?"

"Ready as I'll ever be."

I moved past her to open the passenger door, ignoring the way the familiar scent of her fruity body wash made my brain light up. "Don't sound so excited."

"I'm sorry," she said, pausing to look at me before she lowered herself into her seat. "I don't mean to be a downer. This might be fun. Normally, I love to travel."

I snorted and closed her door, then went to my side and got in. "*Normally*, you love to travel ... but you don't think you will with me?"

"No, it's not that. I guess it's just because I've always traveled with Layla, and we have our routines and stuff. I always know what to expect."

I pulled away from the curb and started the turn-by-turn directions on the car's large screen. "Well, feel free to boss me around as needed. I'm great at taking orders."

"I'm sure you are."

"Oh, and if you need anything, check the glove box."

She quirked a brow and reached forward, opening it to find tiny water bottles, candy, breath mints, tissues, meds for motion sickness, and a few other random comforts.

"Is your car always stocked for a road trip?"

"I take them a lot for business, remember? Plus, I like to have some extra amenities on hand for my clients."

"Got it." She shut it with a snap and leaned back. "You really are thorough."

Unsure how to take that, I lifted a finger to connect my phone's music app to the car. "You wanna listen to music or are you gonna read?" I looked over at her, dropping my hand when I saw her wrinkled nose. "What?"

"Would you be offended if I wanted to read?"

I snorted. "No. You do you."

"What are you gonna do?"

Looking around, I held out my hand toward the road. "Drive the car."

"*Besides* driving the car."

"Uh, I should probably just stick to that if you want to arrive safely. I can't read and watch the road at the same time."

She let out a laugh, shaking her head. "No, I mean, do you want to listen to music?"

"Will it bother you if I do?"

Her lips turned down like it surprised her I'd asked. "No, it's okay if you do."

I slid my gaze to hers, nodding. "Right. Earbuds it is."

"Beau—"

"Hey, relax. It's a long drive. You're allowed to want it to be quiet, and I don't mind putting in an earbud so I can listen to music. We can both be comfortable here."

Slowly, she tucked her legs under her and reclined the seat, then pulled out her Kindle. When she was settled, she gave me a small, "Thanks."

And for the next ten hours—save for a few pit

stops and a handful of light conversations, that was how we stayed. Me, listening to my road trip playlist through one earbud and her peacefully reading beside me.

It could have been weird. It could have been annoying. It could have been a lot of things.

But instead, it was nice.

"So, we're about an hour out," I said, changing lanes as we made our way down I-10 in the fading light.

She looked up from her Kindle and watched the trees outside her window. "That went fast."

"Yeah, it did. And uh, I feel like there's something you should know about my pops before we get there."

"What do you mean?" she asked, and I felt her turn toward me as she sat up straighter.

But I couldn't look at her. I kept my eyes on the road, blinders up. "Well, he's ... *not well.*"

"What do you mean?"

"He's got lung cancer. Stage three."

The Kindle slipped from her fingers, and she scrambled to catch it before it slid between the seat and the center console. "What? Are you serious?"

"Yeah. The doctors think he has a decent chance of survival—something like thirty percent, I think. But if you ask him, he's pretty sure he's dying. Doesn't let me forget it, either."

Lyndi's hands shot out, and she waved them in the air in front of her. "Wait, wait, wait. Stop the car."

"Lyndi—"

She gripped the door handle, breathing deeply. "Beau, stop the car."

Even though I had no idea if this was a car-sickness thing or because she wanted to get away from me and my baggage, I safely maneuvered the car onto the side of the road and put it in park.

Before I could even open my mouth to ask her what was going on, however, she bolted like the car was on fire and slammed the door behind her.

"Lyndi," I yelled, checking my mirror to make sure it was safe to get out on my side before launching out after her. "What are you doing?"

She spun, arms outstretched. "What are *you* doing? Did you seriously tell your dying father that you have a girlfriend because he made you promise to find love so he wasn't afraid to leave you alone? Is that what happened?"

"Whoa, hey ..." She was absolutely right, but I was surprised she'd drawn the conclusion so fast or was this upset about it.

"Of course, you did. It's pretty freaking obvious that's what this is."

"Hang on."

She charged up to me, one finger stabbing the air. "No, *you* hang on. This is *not* okay. We're not going to spend the weekend at your father's house and *lie* to him like this."

"We're not lying," I blurted, stepping closer, palms out.

She sputtered and shook her head. "Uh, I'm sorry, did I miss something? Are we or are we not in a completely one hundred percent *fake* relationship?"

"We are, technically."

Crossing her arms over her chest, she narrowed her eyes at me. "Okay, then I don't see how we're not lying."

"Because I didn't *necessarily* say it was a relationship when I told my dad about us."

"What?"

My throat tightened, her judgy tone mixed with my own stupidity wreaked havoc on my senses. "I simply said I was seeing someone."

"I don't get it."

I blinked at her, gesturing to her standing in front of me. "I'm lookin' at you, aren't I?"

Her mouth fell open in tiny, smooth increments, so low that I thought it might actually disconnect and fall at her feet. "Beau Devereux, that is a stretch, and you *know* it."

I groaned and paced away from her, dragging my

hands through my hair. Then I turned back and stepped toward her again, hoping she could see—or maybe feel, I didn't know—how freaked out my dad's promise had made me. "Okay, okay, listen. He asked if you made me happy. I told him you do. Does that count?"

This made her step back. "That I—what?"

"There are little truths here, Lyn. Okay?" I moved forward again until we were inches away, not touching, but pretty dang close. "Little truths. I'm seeing you. We're in a relationship, it just happens to be a fake one. You make me happy, even though I know it's temporary. If we stick to the little truths, we're not really lying. We tell him how we really met, we tell him we've had a connection for a year but didn't want to act on it. But we don't make any promises for the future."

"That we ... Those are little truths?"

"Yes. But even though those things might be true, this is ending, and we both know it. Right?"

She stared at me for so long I thought the ten-hour drive seemed like minutes. Then she furrowed her brow and backed up, hands in the air. "Whatever. Let's just go."

Without waiting for me to reply, she moved around me and got back in the car. I let out a long breath and took my own seat, but I didn't move back onto the road. Instead, I turned toward her, willing her to look at me.

"I'm sorry I didn't tell you he was sick," I said, my voice breaking a little.

Reluctantly, she finally met my eyes, hers pulling down at the edges. "Why didn't you?"

"Because ... I don't tell anyone. I don't talk about this stuff."

She bit her lip and nodded like she got it. "Does anyone else know about your mom?"

"No."

"Why do you do that?"

I swallowed hard. "What? Keep this stuff to myself?"

"Yes. You're like a completely different person depending on the situation. I've known you for a year, but I don't really *know* you."

I didn't expect the pain that shot through me at her words, and it took my breath away with its intensity. "Wait, really?"

"Kind of. I don't know. I think maybe I get glimpses."

Straightening in my seat again, I thought about all the conversations we'd had over the last year and how vague and surface-level they'd been. I'd noticed a lot of stuff about her just from existing in her world, but I had no idea how much she'd noticed about me. And yeah, real truths between us were few.

I didn't know why it mattered, but for some reason, I felt I needed to tell her about my brother. She'd likely find out this weekend anyway, since there were photos of us as kids hanging on the walls in the living room. My gut ached just thinking about seeing them again, let alone having to explain him to her in the same crazy, blindsiding way.

I sighed, turning back to her again. "In the interest of only having one fight like this—"

"We're *not* fighting."

"Okay. In the interest of only having one *conversation* like this, there's something else."

"What?" Her eyes were beyond wary as she looked me over, and it made the guilt even heavier on my shoulders.

"I had a brother. He died when I was five."

She closed her eyes and leaned her head back against the headrest. "Beau."

"I know, I'm sorry. I just didn't want you to see the photos or have my dad say something in front of you if you didn't know."

What I didn't add was that I knew it would probably hurt her to find out about yet another thing I'd kept locked away. Because that shouldn't matter to either of us. But for some reason, it did.

I cleared my throat, trying to force out a lighter tone. "That'd be pretty hard to explain if we're a couple, right? We would have talked about it or something."

"Yeah. We probably would have. Because people who are in a real relationship aren't afraid to open up to each other."

Since she still had her eyes tightly closed, I adjusted in my seat again and faced the road ahead of us. "Well, I guess it's a good thing this isn't a real relationship, then. Like I said, let's just stick to the facts, and we'll be good."

"Fine," she gritted out.

"Can I drive now?"

As soon as she nodded, I made sure the coast was clear before zipping the car back onto the road. We spent the rest of the ride in utter silence—including me, no earbud this time. And she didn't even read. We just stared ahead and digested that "not a fight" in our own ways.

And even though we didn't say a word, I could feel the tension leaking out of the car with every mile. I had no idea what was going on in that beautiful brain of hers, but with each time I felt her look at me while I continued to stare straight ahead, the knot in my chest loosened.

13

LYNDI

Beau used his key to let us into the quaint house in the suburbs of New Orleans, the smell of cleaning products and air freshener slammed into me the second I stepped in.

The living room was minimally decorated, but it looked like none of it had been updated in at least twenty years. And though I could tell his father had made a good effort cleaning up before our arrival, the home was very clearly occupied by an older, single man.

It lacked a sense of unnecessary frill that seemed to fill the house I shared with my sister. No flowers on the table, no color-coordinated throw pillows on the couch, no bits of random clutter on the counters.

And yet, with old family photos lining the walls and shelves, a plethora of what looked like crime thrillers in stacks around the room, and the inviting sense of "come as you are," it immediately filled me with a surprising amount of ... *peace.*

"Well, there he is," Beau's dad said with a wide smile as he looked up from his book. He sat in a ratty old recliner with an oxygen tank at his side, tubes in his nose, and reading glasses perched just above them. "Welcome home."

"Hey, Pops," Beau greeted his dad, then shut the front door behind us before placing his hand on the small of my back. "This is Lyndi."

I stopped myself from jumping at his touch just in time, forcing on a warm smile instead. "It's nice to meet you, Mr. Devereux."

"It's a pleasure to meet you, Lyndi. Call me Louis. How was your drive?"

"Louis," I repeated in my head, loving his French-sounding name and buttery Cajun accent. It was similar to French, but with a touch of a Southern drawl. It was a shame Beau had mostly lost his, if he'd ever had a strong one to begin with. I made a mental note to ask him later.

Then again, it might be better *not* to ask him about his past or his childhood. I wasn't sure I could handle hearing more about what this man had lived through. I'd already known he'd suffered a great loss at a young age, but *two*? And now with his dad being sick ... Beau's suffering seemed endless, and he kept it locked so tight it was a wonder he could even breathe.

Which was why as much as I'd wanted to give in to the overwhelming sense of betrayal I'd felt on the road out here, it wasn't right. He hadn't owed me anything. He hadn't needed to tell me about his family or the losses he'd suffered. We were barely friends—more like acquaintances—before all of this, so really, I should just be grateful I gave him a reason to open up in general. He clearly needed it. Anyone would.

"The drive was good, thanks," Beau replied. He dropped his hand from my back and moved around the living room, looking at the walls and furniture with a small smile. "The place hasn't changed at all."

"If it ain't broke, don't fix it," Louis said with a laugh that quickly morphed into a cough.

Beau lifted my suitcase and gestured down the hall. "Uh, Pops, do you mind if I show Lyndi to the bathroom and guest room? I'm sure you want to get settled, right?"

I nodded. "That'd be nice, thanks."

"Make yourselves comfortable," Louis said with a wave of his hand.

Beau headed for the hallway, and I followed him into the dark space, pleased when he pointed out a small but clean bathroom.

"And here's the guest room," he said, stepping into a simple bedroom with one full-size bed, a bench at the foot of it, and two end tables but not much else.

He put my suitcase on the bench, then headed back out, so I followed him with my heart in my throat. Was that the only bedroom? Was that the only bed? Did that mean we were supposed to—

I stopped spinning out when he flicked on the light of another room. It appeared to be *his* bedroom. One twin bed was pushed against the far wall, the bedding black and navy blue. There were posters of fast, shiny cars, and one that looked like it'd come from a Marine Corps recruiting office.

There was no other furniture except for a small desk in the corner, and even though there were no clothes in the closet—or strewn around the floor—I could almost picture teenage Beau living here before he left for the Marines.

"I'll be staying in here if you need anything during the night," Beau said, his eyes straining like he was trying very hard to appear unaffected by his surroundings.

Unable—or unwilling—to dive into his feelings, I put my practiced smile back in place and hooked a thumb over my shoulder. "Thanks. Do you mind if I shower? I have to shower before I go to sleep. It's kind of—"

"Your thing," he finished, a ghost of a smile on his full lips. Then he led me back to the bathroom. "There should be towels—ah, yep. Right here."

I accepted the towel he'd taken from under the counter and held it against my chest like a shield. "Thank you."

"You're welcome."

For a long moment, we just stood there, me blocking his exit with my towel shield and him looking down at me. The bathroom's size kept us within arm's reach, and every single cell in my body wanted to step closer.

I wanted to tuck up against his chest and have him wrap his arms around me, rest his cheek on the top of my head, and just breathe through whatever storm was raging inside him.

But I didn't.

I couldn't forget that he didn't want this to be real. He'd made it clear on the side of the road that even if I somehow managed to make him happy—though I still wasn't quite sure what to make of that confession—this was going to end.

He was doing what he had to do so his dad would leave him alone about finding someone, all while helping me do the same with my family. Nothing more, nothing less.

Stepping out so he could leave, I tried not to take his hasty exit personally. Then I went back into the bathroom and closed the door behind me, leaning up against it with my forehead pressed into the cold wood.

⚭

The next morning, I woke up in a panic, totally forgetting where I was. Then it hit me like a ton of bricks and I shot out of bed, scared that I'd slept through ... something. I didn't even know what. But since I was here for a reason and not for leisure, it felt like I needed to get out there and make sure I was doing what I came here to do.

I pulled a hoodie over the tank top and shorts I'd slept in, then opened the door and was immediately met with the smell of fresh coffee and bacon. My feet carried me through the hall and into the living room, and a genuine smile popped onto my lips the second Louis looked up from the newspaper he was reading.

"Good morning, sunshine," he said. "How'd you sleep?"

"Great, thanks."

And I had. I'd slept surprisingly well on the probably-twenty-year-old mattress. I'd expected to toss and turn all night without the familiarity of my room at home. My bed. My sheets. My pillows. The soft glow from my twinkle lights that hung around the edges of my bookshelves or the sound machine I sometimes used when I had too much on my mind.

"Glad to hear it," Louis replied. "You hungry?"

Normally, I didn't eat breakfast. I was rarely hungry right when I woke up, and I needed two cups of coffee just to focus on a new day. But I couldn't deny the rumble in my belly at the mention of food. Beau and I had gotten here so late that we'd gone straight to bed, and even though we'd grabbed a quick bite on the way in, I'd been too nervous to eat much.

"I am, and it smells amazing," I said, looking toward the kitchen where I could see only a sliver of Beau's torso between the low-hanging cabinets and the counter.

He was at the stove. Was he the one cooking breakfast? *Shoot.* I loved a guy who could cook. In my books, obviously.

"Ah, that's my boy, probably showing off," Louis said with another one of his laugh-coughs. "I'm not much of a cook. That kid's been making my food since he was about ... ah, well. Long time."

He didn't have to say it. I already knew. Beau had

probably been cooking for his dad since his mom died, which was hard to imagine. That was practically *Grayson's* age.

Even though my nephew had also lost his mom, he'd been three when it happened. He didn't remember much about her as far as I knew, but if he'd lost her at this age? I pictured his sweet face, and my chest grew heavy. The idea of him going through something so horrible made me want to run from the room.

But I stopped myself, because Beau didn't need me to have another emotional outburst like I'd done on the way out here. He needed me to put on a show for his dad.

And now that I knew more about him—about how he'd not only lost his mom at that tender age, but also his brother—it felt just as important to help him as it felt wrong to do so.

"Yeah, you never could get the timing of a full meal figured out, huh, Pops?" Beau asked as he walked out of the kitchen with two plates of food in hand. I hadn't thought he could hear us over the fan above the stove.

Louis harrumphed.

"But thankfully you know how to make the basics and just survive on those, right, old man?"

I heard the words coming out of his mouth, but I couldn't focus on their meaning. I was way too busy staring at the way his biceps flexed when he put the plates on the table and reached out to straighten the silverware beside them. He wore a simple white tee, stretched tight across his broad chest, and the sexiest pair of gray sweatpants I'd ever seen in real life. Turned out, that whole trend on TikTok book review videos about gray sweatpants being hot wasn't limited to fiction.

Why did this man have to be so dang perfect?

Okay, no. Beau was *not* perfect. But dang it, he was flawed in that ridiculously perfect way, where you couldn't help but want to hit him for being such an idiot and also hug him for everything he'd been through. It killed me.

"Yeah, I get by. Anyway, let's eat."

Louis's words brought me out of my tailspin, and we all moved to the table, then I pivoted and pointed to the kitchen. "Coffee?"

"Have a seat, I'll grab it," Beau said with a wink. "How do you want it?"

This man and his winks. Knock it off already, Devereux.
Oh, right. The show.

"Is there creamer?" I asked, hoping beyond all hope there was.

"Oh, you mean that bottled garbage that's supposedly terrible for you?" Louis asked.

I grimaced. "Yes, that."

"Caramel macchiato is the flavor of the week. I love the stuff. What do I care if it's bad for ya?"

Beau snorted and went to get me some, and I settled into my chair across from Louis with a grateful smile.

"So, Lyndi, I hear you're a photographer," he said, digging into his bacon.

I thanked Beau for the coffee and refrained from staring at him as he sat down next to me in those darn sweatpants. "Yes, sir."

"That sounds like a fun job. What made you want to do that?"

I started to give him a simple answer. But then I remembered how at peace I'd felt in his home so far and how there was something about it that had me feeling like I could be myself, so I decided to be honest instead.

"I've always been more comfortable out of the spotlight, but I like to watch people. I don't even remember how old I was the first time someone gave me one of those old wind-up cameras and told me to go wild at a family gathering. It was so fun to slip into the room and take photos of my family laughing and talking together. But I didn't feel like I had to join them. It was like I could be there, but not. And, I don't know, I like taking photos of the moments that people are usually too busy to appreciate."

Louis's kind, hazel eyes sparkled, reminding me so much of his son. "Hmm. Yeah. I definitely wish I'd taken more photos back in the day. Something you don't always think about until you're staring at the same few every day."

Beau cleared his throat, shifting uncomfortably beside me. "Anyway, Pops, what do you wanna do today? You up for anything?"

He scoffed. "Me? No. I'm not getting around too well these days. But you two should go to the festival I told you about. Get out and enjoy the fresh air. Have some fun."

"You could use a little fresh air, yourself," Beau said with a pointed look.

"Did you see I got me a new front porch rocker? I'll be out there, doing my thing. You two go. Seriously. I need to rest."

Beau put down his fork and sighed. "We're here to spend time with you, Pops."

"Yeah, well, I'll be more use to you later if I've got the energy for it, right?" he fired back, not budging.

"It's okay, Beau," I said, reaching out and touching his forearm before quickly pulling my hand away. "Um, we can go explore."

He didn't look too sure. "The festival's pretty chaotic.

If you don't want to do that, we can find something else to do."

"We can play it by ear," I suggested with a shrug.

It was something Grayson always said for some reason, and we both knew it. I was fairly sure it was because he was trying to get his dad to let him do something and didn't want to hear no right away, but either way, it was cute.

Beau recognized the line and looked up with a smile, our shared fondness for Grayson releasing some of the tension between us. But then I caught his dad looking between us with a wide grin and I focused on my coffee again.

I'd thought Beau was tentative and kind with Grayson because he was his best friend's kid and he was sweet like that. I hadn't realized it was because they'd had so much in common until recently. And the reminder of that made me tread carefully.

"Okay, well, I'm stuffed," I said after eating most of the food on my plate. "This was really good, Beau."

He shot me a crooked grin. "I aim to please."

"Hush." I stuck my tongue out at him automatically, really starting to hate that simple phrase and what it did to my insides. "I'm gonna go get ready."

"You do that," he replied to my back as I carried my dishes to the sink.

Then I slipped down the hallway to get ready, and thirty minutes later, we pulled up to the festival. The dirt parking lot was crowded, and dust clouded the air around us. People were everywhere. My fingers tingled, knowing already this wasn't my scene.

A parking spot opened up ahead of us, but instead of pulling into it, Beau made a quick maneuver and pulled right back out of the lot.

"What are you doing?" I asked, looking over my shoulder to see if I could spot the issue.

"New plan."

I tilted my head at him, but when he simply smiled that sideways smile again, I sighed. "Beau, it's okay. We can go to the festival."

"Lyndi, is this your idea of a fun way to spend your Saturday?" he asked, and when I opened my mouth to tell him it was, he held up a warning finger. "Don't lie to me."

With a long sigh, I relented. "No, it's not."

"Exactly."

"But it's fine, I can manage."

He slid his gaze to me as he drove through the city streets. "Why do you always do that?"

"Do what?"

"*Manage*. You do it all the time. You're always trying

to act like stuff doesn't bother you when it clearly does. Why not just be yourself?"

I let out a burst of laughter, complete with a thigh slap. "Ha. You're one to talk."

He joined me in laughing as he shook his head. "Oh, so it's like that, huh?"

"Sure is, *Mr. Fake Date*."

"Mm-hmm. Careful with that flirty banter, trope queen. You wouldn't want this fake relationship story to drift into enemies-to-lovers territory, would you?"

"I mean, without the lovers part, obviously."

At this, he shot me a wicked grin. "Book ain't over yet."

"*Beau,*" I yelled, totally shocked. I swatted him on the arm. "You did *not* just say that."

"Ow, I'm kidding, I'm kidding. It's not my fault you walked right into that."

"Whatever," I said with an eye roll, still chuckling. "Where are we going?"

He seemed so relaxed this morning. All of yesterday's tension had melted away after one night in his childhood home. It was a good look for him, as much as it pained me to admit it. Happy Beau. Not fake happy, but just ... *happy*.

It was nice.

And it kind of made the glimpses I'd gotten through his fake persona for the last year seem even smaller when compared to the canyons of space through his mask now. Maybe it was because he'd told me about his family.

"A daytime ghost tour," he said after a minute. "New Orleans is haunted, you know."

I stilled. "You're kidding, right?"

"Yes."

"Where are we really going?" I asked again with a huff of impatience.

"You'll see."

14

BEAU

"So, tell me more about your cousin's wedding next weekend," I said as we walked along the path next to Lake Pontchartrain.

Breakwater Park was one of my favorite places in New Orleans because of its views and overall relaxing vibe. It was the perfect place to take Lyndi if she wanted to avoid noise and chaos. But I didn't realize until we got here that I'd only ever come out here alone, and there wasn't much to do besides walk and talk and look at the scenery.

"Well, it's in Charleston," she said. "Clara is going all out, making it the most picture-perfect Southern wedding she could ever dream of."

I bit my lip, hoping it was safe to ask the question that'd been on my mind since I first heard the wedding was out of town. "Is there a reason she's not having it at Starlight?"

"It's not a diss against Aria or anything, if that's what you're asking," she said with an easy laugh.

"Just checking. Seems like everyone you guys know gets married there, that's all."

"Well, since her wedding is the *first* week of May and Aria was supposed to have the baby the *second* week of May, she told Clara it might be better to find somewhere else. Plus, her husband's family is in Charleston. So now it's an out-of-town wedding for our family but a local one for his."

"Gotcha."

"So," she went on, eyes on the lake, "we'll get there Friday night and probably go straight to bed, then Saturday she's got some 'family bonding' activities planned."

"That you're *super* excited about," I guessed.

"Oh, *super*. And then that night is the bachelorette and bachelor parties."

I frowned. "The night before the wedding?"

"Yeah, I guess because most of their bridal party is from out of town, they didn't want to make everyone come out multiple times. But I'm sure we'll keep it low-key. Knowing Clara, she'll want to get her beauty sleep."

"Zac isn't in the wedding, is he?"

"No, he doesn't know the groom. So the two of you can hang that night with Grayson while Layla and I go out with the girls."

Relieved that I wouldn't have to tag along on a bachelor party for some dude I didn't know, I relaxed slightly. I hated it when my client was in the wedding party and insisted that meant I had to bro-it-up with the guys. I had my circle of friends, and I was good with them. I didn't need fake ones.

"Cool. I'm sure we can find something to keep us busy."

"I'm sure you will," she replied, then she looked up at me and bumped my shoulder with hers as we walked. "You really like my nephew, don't you?"

"Grayson? Yeah, he's a great kid."

"And um ... maybe you kind of ... relate with him a little?"

My stomach turned and I held up a hand. "Hey, whoa. I didn't tell you that so you could use it against me."

"Ah, right, because talking about real feelings is off-limits with you."

I started to say that it was, but then something about her tone had me deciding it was too late to clam up now. "Fine. Yeah. I guess I feel for the kid. Though, I'm also a little jealous of him."

"Because he was so young?"

"Yep. I wish I didn't remember her, but I do."

Lyndi stopped walking, so I reluctantly turned to face her as she stood there fiddling with the strap of her cross-body purse. "Do you remember your brother?"

"Not really, no," I said in a low voice. I looked out over the water, unable to meet her eyes. "Sometimes I'll remember little things. But I'm not sure if they're real memories or something my mind is tricking me into seeing." I laughed dryly and jammed my hands into my pockets. "Sorry, that probably sounds really dumb."

She took a step closer. "No, it doesn't. If I had a dime for every time I thought something would sound dumb if I said it out loud ... well, okay, I'd be rich, but regardless, I'd continue working as a photographer. But still."

I grasped at the chance to change the subject. "That's really great, you know. The fact that you love what you do."

"Don't you?"

"Yeah, I guess I do. I don't love that being a Marine has kept me away from home for so long, though."

Which, now that I thought about it, was a good reminder for both of us that being a Marine kept me away from a lot of stuff, whether I wanted it to or not.

"Yeah, I would hate that," she said, gesturing for us

to start walking again. "So, can I ask what happened? To your mom and brother, I mean."

"I'd really rather you didn't," I whispered, not trusting my voice.

"Okay."

For a few minutes we walked in silence, the only sound from the lake or the birds or the breeze. Then I hung my head and sighed, the words pouring out before I could stop them. "My mom's is pretty simple. It was breast cancer. She was older—had us later in life because they couldn't get pregnant for a long time after they met. And Rene ... well, he died in a car accident."

Lyndi gasped beside me and then covered her mouth with her hand. "Oh, Beau. I'm so sorry."

"It was my fault. I distracted my mom. I was mad that he wouldn't give me back some stupid toy or something I had with me. I don't even remember what it was. Which is ridiculous, because how important could it have been if I can't even remember what it was now?"

Why was I telling her all of this? I'd thought I was in the clear as we walked in silence, but then it was like someone had taken a giant sledgehammer to a dam, and now the stuff I'd kept to myself couldn't stop flowing out.

"It wasn't your fault, Beau. You were just a kid."

"Yeah, that's what my mom said. Pops, too. But still.

It's not really something I ever believed. Not fully, anyway."

Lyndi reached out and stopped me, turning me to face her. I wasn't sure what she planned to say, but it freaked me out. Only, she didn't say anything. She simply stepped closer and slid her hands around my waist, wrapping me in a tight hug. All of the air left my lungs in a quiet stream as I circled my arms around her back and leaned down to rest my cheek on the top of her head. I hadn't even intentionally done it. It just happened.

For a long moment, we stayed that way. I hugged her like this hug had always been inside of me, begging to happen. It wasn't like that day at the hospital when she'd all but hurled herself against me. I'd known it was for her. She'd needed it. I'd needed it too, but it wasn't the same as this. *This* was meant for me. A purposeful act of comfort on her part, and I couldn't remember the last time I'd been hugged like this by anyone.

When she finally shifted and brought her chin to my chest, and I put my forehead against hers, I had to actively tell myself not to kiss her. I repeated it over and over in my mind.

Do not kiss this woman. Do not kiss this woman. You cannot *kiss this woman.*

And yet I felt my chin dip, my heartbeat racing as my

lips sought out hers, all seemingly against my will. Her hair whipped wildly around us, and I used one hand to draw it away from her face while the other found her hip. Her light-brown eyes caressed mine before lowering to my lips, almost giving me permission to—

"Yes!" a kid screamed from behind us, breaking the spell and causing us to jump apart.

My eyes scanned the park for the source of the shout, landing on a boy about Grayson's age jumping for joy after one of the bean bags he'd just thrown into a portable cornhole board had landed in the hole.

Looking down at Lyndi with disappointment and relief butting heads in my gut, I couldn't help but be grateful to that random kid and his wild shout of victory. Then I slid on a familiar, easy-going smile to mask the turmoil inside me. "That was close."

"What?" she whispered.

"We almost kissed."

She brought her fingers up and gingerly touched her lips. "Did we?"

"Yep. And we can't let that happen."

Her eyes steeled and she stood straighter, but there was humor in the way she was looking at me. "Why, are you afraid you might catch feelings?"

"Nah, I'm afraid you'll tell me it was gross," I joked, jerking my chin toward the parking lot. "Let's go grab some beignets. Can't come to New Orleans and not get some."

She brightened. "Café du Monde?"

My hand went automatically to my chest and I gave her a teasing bow. "Yes, my little tourist. Where else?"

"Aw, sad. Is Café du Monde one of those tourist traps the locals hate?"

"No. But if there's a line, we're not waiting. Most locals don't," I replied with a sly smile. Lyndi's face morphed into one of horror, and I chuckled, backing toward the car. "Come on."

"It was so good to meet you, Lyndi," Pops said, shaking her hand as I loaded the car.

After we'd spent Saturday exploring, we'd come home for dinner with Pops, where he'd regaled us with stories from his good ol' days in the navy. Stories I'd heard about a million times, but Lyndi'd seemed to love it. Especially when he'd told her the story about singing the song from *Top Gun* to my mom.

It should have felt weird to have her in my childhood home, at the kitchen table with my dad, talking about my family like I had nothing to hide. I'd spent the last decade keeping everyone away so I didn't have to share moments like that with them, and yet there she was, feeling like a missing piece to the puzzle instead of an outsider.

"You too, Louis," I heard her say behind me, picturing the warm smile I was sure she was giving him.

"Take care of my boy for me," my old man said in a low voice that wasn't quite low enough. "He's a bit hard to crack, but I think you'll manage."

There was a long beat before she answered, then when she finally did, the two little words made me cringe as I approached, wishing they were true. "I will."

"I'll meet you at the car in a minute," I said when I reached her, lightly touching her back.

I waited for her to give my pops one last smile and wave before getting in the car. When she shut the door, I turned to him and gently closed my arms around him.

He seemed so fragile, but I still had hope. Thirty percent wasn't zero, and if he didn't believe he'd beat this, I'd believe it enough for the both of us. I had to. Because otherwise, this could be the last time I saw him. And I couldn't handle the thought of that.

"Good to see you, Pops," I said as I stepped back.

"You too, son." He nodded toward the car before looking back at me with a bright smile. "She's a keeper, that one."

The words he'd spoken during that horrific phone

call sang through my mind. *Love her, son. Don't let her get away.*

Desperate to smash down the lump in my throat, I shrugged. "Eh, I'm undecided." He glared at me before chuckling quietly. "I'll see you later, old man." Patting his shoulder, I went for the car.

"Beau."

I swallowed and turned back around. "Yeah?"

My dad waved me over to the porch, and when I got close enough, he swatted me upside the head like I was a kid again. "Ow. What was that for?"

Thankfully, Lyndi was looking down—probably at her Kindle already—and hadn't seen it.

"Boy, what makes you think you can bring a *fake date* to my house and try to pass her off as real?" he asked, tone icy. When all I could do was gape at him, he scoffed. "Oh, don't look at me like that. I was born on a Tuesday, but not last Tuesday."

"Pops. Sh-she's not a client," I stuttered.

"What's that mean? She's not paying you? Fine. But that doesn't mean this isn't some kind of charade. I know what real love looks like—"

I snorted and shook my head. "What, and you're saying *this* isn't it?"

"Did I say that?" he growled. "No. I'm *saying*, this *is* it —but you haven't held that woman's hand any earlier than a week ago judging by how jumpy it made her every time you touched her. Shoot, practically every time you *smiled* at her."

I felt my cheeks grow hot at his observation, then a smile worked its way onto my lips before I could stop it. "She's jumpy by nature."

He shook his head. "You always were a stubborn fool, weren't you? Fine, don't admit it. I'm just sayin,' I see what you tried to do here, and I don't like it. But at the end of the day, I can't say it matters much."

My heart pounded in my chest, guilt and grief and shame swirling through me. "What do you mean?"

Then he surprised me by giving me the wink I'd learned from him, a wide smile stretching over his leathery face. "I don't care how it started, son. I still got my way. Drive safe, now."

Then he turned and left me standing on the porch as he went back inside and closed the door behind him.

What just happened?

Numbly, I made my way to the driver's side and got in. Lyndi looked up from her book and gave me a small smile before wordlessly going back to it.

I cleared my throat and reached up to put the navigation on my car's screen, clenching my fist a couple times when I realized my dang hand was shaking.

What was I supposed to do now? I was beyond

rattled, sitting beside a woman who I couldn't seem to fake it with no matter how hard I tried, leaving the home that made me both remember too much that I wanted to forget and forget things I wanted to remember.

Over the course of this weekend, I'd been more real with Lyndi than I'd ever been with *any* woman, and despite the fact that my dad thought he would get his way, I knew the truth.

Having feelings for Lyndi would do nothing but make everything worse in the end. Despite how much I might want to get out of my orders to Hawaii, they were *orders*. As Marines, we were all cogs in a machine, and you couldn't just request a change like that when you were only a few months out from leaving.

Yeah, no doubt about it. Someone already had orders to come take my place, and they probably wouldn't have time to fill the spot I'd leave vacant in Hawaii. This whole thing was completely lose-lose.

My gaze drifted to Lyndi again as I shifted the car into reverse, and my heart squeezed painfully in my chest. All of that may be true, but I'd already screwed up. I'd already fallen for her.

But I wasn't what she wanted anyway since I was leaving, and honestly, it was probably also because she was too scared to let anyone see the real her, just like she always accused me of. I could tell by her expression and body language when she let her perfect mask slip. I was good at reading people, and Lyndi didn't want to be read. Not really.

So, as much as it killed me to know I had to pull back, I had to do it for both of us. "All right, that's that, then," I said, backing out of the driveway where I'd played basketball as a kid without sparing the house another glance.

She didn't look up from her book. "What's what?"

"Well, mission accomplished here. My dad's happy he got his way," I said carefully, knowing I was leaving out a key detail about the *how,* "so I'm in the clear. All we have to do now is put on a good show for your family and we'll be good. We're pretty great at this faking-it-for-family thing, don't you think?"

Please believe it's all for show, please believe it's all for show.

This time, she did look up. But it was to stare out the windshield for a second before looking back down again. "Yep. *Super* good at faking it. Oscar-level, for sure."

Okay, yeah. This sucked. But instead of poking the bear, I simply put in my earbud and started my playlist. She continued to read, still not looking at me. And with that, we started the longest drive of our entire lives.

15

LYNDI

Layla came through the door the next day with a sigh. "I'm exhausted. Remind me never to go back to work the day after flying home from my honeymoon again."

I laughed and put down my phone. "Uh, since you likely won't be taking any other honeymoons, that shouldn't be a problem."

"Traveling, in general, then." She flopped down onto the couch next to me and laid back, putting her long legs over my lap. "Can we skip book club?"

"Uh, no." I pointed to my shirt, which read, *Sorry, can't. I have book club.*

I'd gotten one for all of us last year and each was a little different but all book club related. Layla's said,

What happens at book club, stays at book club, because she was the one who always brought up the controversial topics that got us spilling our guts.

Aria's said, *Book Club: Where we read between the wines,* because she rarely had time to read due to her business, but she never missed our monthly meetings because wine time with her girls was too hard to resist.

I insisted that all of our members wear it each meeting, and because they loved me, they usually did. Even Ms. Hattie had one, but hers was simply a mix of beautiful flowers coming out of an open book with the words *Book Club Babe* scrawled underneath.

"Fine," Layla groaned, "but I think my shirt is packed. I'll have to wear this."

I gulped, shrugging like it was no problem. It wasn't, of course. I mean, did it matter if she was missing the uniform so long as she came? No. Not in the grand scheme. But it was a reminder that this week she was moving what was left of her stuff into Zac's apartment, taking the first step toward leaving me for good when they inevitably got orders, and I hated it.

"Oh, shoot. Before we go, you have to tell me about your trip." She sat up and tucked her legs under her, eyes wide. "How was meeting Beau's dad?"

"It was really nice. He's so sweet. Charming, just like

Beau. But also funny in this quick-witted kinda way. I guess also like Beau. And he was—" I stopped short, taking in her stony glare. "What?"

"Lyndi, did you kiss him or something?"

I reared back. "His dad?"

"Girl, no. Beau."

"Oh. No, why would you even ask that?"

One eye narrowed into a slit. "Because you're so ... I don't know. I feel like something happened."

"I guess a lot happened, but we didn't kiss."

Not unless an almost-kiss counts.

She bobbed her head slowly. "Okay. So, what's 'a lot'?"

"Well, he told me more about himself and why he doesn't want to date anyone for real. I'm not going to go into details because it's his business, but let's just say I don't foresee any of this fake stuff turning real for him. It's pretty cut-and-dried."

"Doesn't sound cut-and-dried. It sounds messy."

I rolled my eyes. "It's not messy. It's real. Which, okay, yeah. Maybe means it's messy. But either way, you don't need to worry about me thinking it can be more than it is because I understand why it can't be, so I'm not letting myself go there."

"Right, because you're so good at taking logic and applying it to your emotions."

"Rude."

"Accurate, though. Honestly, how many times have you told me you understand why something is happening *logically,* but you can't get your feelings to catch up? I'm talking about getting offended or taking things personally that you know have nothing to do with you, yet you still obsess over it. Or feeling guilty for something you said even though you knew you couldn't have known it was an issue when you said it. Stuff like that."

"What's your point?"

She shifted on the couch, looking at me with nothing but kindness in her knowing eyes. "Don't you think *logically* knowing why Beau won't let himself fall for you isn't going to keep you from falling for him and getting hurt anyway?"

My phone screen lit up on the coffee table, taking my thoughts from her words to the notification bar there. It wasn't a text from him, like I'd hoped it would be, but instead a notification from TikTok that a BookTok-er had replied to my comment on her video.

I picked it up and swiped the screen, grinning when I read her response. I'd commented on a post about the latest book she'd reviewed, and she liked my perspective on it.

Layla sighed. "Uh, did I lose you?"

"Yeah, sorry." I put down the phone and grimaced. "What were we talking about?"

She chuckled and nodded at the phone. "What was that, anyway?"

"Oh ... well, I was talking to this lady who does book reviews on TikTok, and she liked what I said about a book she'd reviewed."

"Cool." Layla lifted one perfect brow and angled her head at me. "Why do I feel like there's more to it than that?"

"Well, I've been participating a little more in the BookTok community lately. You know, instead of just lurking."

"Okay ..."

"Beau said he loved my passion when I talk about books and that I should have my own review channel on YouTube. Obviously, if I was going to do anything, it'd be on TikTok, but—"

My big sister held up a hand. "Wait. You hate being in front of the camera."

"Yes."

"So, what, your fake boyfriend tells you to start a book review channel and suddenly you *don't* hate being in front of the camera?"

I frowned. "No, it's not like that. It was just cool to hear I'd be good at it."

"Lyn, of course, you'd be good at it." Her face softened and she reached out and patted my knee. "I'm not saying you wouldn't be good at it. I guess I'm surprised you'd consider it, given the way you've always felt about being anywhere but *behind* the camera."

"Me too. It's probably not something I'd actually pull the trigger on. I just started thinking about how a lot of the videos don't even show people's faces, just the books themselves with text or music. Or I could even do those ones where they only show the pages flipping and inlay excerpts or things you like about it. You know what I mean?"

Layla blinked at me, a small smile tugging at the corners of her lips. "Huh."

"What?"

"You do seem really passionate about this."

"Well, I mean, it could be fun. But I probably won't do it." I shook my head and got up, sliding my phone into my back pocket as I headed for my purse. I picked up my paperback copy of the book we'd be discussing tonight and tossed it in, then put the strap of my bag over my shoulder. "Come on. We're gonna be late."

Layla's eyes flared a little, her lips pulled into a tight line. I could tell she wanted to say something but was working very hard not to, and I found myself hoping she didn't fail and let it out. I had a feeling it would only be more discouraging words about this Beau situation, and I'd had enough of them swimming around in my already cluttered brain as it was.

16

BEAU

Since I was still on leave, I decided to drive down to Bluffton to hang out with the guys while all their women—and Lyndi, too—had their monthly book club meeting with a few other friends. Including Ms. Hattie, of course, who I hoped wasn't bugging Lyndi too much about us.

Paul, Will, and Trevor were involved in an intense F1 race with Grayson on the PlayStation, so Zac and I were cooking dinner without their help. Which was good because I wasn't used to having a lot of cooks in the kitchen.

"So, you haven't said much about your trip to see your dad," Zac said, chopping up a head of lettuce on the other side of the counter.

I wasn't much of a salad guy, but Zac was our resident

health-food nut ever since he'd had to learn a ton about ingredients thanks to his son's nut allergy, so dinner at his house was always a lot healthier than anywhere else.

"Not much to talk about. We hung out with Pops, did a little sightseeing, got some beignets."

As I added a final layer of barbeque sauce to the six racks of ribs Zac had slow-cooked all day, all of the other stuff we did flew through my mind like a movie reel. All vivid and bright, the images tortured me with their intensity despite how hard I tried not to remember.

Sitting in comfortable silence while we read, my dad too—while also wheezing steadily in his recliner.

Sharing meals together at my kitchen table, joking about silly stuff and bonding over the best '80s action flicks. Apparently, her dad and my dad would get along great.

Talking late into the night on Saturday while my dad slept, neither one of us ready to call it a night despite the long drive we had ahead of us on Sunday.

That freaking almost-kiss at Breakwater Park that could have ruined everything.

Not that it wasn't already ruined on my end. I was totally and utterly into that woman, and there wasn't a thing I could do about it without asking her to compromise on what she wanted in a man.

"Uh-huh. Sounds charming," Zac said dryly. "And did your dad buy it?"

The brush I held slipped out of my hand, but I caught it before I splattered barbecue sauce all over myself. "What? Did he buy what?"

"You and Lyndi. As a real couple."

I stared at him, eyes unseeing. "You *know?*"

"Of course I know." He leaned forward and spoke in a low tone. "Bro, do you know who my wife is?"

"I mean, I knew Layla and the girls knew, but I didn't think *you* knew," I whispered, conscious of how close we were to the rest of the guys.

"Of course I know. So do they." He jerked his chin over his shoulder.

I looked into the living room at our friends and his son, then my eyes zipped back to his. "No way. They haven't said anything."

"Yeah, and if they know what's good for them, they won't. All of our wives have sworn us to secrecy. So you'd better not let it slip that we know, or we'll all be dead by the end of the day."

I let my head fall back and stared at the light fixture on the ceiling. "Ugh, well, since you know … what do you think of the whole thing?"

I shouldn't have even asked because I probably

didn't want to know, but I wasn't on a winning streak as far as decision making lately.

"I don't know. It's dicey."

"How so?"

He shrugged. "She doesn't want to be with someone who's leaving, and you are. Layla's worried about her falling for you and then getting hurt when you leave."

I had the same fear, since I already knew how much it was going to suck for me, and I didn't want the same thing for her. "Well, at least she isn't trying to change her mind."

"What do you mean?"

"I don't know. Not that it matters, because this isn't going to turn into a real thing, but I guess I'm glad she's not trying to convince her she should go to Hawaii with me. It wouldn't be right."

He stopped chopping the lettuce and furrowed his brow at me. "Wouldn't you *want* Layla to convince her to go with you?"

"I don't want Lyndi to be *convinced* of anything she's not comfortable with. Even that. But again, it doesn't matter."

"Liar."

"That's not exactly breaking news, is it? Kind of my thing." The second I said it, the familiar words reminded me of Lyndi.

Man, I'm in deep.

"It *could* matter," he said, resuming his chopping.

"Of course it can't."

Zac picked up the cutting board and slid the lettuce into a large bowl. "Why not? You should tell her how you feel."

"I can't."

He added some carrots to the salad. "Again, why not?"

"Because," I said, gesturing with the brush and wincing when I accidently flicked barbecue sauce at him. "Sorry, but you said it yourself, she doesn't want to leave, and I'm leaving. And even if she did, I don't want this either. I don't want something *real* with Lyndi. My life was fine before all this. In fact, so was hers. Everyone else just needs to butt out."

"You're a mess, dude," he said, wiping barbeque sauce off his arm.

"Tell me about it."

"And even with all that crap you're telling yourself, you wound up feeling something real anyway."

I sighed. "Lucky me." Finished with the ribs, I nodded at the salad. "You done prepping the rabbit food? Maybe we can eat these ribs before they fall off the bone by themselves."

"Come on, man, you're telling me if she suddenly

didn't care about leaving, if that was *never* an issue, you wouldn't just push through whatever it is that's keeping you from wanting a real relationship?"

I glared down at the ribs like this was their fault. "It's not that easy."

"Take it from me. It *is* that easy. I think people would rather hold onto the feeling that they're right than let go and be happy. And I know this because I freaking *learned my lesson*. When I think about everything I put Layla through because I thought I was right about how it would end ... man, I'd kill for a do-over."

Grayson must have won the race, because he jumped up from the couch and started doing a victory dance, calling all of his uncles "big fat losers." I watched as they pushed him around and they all laughed, the carefree smile on Gray's face hitting me right in the chest.

Zac was right. I was a mess. And since I'd already told Lyndi about my family and my repeated losses and it had actually made me feel surprisingly better the next day, I figured maybe it was time I told my best friend, too.

I put my hands on the counter between us and braced myself. "My dad's sick, Zac."

He froze, his jaw clenching tight for a second before his face morphed into that pitying expression I'd spent years avoiding. "I'm sorry, dude. How sick are we talking?"

"Stage three lung cancer. He thinks he's a goner, but the docs still have hope. I'm with them."

"Well, me too, then. But still, even *with* that, you gotta be honest with Lyndi. Doesn't that tell you life's too short?"

I rolled my eyes, annoyed that he was missing the point. "*No.* Listen, I'm not gonna get into it, but I've already lost my mom and brother. And now with my dad ... all this just tells me life's short, end of story. I can't ... I *won't* get close to someone only for me to lose her too."

The surprise followed by utter sympathy all over his face was almost enough to make me take it all back and say I was joking. He stepped around the counter and reached out a hand, then thought better of it and crammed it into his pocket instead. "You don't know you'll lose her, man."

I stood straighter. "I do. Trust me, I see a lot of breakups in my line of work."

"Yeah, but you also see tons of examples of it working out. All I'm saying is, next time you're around her, try to hang out with her without all the rest of this weighing you down. And yeah, by *this* I mean all that loss that I know you don't want to talk about, so I won't even try. But just do me a favor and try to imagine what it would be like if the only obstacle was your orders."

"Yeah? And what am I supposed to do about those?"

He pursed his lips and thought about it for a minute, then shrugged. "I don't know. But even if you had to have a long-distance relationship until you got out, wouldn't that be better than nothing?"

I turned away to bring the ribs to the table, unwilling to entertain it. I had no idea if Lyndi would be down for something like that, and even if I wasn't burdened by my past, I wasn't sure I wanted to put myself out there like that only to get shot down.

Realizing the conversation was over, Zac picked up the salad he'd mixed and set it down next to the ribs. "Well, play it by ear."

17

LYNDI

As soon as we arrived at the beautiful, Southern resort for Clara's wedding, my mom and grandma met us at the car, cheesy grins on both of their faces. They greeted Grayson first, of course, but then completely ignored Layla's complaints that she was chopped liver as they zeroed in on me.

And not just me, but Beau too. My *boyfriend*.

The man with the fake wedding date business I'd never been brave—or stupid—enough to hire, who was now here for that very reason without the money attached.

The man who hugged my mom and grandma like we'd been together for years instead of days, because he was so good at reading people he could tell that was the level of enthusiasm and comfort they were hoping for.

The man who'd managed to fake it so well in Louisiana that even I had started to question the nature of his feelings, even though I knew he didn't want to have something real with me.

It was that day at Breakwater Park that clicked it all into place. When he told me about his brother, and I looked at the big picture of what he'd lost, I could see why he didn't want this. I could feel it. So many things about him made more sense, but the thing that stood out most was how badly he needed me to respect it. If I wanted him—or *anyone*—to understand and respect me for who I am and what I want, I had to respect the fact that he never wanted to let anyone close to him again.

Even if he openly admitted I made him happy. Even if he made me happy, too.

For ten minutes that felt more like ten years, I chatted with my mom and grandma while Beau behaved like the perfect boyfriend. He was a total charmer, saying all the right things, and even putting his arm around me like it was the most natural thing in the world.

But then he leaned down and pressed a quick kiss to my temple, and it felt like I'd been cracked with a waffle iron. I jerked back, then tried to play it off. "Sorry, I just have a headache," I said, sliding out from under his arm and pointing to the check-in desk. "I'm going to go help Layla check us in."

"I'll be here with these two lovely ladies," Beau replied easily, causing my mom and grandma to smile and giggle. Yes, *giggle*.

Turning away before they could see me curl my lip, I stomped up to Layla. "How's it going?"

"Good. She's making the keys," Layla replied.

"Here you are," the woman behind the desk replied, handing them over. "Your cottage has two bedrooms, each room with one king bed."

Layla tried to hand her back the cards while my stomach hit the floor. "Um, sorry, there must be some mistake. I reserved a three-bedroom."

"Oh, I'm sorry, ma'am. Let me take another look here." She typed on her computer for a moment, then gave us an apologetic smile. "So, it appears that you did have a three-bedroom for the original booking, but we must have oversold. The best I can offer you is a two-bedroom."

Layla let out a short laugh. "Oversold? How does that even happen?" Then she turned to me and whispered, "This would have never happened at Starlight."

"What about single rooms?" I asked meekly.

She cringed. "Sold out."

"Okay, thank you," I said, pulling Layla away before she said whatever she'd just opened her mouth to say.

We didn't need to make a scene, we just needed to regroup. And I needed to get away from that woman so I could collect myself before I started crying all over the check-in desk.

"I have no idea what happened," Layla promised me as I led her away. "I intentionally made sure to book a three-bedroom. Even before we knew Beau was coming, I did it so Grayson could have his own room."

"Okay, well, it's not like Beau can share with *me*. So, what are we supposed to do now?" I hissed.

"What's wrong?" Beau asked, walking up with that ridiculously nonchalant demeanor he always adopted at weddings. *Chameleon at work.*

I held up my hands, then let them fall with a sigh. "We have a two-bedroom cottage even though Layla booked a three-bedroom. Apparently, they oversold. Zac, Layla, and Grayson can take one room …"

"I can book myself a single, no worries," he said like we hadn't already thought of that.

"They're sold out of those, too," Layla told him.

Beau put his hands on my shoulders, forcing me to look at him. The mask slipped a bit as he looked into my eyes and tried to reassure me. "Lyndi, it's fine. Don't overthink it. I'll sleep on the couch."

Relief coursed through me. "You sure you don't mind?"

"Not at all."

And just like that, he was cheery Mr. Fake Date again in a flash, taking both my suitcase and his and walking us to the cottage. I steamed the whole way there. I was angry at myself for falling for this award-winning actor. And for the level of sarcasm I hurled at him in my own mind. But mostly, I was angry at myself for also being irrationally angry at *him*.

When Zac unlocked the door of the cottage and we stepped inside, however, all I felt was guilt. The couch was nothing more than a love seat. And not even a comfy one. It was one of those wooden ones with thin cushions against the back and bottom. It would probably be terrible if Grayson had to sleep on it, let alone the six-foot hunk of a Marine looking down at it like he was trying to figure out how to get out of this mess he'd stepped in.

"This will be great. If anything, I'll line the cushions on the floor and make a pallet," Beau said, all charm.

I swallowed. "Great."

"Who's hungry?" Zac asked, coming through the door with a bag of fast food and a cardboard container of milkshakes.

"Me," Grayson replied, running for a milkshake.

I wasn't the slightest bit hungry. I was *this close* to crawling out of my skin. Or maybe calling this whole thing off and taking an Uber the two hours back to Bluffton. But I pushed all of that down and made it through dinner, feeling a little better after I got some food in me.

Later, after I'd gone outside to read on the patio, Beau came and sat down next to me without a word, taking out his own book. It reminded me of our time together in Louisiana—the way I'd spent the whole time there trying to decide if we could actually make this work between us even though I wanted to respect his choice not to try.

And that only made me feel worse.

I wasn't angry at Beau. I was angry at the situation.

I looked up, intending to apologize to him for the way I'd been acting—even though I wasn't even sure if he'd noticed—but then I caught movement out of the corner of my eye and gasped.

"What?" he asked, closing his book and looking behind us. "Oh, crap."

Oh, crap was right. That giant milkshake that Zac had admitted might be a little too much for Grayson to finish was now absolutely *covering* the cushions of the love seat that was trying to pass for a couch.

"It's okay," Beau said, holding his hand in the air

between us. "Look, Layla's already cleaning it up. I'll put a towel down if I need to."

"Are you sure? That couch is so tiny ... and now dirty. I feel really bad."

"No worries. It's not like I'm gonna make *you* sleep there."

He hadn't said it, but I'd heard what he'd meant. It wasn't like there was anywhere else for him to sleep. You know, since he sure wouldn't want to sleep in the same bed as me since this is fake, so that would be weird.

I turned back to my book and chose to focus on the love story between two people whose obstacles were sure to be solved by the end. An hour later, my alarm went off on my watch, telling me it was time to get ready for bed so I wouldn't be tired tomorrow.

"I'm gonna head to bed," I told Beau, standing.

He stretched his long arms over his head, causing the hem of his polo to ride up just enough that I needed to quickly avert my gaze. "Me too. You're gonna shower, right?"

"Yeah."

We headed into the cottage, and he gestured to the bathroom on my side of the living area. "Mind if I brush my teeth and stuff real quick before you get in there? I'll be fast."

"Go for it."

He nodded and grabbed his toiletry bag, then headed into the bathroom while I went for my room. I dug around in my suitcase, trying *not* to look at how absolutely massive this bed was compared to the rickety couch Beau would be sleeping on tonight.

"Hey, check out this tub," he called from the bathroom.

Curious, I went down the hall, leaning against the doorframe. A white claw-foot tub sat in the corner of the room, its gold fixtures and feet gleaming in the light from the Edison bulbs over the sink. "Pretty."

"You should skip the shower and put it to good use. You can bring a book in here and relax. Total vacation vibes."

"Ew, I'll pass," I blurted, then instantly regretted it.

Slowly, he turned around, his toothbrush halfway to his lips. "*Ew?*"

"I don't like baths, okay?"

Why did I keep telling him all the stuff I usually kept to myself? It felt like investing my life savings in a snow-cone shop at a ski lodge. Pointless and dumb.

"Why not?" he asked then started brushing those perfect teeth of his as he watched me.

Figuring I might as well tell him at this point, I pointed to the tub and swirled my finger. "Because it's like soaking in ... *human soup*. I don't want to stew in a pot of dirt and ..." I trailed off, distracted by the way he was listening while he brushed without even a hint of amusement in his eyes. Man, this guy was good. "Okay, I'll shut up."

Now, he chuckled and turned to spit. "You're not wrong, though. And that's funny. I've never thought of it that way."

"Are you a bath person then?"

"No. They don't have bathtubs in the barracks. But I guess I liked the idea of it. Seemed relaxing. *Until now,* of course."

"Sorry to burst your bubble," I said with a quiet laugh. Then I shuddered. "Dirty water is the opposite of relaxing for me."

"Fair. What *is* relaxing for you?"

I thought about it as he returned to his oral care, looking at the ceiling. "Reading. Ice cream after a long day. Oh, and watching endless book recs on TikTok, which only make my TBR list longer and longer."

"Book recs *you* should be making."

I snorted, wondering if I should tell him I'd been considering it. "Ha."

"You're already a photographer. I bet you'd be great at it."

Waving a hand, I blew it off, just like I had the last time he'd brought this up. Just because I'd been thinking about it, didn't mean I'd ever have the guts to put myself out there like that. "Yeah, yeah. Hurry up and finish so I can shower."

He smirked. "Yes, ma'am."

I started to head back to my room, then stopped and turned back around. "Wait, you're not gonna take a bath, are you?"

He pulled his toothbrush out of his mouth as a full-blown grin appeared, complete with a mouthful of foamy white bubbles. "Why, you thinking of joining me?"

I stepped toward him ever so slowly, deciding that if he was going to say things to get a rise out of me, he deserved to get the same treatment in return. "*Beau*, the only thing more disgusting than soaking in my own dirty water, is soaking in somebody else's."

His smile dropped and he spit out the toothpaste, then he wagged his toothbrush at me. "You sure know how to make a guy feel gross, you know that?"

"Sorry," I said with a shrug.

"Don't be. Now quit distracting me. I'm supposed to be finishing up so you can shower."

I woke up around two in the morning feeling restless. The bed was comfortable, but there was something nagging at me and no matter how hard I tried, I kept waking up every thirty minutes or so.

I knew exactly what it was, too, but I tried to ignore it.

Him.

And since I probably wouldn't look very good tomorrow unless I got at least a few hours of sleep, I finally decided to go out and check to make sure he was okay. That couch had to be a nightmare to sleep on, and I kept picturing him sleeping while sitting up. Or not sleeping at all, like me.

When I opened the door and stepped into the living room, I almost groaned out loud. Not because he was shirtless, which okay, yeah, was worthy of such a reaction. No, it was because his head was tipped over the arm of the love seat with his pillow resting on the end table, bent back at what had to be a painful angle.

His carved-from-marble torso was crooked so he could rest his long legs on the ground instead of on the couch itself, likely because they didn't fit all the way across.

And because of the strange position he was in, his arms were slung off to one side, the sheer weight of them hanging toward the floor making me think he was seconds away from slumping right off the couch.

Sighing, I tiptoed over and sat on the coffee table, pushing his shoulder to see if I could straighten him up a bit without waking him.

But the second I made the first little shove, he woke with a start and jumped forward, slamming his forehead right into mine.

"Ow," I cried, grabbing my already throbbing head.

"Lyndi, I'm so sorry, I didn't mean to—"

I held up my hands and tried to blink the stars from my vision. "It's fine. It's my fault. I was trying to fix you without waking you up, but now I see that was a stupid idea."

"*Fix* me?"

"Yes, you were about to fall off the couch. Or even if you weren't, you looked really uncomfortable. I was trying to see if I could get you to ... you know, scoot."

He chuckled. "Ah, yeah. It was the best I could do, given the milkshake disaster."

"But I thought Layla cleaned up the mess." I looked toward the towel, seeing no evidence of chocolate milkshake.

"Yeah, she did. But she used a ton of water. It's still wet."

I patted the towel then pulled my hand back and

wiped it on my pajama pants. Then I winced. "Ew. I'm really sorry, Beau. We should have called to confirm we had enough beds once you decided to come."

"Lyn, I'm a Marine. This is no biggie to me. I've slept in a lot worse places than this. Including a muddy hole while getting eaten alive by mosquitos."

"Sounds pleasant."

"Quite."

I tapped my forehead, sucking in a breath when I felt a lump.

"You okay?" he asked, eyes tracking my movements.

"Yes. But listen, this is ridiculous. We're adults, and we both know nothing is going to happen between us because neither of us want it to, right?"

He gulped, nodding quickly. "Right."

"Exactly. So, you can sleep on the other side of the bed. It's a king. There's plenty of room for both of us—with a line of pillows between us."

He chuckled, but then he shook his head and reclined back onto the couch again. "No, I don't think that's a good idea."

Lowering his head to the table pillow again, he winced like the motion hurt his neck.

I rolled my eyes and tugged on his heavy arm. "Come on. I'm not taking no for an answer. But you need to put on a shirt. And I get the side away from the door."

"Anything else?" he asked as I pulled him along.

"Yep. Door stays open and you stay above the comforter. I think that about covers it."

I'd turned toward the bed, but he reached out and grabbed my arm, forcing me to look up at him in the dark room. His eyes bored into mine, searching for any hint that I was doing that thing where I pretended to be comfortable with something when I wasn't.

"Are you sure?" he asked in a gravelly tone, so quiet I could barely hear him.

"Yes. Don't make a big deal out of it and it won't be."

He dropped my arm. "Okay."

He went to the closet and pulled down a spare blanket while I arranged two of the extra-long king pillows in a line down the center of the bed. Then I climbed in, pointing at his chest. "Ah-ah. Shirt."

"Right, sorry." He left, and I heard the bathroom door close with a quiet snap.

Why did he need to go in there to put on a shirt?

A minute later, he was back, and he was wearing a black shirt with a different pair of sweats than he'd been wearing a moment earlier. "Better?"

"Better. But um, why did you change your pants?" I probably shouldn't have asked, but whatever. I'd apparently lost my ability to filter myself around this guy.

He laid down on top of the covers, and I heard him

shaking out the blanket and covering himself with it in the dark. "Like I said, Layla used a *lot* of water. That's why I didn't have a shirt on before. It's like she cleaned the mess with a fire hose."

I narrowed my eyes at the nearly black ceiling, making a mental note to ask her if that was an intentional move to stick it to Beau. She wasn't his biggest fan, and I wouldn't put it past my crazy, overprotective big sister.

And if it *had* been intentional, she probably hadn't considered he'd wind up here.

Not that he particularly *wanted* to be here. I'd gotten the impression it was the last place he wanted to be. And because of that, I felt the need to get something off my chest so he could relax about my intentions of inviting him to sleep here.

"Beau?" I asked quietly, wondering if he'd already fallen asleep.

He cleared his throat, answering that question. "Yeah?"

"I just want you to know that I get it."

"Get what?"

"Why you're so fake."

I felt the bed rumble with his laughter. "Whoa, shots fired."

"I'm sorry. That came out wrong. I told you, I'm

bad at—"

He held up a finger, silhouetted against the light coming through the open door to the hallway. "Don't say it."

"Sorry. What I meant to say is that I get why you don't want to have a real relationship with me. Or anyone. I know it's because you think you'll wind up losing someone else who matters to you."

There was a long silence, and if it hadn't been such a delicate topic, I might have thought he'd fallen asleep. Finally, he sighed. "How do you know that?"

"I don't know. I just see it, I guess."

"Uh-huh."

I fidgeted with the sheet. "And I want you to know it's understandable. And it's okay. I don't blame you, and I'm not going to try to change your mind."

"Um." Another long pause. "Really?"

"Yes. Why is that surprising?"

"I don't know, I guess I just figured you'd tell me to man up and get over it."

I sat up, looking down at him in the dim light. "I think you probably know me well enough by now—the real me, I mean—to know I hate it when people try to get me to *woman* up and get over my stuff. It's exhausting. So, I wouldn't do that to you. Sometimes I think we all need someone who's going to let us have our things and not try to fix us, you know?"

He stared back at me, his expression completely blank. "Yeah. Makes sense. It is what it is, right?"

"Right."

I laid back down, this time turning on my side and putting my back to him. His answer to that could only mean one thing: all the little things I'd thought I'd felt between us were either really in my head, or not important enough to him to make a difference in the way he felt.

Which was honestly exactly what I expected. I wouldn't have invited him in here if I'd thought he'd finally admit that we could try to make this work despite everything that stood in our way. At the end of the day, Beau Devereux was just as unattainable now as he always had been, so he might as well be a paperback book on the other side of those pillows rather than a real man.

"And it's the same for you too, then," he said, causing my eyes to pop open in surprise. "With not wanting to date someone who's leaving, I mean. I get it. And I don't think you need to worry about how anyone else would perceive you for feeling that way. Because you're right, this isn't a romance novel. I'm not the hero and you're not the heroine, so you don't need to worry about readers thinking you're being unsupportive of my job. We're just two people doing each other a favor, and that's it."

I'd never felt so seen in my entire life, and I knew he felt the same way. Which was why the tear slipping down my cheek was so confusing. Why did it matter? He was still the same old Beau I'd had a crush on for over a year with no chance at cracking. Nothing had changed, no matter how much his dad or my family or I might want it to.

I heard him shift behind me, then felt the bed move under his weight. "Lyndi?"

Turning, I jumped when I saw him leaning over the pillow divider. "Yeah?"

"Just so you know … if things were different, if there was ever a right woman … it would be you."

My mouth fell open before I could even think about clamping it shut. He'd heard my quiet slipup at Layla's wedding about there being a right man who could get me to leave. I'd wondered but hadn't known for sure. And now I did.

He reached out, slowly tucking a stray piece of hair behind my ear. Then he leaned back and disappeared into the dark on the other side of our makeshift wall.

"Good night, Beau," I said, turning away once again.

"Good night, Lyndi."

18

BEAU

The next morning, Lyndi and I barely spoke when we were in the privacy of the cottage. But outside with the family, we had to play nice. We had breakfast with her parents and grandparents, did team-building activities like the bride had arranged, and even made it through a round of mini-golf with her parents, Zac, Layla, and Grayson.

I was fine since this was my job, and I was a master at putting on a good show. No matter how frustrated I might be on the inside, on the outside I was cool as a cucumber.

Lyndi, on the other hand, not so much. But oddly, I didn't think it had anything to do with me or our fake relationship. If I wasn't mistaken, it was simply the setting. I could practically feel the tension coming off her in waves, so I needed to pull her aside and make sure she was okay before she took off screaming.

"How's it going?" I asked when I was sure we were far enough away from anyone who could overhear us.

"Great," she lied.

I angled my head so I could catch her gaze. "Lyndi. How's it going?"

"I'm freaking out."

Chuckling, I tucked my hands into the pockets of my dress slacks. "I can tell."

"Do you think anyone else can?"

I shook my head. "No." *Not yet.*

"It's just a lot. There's a lot of people here, and I kind of want to go back to the cottage and read. How terrible am I?"

"Not terrible. In fact, more normal than you think. I bet you half the people here would rather be somewhere else, too."

She frowned up at me. "You think?"

"I do. I've been to plenty of weddings with introverts who only hired me to help them make it through the day without going nuts. Don't get me wrong, I think there is a ton about you that's really ... unique." I almost said *special* or *intriguing* or *mind-blowingly interesting*, but it felt like a little too much. I had a point to make, and it wasn't to tell her how I felt about her beautifully different brain. "You'd be surprised how many people have stuff they mask when they're in public. Including *me*, if you remember."

"What, so you're saying I've got issues, but you have them too?"

"Oh for sure, you're a twelve-month subscription. In fact ..." I paced in a circle around her, lifting each arm and looking underneath it, making her squirm and twist to get away from me.

"What are you doing?" she hissed.

"I'm looking for one of those little white cards that falls out of the magazine. It's gotta be here somewhere." I continued to poke at her until—"There it is."

"What? The card?"

"No. The smile you don't think too much about." The blinding smile on her face faltered slightly as she looked away, so I cleared my throat and took a step back. "Anyway, if you want me to stay here and tell everyone you're not feeling well so you can take a beat to recharge, I will."

"No, I should stay. I'll regret it if I don't."

"Okay. But the minute you're done, say the word, and I'll get you out of here."

"Thanks."

"Hello, you two. Are you having fun?" Ms. Hattie

asked, seeming to materialize out of nowhere with her husband on her arm.

"Yep," Lyndi said, a smile coming quickly now, "lots of fun."

She stepped closer to me, so I put my arm around her for probably the twentieth time that day. But my reaction to having her so close was just as potent now as it had been the first time I'd done it.

"Hi, Thatcher," Lyndi greeted him, "good to see you."

"You too, Lyndi. Hey, Beau, how's it going?" he asked me, shaking my hand with a kind smile.

"Great, sir, thanks."

"Where's Brett?" Lyndi asked.

I poked her side in a funny *why do you care?* kind of way, but she only pinched the back of my arm in return.

"He's at the shop, running it for us this weekend," Ms. Hattie explained. "He said one wedding was enough for him on this trip."

Thatcher tugged on her arm. "Come on, Hattie, let's go find me some food."

"You got it," she replied, then peered at us with a mischievous smile. "Have fun, lovebirds."

We kept our phony smiles in place until they were gone, then I turned back to Lyndi. "You know the whole thing with Brett was a setup, right?"

"What? How so?"

"Apparently, we've had targets on our backs the whole time. She thought trying to set you up with him in front of me would push us together."

Eyes wide, she slowly shook her head. "Wow. I should have known. Joke's on her."

Pain sliced through me, but I played it off. "Yeah. For real. And it's a good thing we're going to keep up the illusion after I leave. If she thinks she's won, she won't mess with you again." I looked over my shoulder and laughed. "See? Look at her. She's probably talking to whoever that is about her dating life."

Lyndi followed my gaze and nodded. "That's another one of my cousins, and you're totally right. She probably is."

"Everything's running like clockwork. All *we* have to do is play our parts."

Zac appeared behind Lyndi, waving to get my attention.

Frowning, I held up a finger to him before looking down at her. "I need to go see what Zac wants. You gonna be okay?"

"Yes, Beau. Your little magazine thing loosened me up. I'm good."

"Okay, be right back."

I crossed the grassy lawn to where Zac stood, nodding at him as I approached. "What's up?"

"Hey. Are you doing what we talked about?" he asked, jerking his chin toward Lyndi.

"What, putting aside my wounded little heart and trying to have real feelings for her?"

He smirked. "Yes. That."

"It's not a good idea."

"Why not?"

"Because we talked last night, and she said some stuff … I don't know, man. She said she gets why I don't want to have a real relationship with her, given my history. And she doesn't blame me."

"Did you tell her it was too late? You already want to have a real relationship with her?"

I looked around, feeling oddly exposed. "No."

"So, she still thinks this is all fake to you, even though it's about a million miles from that?"

"I don't know if I'd say *a million*. That's a little extreme."

He patted my shoulder. "Tell that to your face when you look at her."

"When did you turn into such a sap, Zac?"

"Marriage did it, I think. I'm pretty sure I'm screwed now."

"Great."

"So, why didn't you tell her how you feel? Sounds like the conversation last night would have been the perfect time."

Actually, it wouldn't have been because I happened to be sharing her bed at the time. I adjusted my tie, suddenly feeling like it was a little too tight. "Because then I asked about her not wanting to date someone who's leaving, and her answer pretty much told me she wasn't letting herself be into me either. I think maybe some things just aren't meant to work out, you know?"

"Nope. But again, I'm a sap now, so what do I know?"

"Uh-huh." My gaze wandered back to Lyndi, finding that she was talking to an older woman who looked a lot like her mom. I needed to get back there and do my thing. "Anyway, abort mission. I'm gonna keep doing what I'm doing and call it good."

He hung his head. "Your loss, man."

"No," I disagreed, backing up to rejoin her, "because you can't lose something you never had."

I hurried over to Lyndi and pasted my professional smile in place, sliding next to her and resting my hand on the small of her back. "Hi."

"Aunt Rose, this is my boyfriend, Beau," Lyndi said, introducing me the same way she had been all morning.

"Nice to meet you. I've heard a lot about you."

"You too," I replied, slightly uneasy.

"How long have you two been together?" Aunt Rose

asked, blinking up at us with an innocent smile on her lips.

"Oh, almost a month now, right?" I asked Lyndi.

She nodded with a grin. "Yep."

"How nice. And how did you meet?"

Lyndi squeezed me tighter against her. "He was at a wedding I was working."

"Was it love at first sight?" Aunt Rose asked, her hands clasped in front of her.

Oh, this is a new one.

I looked down at my fake girlfriend. "What do you think, Lyn?"

She pursed her lips, then shook her head. "I'm not a huge fan of love at first sight. I'd say ... crush at first sight is more accurate."

"I can't blame you," Aunt Rose crooned, giving me a look that had me gulping like a rabbit spotted by a hungry ... well, cougar, actually.

Lyndi gasped. "Aunt Rose!"

"I'm old but I have eyes," she said with a teasing laugh. "Anyway, my daughter said you have a business as a wedding-date-for-hire. Is that how this started?"

I shook my head and slung my arm over Lyndi's shoulders. "No, no. This was completely unofficial."

"I see. And are you still in the business?"

"Not locally," I answered, again, like I had been all

morning. It was a popular question since her family all knew about my side gig and this is what we'd agreed on. "I'll still take out of town jobs, though."

"Isn't that a little *strange* for you, Lyn? Knowing he's out there with other women? I know it's all for show, but still."

If other family members had thought that today, they hadn't had the guts to share their opinion on it yet. And if I were being honest, it was a fair question. Now that I knew how I felt about Lyndi, the idea of going on any more fake dates didn't sit well with me at all.

But what was I supposed to do about my old man's debt? I couldn't just cut off thousands of dollars a month for a woman who openly made it clear we couldn't be together for reasons that were important to both of us. That would be crazy.

And yet, Lyndi gently removed herself from under my arm and straightened her shoulders. "No, it's no big deal. It's just business. I know he's able to separate fake dates from real feelings. He's a master at it. Excuse me."

She started to take off, but there was no way I planned to let her get away that easily. Not after we'd answered that question the same way half a dozen times already and she hadn't reacted like *that* even once.

But before I could say anything, a woman's voice called out from behind us. "Oh, Lyndi, there you are!"

She turned, not even looking my way. "Yes?"

The woman held up her fancy camera. "I'm Joanie. Clara wants me to take photos of all of the couples so you'll have a keepsake. Would you two mind posing?"

I considered telling her it wasn't a good time, but then I saw Lyndi's mom and grandmother watching from about twenty feet away with big grins on their faces.

Stifling a groan, I held out my hand to Lyndi, silently pleading with her to put whatever that was aside so all of this wouldn't be for nothing. I shot my eyes toward her family, and when she spotted them too, she nodded and placed her hand in mine.

We stood together, straight as boards, barely touching. Smiling sure, but I knew without a doubt we looked like the life-size versions of Barbie and Ken.

"Great, that's nice," Joanie said, looking a little like she meant it looked terrible. "Can you do a little more? Maybe try to loosen up a bit? You look … stiff."

Thinking on my feet, I grabbed Lyndi's hand and twirled her, catching her in my arms and lowering her into what I knew would be a picture-perfect dip.

"Ooh, *perfect*. This is amazing," Joanie called. "Why don't you give her a smooch?"

I shouldn't do that.

Definitely not.

Oh, who cared at this point? It already felt like we were at a tipping point, so why not take a leap over the edge?

But the moment my mouth closed over hers—finally, after what felt like years of wanting—I knew I hadn't simply taken a leap over the edge. I'd fallen face-first out of an airplane with no parachute, sure that I'd meet my end as soon as I hit the ground.

And because of that, I decided to enjoy the scenery on the way down. I kissed her slowly and tenderly, taking more time to savor the connection than I ever had with anyone in my entire life. Then at the same time, the fury of desire for her raged inside of me, begging to be let free even though I wouldn't let it.

Kissing Lyndi erased all the doubt and fear I'd bottled up my entire life. Her lips were warm and welcoming, and I'd never felt anything like this with any other woman.

Not with a fake date, where I basically had to step outside my body so I wouldn't have to think about how weird it was that I was getting paid for it.

Not with a real date, when I'd always held back because I knew I'd never let myself feel more than the basics.

Not even with that cheerleader I'd kissed in high school on a dare, even though I knew it was the first time for both of us and I thought it was the coolest thing ever.

I'd always heard kissing caused people to catch feelings, but in all reality, I'd never experienced it on my end. It was just something I was trying to protect myself from in case the woman I was kissing decided to do so.

But this kiss? This kiss shifted something inside of me. If I'd thought kissing her was what would cause us to catch feelings, I was completely wrong. We'd already done that. But now those feelings had been set on fire, and there was absolutely no going back.

19

LYNDI

Kissing is gross.
    Right.
Sure it is.

Maybe kissing other people was gross. Maybe the *idea* of kissing was gross. But kissing Beau Devereux could not have been more opposite of that word.

It was intoxicating. Electric. Consuming.

It was fireworks and champagne and freaking *magic*.

Beau moved his lips over mine in a way that was so gentle and loving while also managing to be coaxing and confident in a way that had my blood boiling.

Some logical part of me knew this kiss wasn't lasting as long as it felt like it was. We were standing in front of a photographer for crying out loud—with my grandmother not twenty feet away. But time and space didn't exist at this moment, because the second his lips touched mine, the entire world fell away.

But all good things must come to an end, so after what felt like a lifetime and also barely a second, he lifted me out of the dip and drew his lips from mine. But he didn't release me, thank goodness. I didn't think I'd be able to stand if he did.

"That was beautiful," Joanie said with a delighted squeal. "You guys are going to love these photos. Thank you!"

I was still trapped inside Beau's eyes as he held onto my arms and gazed down at me, but out of the corner of my eye I saw her prance away like the ground hadn't just split open under our feet.

"Lyndi," he said evenly. My name falling off his pillow-soft lips in such a casual way yanked me out of the moment as if I'd been thrown from a dream.

He was fine. Just like the photographer who got us into that mess, he had no idea how amazing that kiss was. *He didn't feel it.* He may have been holding onto me still, but his face was totally blank.

He didn't have a broody stare that flamed with desire the way book boyfriends always did after an intense first kiss. There was no clenched jaw, or rattled expression, or raspy voice when he spoke his first post-kiss words.

He was simply ... *fine*. Because to him, Mr. Fake Date,

the master of being whoever he needed to be, this was all a sham. Pure and simple. I jerked free, not caring who was watching. Just as Layla said, fake-dating Beau was a terrible idea. Because now that he'd *kissed* me, I knew I was way past the point of being able to let him go without getting hurt, and that knowledge was a crushing weight on my chest as I ran away.

And he didn't even try to stop me.

"Um, hello?" my sister called as she ran to catch up to me. When she reached me, she tugged me into the conveniently close bathroom and let out a noise of frustration. "What part of *no kissing* did you not understand? I saw that."

I put my hands on my hips and paced the marble floor. "I know. I know. It was horrible."

This brought her up short and she looked dumbfounded. "Wait. Really? I figured it was amazing. Ill-advised, yet amazing."

"No, not the kiss itself," I said. Leave it to Layla to give me a reason to let out a short laugh in the midst of heartbreak. "*That part* was amazing. But that's what makes it so horrible."

She nodded like that made sense, then she stopped

my forward momentum and pulled me into her arms for a tight hug. "Okay," she said into my shoulder, "so, I'm kind of at a fork in the big-sister road, here."

"Meaning?" I murmured with my cheek still squished against her neck.

She pulled back and used her thumbs to wipe my tears in such a way that wouldn't ruin my makeup. "Well, I could take the road that leads to me telling you to get out of your comfort zone and maybe try to see what it would be like to leave Bluffton with him. If that kiss—and the rest of it, the stuff that's been building for like a year now—all adds up to you being in love with him, then maybe that's what you should do."

"And the other road?"

"The other road is the one where I don't try to make you do what *I* would do if it were me."

I swallowed, turning to the mirror to clean myself up. "And, if you went that way, what would you say next?"

"That it's going to hurt, but you should probably end things with him now. Call off this whole thing before it gets worse. Because I have a feeling if it goes on any longer, you're going to be absolutely *crushed* when he leaves, and I really don't want that to happen."

I met her eyes in the mirror. "I think it might be too late for that."

Layla's eyes softened even more, making her face look a little bit like it was about to melt off. "Which road do you want me to take, Lyn? I need to know what to say so I can help you."

"Lyndi?"

I spun around at the sound of Beau's voice, widening my eyes at Layla.

"Beau, this is the women's restroom," Layla said impatiently.

"I know it is, that's why I'm not coming in. Lyndi, can we talk? Please?"

Layla looked to me for an answer, and I nodded. "Okay. Good luck. I'll see you later."

I hugged her one more time before checking my reflection again, then we walked out. Beau looked even more gorgeous than ever now that I knew what it was like to feel his lips on mine, and my heart cracked at the sight of him leaning against the wall outside.

I waited until Layla walked away, then turned hesitantly toward him. "Sorry about her."

"It's fine."

Shifting from one foot to the other, I fought to keep my emotions in check. "So, um, what did you want to talk about?"

"I just wanted to make sure you were okay. I know

we said we'd only kiss when prompted, and while that was technically prompted, I know it was ... surprising."

I wrinkled my nose at him, needing to lighten this up before I started crying again. "You're not gonna ask me if it was gross, are you?"

A shocked laugh escaped him, causing him to put a hand on his chest. "Uh, no. I don't wanna know."

Well, it wasn't. Unfortunately for me.

Remembering that I'd only bolted because of his post-kiss reaction, I squared my shoulders and lifted my chin. I needed to gain back a little dignity. "It's fine. I could tell it wasn't a big deal to *you*, so it's not a big deal to me."

"What's that supposed to mean?" he asked, his whole mouth curling up like he'd just tasted acid.

"Honestly? I know I don't have a lot of real-life experience, but after that kiss, you looked ... *fine*. You weren't all lit up with desire or clenching your jaw or feeling rattled. It was just *business*."

I didn't know what I expected him to say, but the bitter laugh that shot out of him wasn't it. He jammed his hands into his pockets and took a step back. "Ah, lemme guess, the heroes in your romance novels always get all lit up and jaw-clenchy, am I right? Little descriptions put in there by the author to let you know how much that kiss turned their whole world upside down in case you wondered if it was just a kiss or *the kiss?*"

I nodded, once again. The man could read people, and he'd read me like one of the very books he thought so little of. "Yep. But don't worry, I get it. You 'aim to please,' right? And this isn't real." I'd used air quotes around his favorite line, and he'd winced like I'd slapped him.

Without warning, he moved right up against me, his breath hot on my face. "You know, maybe if you stopped comparing real-life men or real-life kisses to fictional ones, it might help you navigate dating in the real world a little better."

"I've heard that," I snapped.

"Yeah?"

"Yeah. But you know why I always make things about book boyfriends?"

"Enlighten me."

"Because if I dismiss them for not saying the right things or doing the right things, then it's not *about me*. It's not about how I don't feel like I know how to say or do the right things, and even if I manage to mask that for a little while, deep down I know I won't be able to do it forever. Okay? So, us breaking up for all these non-book-boyfriend reasons is a lot better than all of that. Is that *real* enough for you?"

Movement caught my eye, and I flicked my gaze that way without thinking. Then my eyes landed on my grandma walking over here with her head tilted like she was concerned.

Concerned we were fighting.

Maybe even concerned we were *faking*.

Oh, no. This wasn't going to fall apart after I got my heart trampled. Not on my watch. *We're just a happy couple, nothing to see here, Grandma.*

I reached for his face, pulling him toward me and right into a crushing kiss. He responded immediately, wrapping his arms around me, one hand at the small of my back and one at the base of my neck.

This kiss was different already, only a second in. But I wouldn't let myself experience the contrast between tender and passionate. I didn't need to add such comparisons to my memory bank only to cry over it later.

I snuck a glance over his shoulder to make sure the coast was clear, and when I saw that Grandma had pivoted and taken off in the other direction, I wrenched free of him and stepped back.

"What—"

"My grandma was coming," I said quickly, the burn of embarrassment shooting through my veins. "It was fake."

And then I turned on my heel and left him once again, this time not bothering to look at his expression. I didn't need to see him looking unmoved again, and he didn't deserve to see me looking—once again—like my entire world had been turned upside down.

20

BEAU

"That woman is infuriating," I said to the empty hallway, just barely stopping short of punching a wall.

She'd totally wrecked me, and she was *mad* because I didn't express myself the way she thought I should while I was still trying to figure out which way was up?

How dare she.

There I'd been all morning, *not* hoping while also low-key *obnoxiously* hoping for a reason to kiss her, and in a few minutes, I'd gotten *two*. And then she lost her mind and freaked out after both of them.

See, this is another reason people shouldn't force people into relationships.

As I paced around the hallway and ran through my thoughts, I zeroed in on her confession about why she always chased book boyfriends. Just as I'd suspected, it was because the things that made her so amazing to me scared other guys away, and she wanted to protect herself from that.

It blew my mind. It was wrong. *She* was wrong.

Now, more than ever, I knew I needed to figure out how to stay in South Carolina. Not just for her, because I also had Pops to think about. But if I had any chance at being with her, I had to take it. And it wouldn't be in a way where I had to change her into something that she wasn't. I needed to meet her where she was if I had any hope of showing her this was real for me, and she could be real *with* me.

With purposeful movements, I pulled out my phone to text Grant.

Me: Hey, man. Quick question. Are they hurting for drill instructors right now?

Thankfully, he started typing right away. *Great timing.*

Grant: I mean, usually if given the choice most Marines pick embassy duty or recruiting duty over this, so I guess they're always accepting applications. Why?

My pulse sped up, victory so close I could almost feel it. But there was one more consideration.

Me: I think I might put in a package. But only if I can request to be at Parris Island. Is that a thing?

Grant: Yeah, they give you a preference on East or West. But it's not a guarantee. This is still the Marine Corps.

I fist-pumped the air, then looked around to make sure no one was watching. Clearing my throat, I went back to my phone.

Me: Yeah, I hear you. Still, might be worth a shot.

Grant: Why would you want to be a DI? Didn't you hear me when I said how rough it's been?

Me: I heard you. But it's the only way I can think of to get out of my current orders so I can stay here.

Grant: Okay. Well, if you put in a package, expect it to roll fast. You'll probably be sent to DI school pretty quick. And that, my friend, is rough.

I frowned. How bad could it be? I'd already gone through boot camp, which was thirteen weeks of chaos and mind games. Then I'd been on a combat deployment and several other training detachments. I could handle DI school.

Might as well bite, though.

Me: Why? What's it like?

Grant: Imagine going to boot camp again, only this time you're ten years older, more set in your ways, more salty. And the DIs are literally trying to break you down to feeling like a worthless piece of dirt only so they can build you back up into someone who knows how to do that to other people.

This dude knows how to paint a picture.

Me: Wow.

Grant: Yep. Choose carefully, man. It's intense.

Me: I will. Thanks for the info.

I put my phone away and headed back out to the grass where the guests were mingling. Zac took one look at me and left Grayson with Thatcher, jogging over. "What's up? You look like you're on a mission."

"Yeah, the one I told you we were aborting."

He snorted. "I figured. How can I help?"

"I just talked to Grant. I'm putting in a package for drill instructor duty."

His face soured. "You're *what?* Why would you do that? You know they'll make you do a B billet eventually, and you would make a killer recruiter."

"Because I can request to be stationed at Parris Island."

"So you won't have to leave Lyndi."

"Or my pops. I mean, I'd be closer to him than if I were in Hawaii."

He let his head fall back while he thought about it, then he sucked in a breath. "Okay, well, that's a good plan. So, I guess that means you're giving up all that crap about not wanting something real?"

"I don't have a choice, man. It's too late."

Zac raised a hand and pointed at me with a massive smirk. "Now who's the sap?"

"Shut up," I said, swatting his hand away with a laugh.

"So, now what?"

"Now, I'm gonna take your advice and treat the rest of this weekend like I would if it were real. She's under the impression I'm a total psycho with no feelings, so I need to prove that's not true."

"Good luck."

I rolled my shoulders, trying to release some of the stress of the last hour. "Maybe tonight I'll take her on a date. Something she'd love ... maybe—"

"You can't tonight. She's got that bachelorette party thing."

"Oh, that's right. Where are they going, anyway?"

I pictured Lyndi being out bar hopping and wondered how she'd feel about all the chaos of a party bus or a bicycle trolley through downtown Charleston. If she didn't like the looks of the festival in New Orleans, she definitely wouldn't like any of *that*.

"Well, Layla was put in charge of planning it, so she picked some little hole-in-the-wall karaoke bar. I guess she thought it would be best to keep it as chill as possible, plus her cousin has gone with them to Mickey's a few times, so they found a place just like it here."

Relief flooded me. "Really? Interesting choice."

It's funny how despite the noise, Lyndi was cool with karaoke. She must distract herself with the singing or something. Either way, it was a good thing I wouldn't have to worry about her going along with them because she felt like she had to.

Then as I pictured her in a karaoke bar, an idea snapped into my mind. "Hang on, you know what we should do?"

"What?"

"First, do you think Gray can chill with Ms. Hattie if we pop over to the karaoke bar for a few minutes during the thing?"

He furrowed his brow. "Uh, I guess, but why would we crash the bachelorette party?"

Because if I wanted to show Lyndi that I had real feelings for her, there was something I could do to make it perfectly clear in a way that only she would get.

But instead of saying that to Zac, I grabbed his arms and hoped he'd get my movie reference as I pulled out the cheesy *Top Gun* quote. "Because, man. She's lost that lovin' feelin'."

It only took him a second, but then he grinned. "No, she hasn't."

"Yes, yes she has."

I walked away to start putting my plan in motion, grinning and raising my fist toward the sky when I heard him yell, "I hate it when she does that!"

21

LYNDI

Our group was pretty much the only crowd at the tiny karaoke bar Layla had found, and I was so happy I could scream. It was exactly what I needed to stop feeling sorry for myself. A little night out with the ladies, a cold seltzer in my hand, and everyone but me singing their heart out to our favorite girl-power songs.

Layla got up there and wowed everyone with a few songs by herself—she really had an amazing voice. Then she and Clara had chosen to sing "Girls Just Wanna Have Fun" together, and I sat cackling at Clara's off-tune singing the entire time. As gorgeous and sweet as she was, our cousin couldn't sing to save her life.

"This was such a great idea," I told Layla when she sat back down after her sixth song of the night.

She flipped her hair and took a sip of her beer. "I

know, I'm brilliant. Plus, I knew you'd enjoy it a lot more than some of the other stuff we could have done around here."

"Well, yes," I replied, bumping her shoulder with mine, "I am. And that's why you're my favorite person ever."

"Good. It's nice to see you loosen up and forget about Beau for a while."

The idea that I could *forget* about him was laughable, but the distraction of being here definitely helped. I loved watching the words on the screen while people sang, tracking to see how on or off they were. I loved how confident they looked even when they were scared. And if it wouldn't be incredibly weird, I'd bring my camera to stuff like this so I could capture all the little things I was lasered-in on to drown out the rest of the noise.

"I really wish Aria and Shelby could have come to Charleston with us," Layla said with a pout. "I miss them."

"I miss them, too. But I'm sure Aria is exactly where she wants to be now that they have Oliver."

Just as Will had predicted, Oliver proved to be the perfect distraction for workaholic Aria—she now had more important things on her mind and holding her newborn son was a beautiful reason to stop and smell the roses. She seemed to be in no rush to go back to work, as much as she still loved it. But I had a feeling when she returned it would be with much more delegation in place, which would work wonders for her work-life balance.

"You're right. I can't wait to get back to town and snag some squishy baby snuggles. I have serious baby fever these days," Layla said with both hands pressed to her chest. "I can't wait to add another little one to our family."

I rubbed her back. "I can't wait to become an auntie again."

"I'll try to make it happen before he gets stationed somewhere else so you can be with me. I can't imagine going through pregnancy and childbirth and new motherhood without you with me."

Nerves swirled within me, but I pushed them away, focusing on my happiness for my sister. "Fingers crossed. But if not, I promise I'll come visit."

As soon as that thought left, another one showed up. Why the heck was I so determined to stay in Bluffton without Layla? Fear. Fear was why. It was an easy answer, but that didn't mean it would be easy to overcome.

"Speaking of topics that remind me of Beau," Layla said, looking pointedly at me, "despite the fact that I'd love nothing more than to keep encouraging you to pursue him like I have been all year, I've chosen which big-sister road to take."

"You have? I don't remember answering you when you asked me which one I wanted you to take."

She waved a hand. "Yeah, well. Take it or leave it, sissy, but I'm choosing the one where you shut this down *now*. It'll be better in the end if you really don't want to leave."

I hated to admit it, but she was probably right. Just because I could acknowledge that fear was what was keeping me in Bluffton and self-consciousness was what made me compare everyone to book boyfriends didn't mean I was strong enough to overcome either of those things.

When I didn't reply, Layla put her arm around me and rested her cheek on my shoulder. "I'm really sorry, Lyn. I wish things could be different. I wish he was just some local guy, some dude who wasn't in the military, and could choose to stay. But he's not. And I'm sure you'll find the right guy someday. So, the sooner you can start getting over Beau Devereux, the better."

I started to reply, but then the first notes of "You've Lost That Lovin' Feelin'" by The Righteous Brothers began to play, and I sat up straight. "No way."

Layla hadn't even been fazed by the way I'd pushed

her off my shoulder. She clapped her hands and screamed, "Ah, I love this song!"

"Me too," I whispered, eyes searching the dimly lit bar for something I almost couldn't believe I was crazy enough to be looking for.

And then I saw him, microphone in hand and Zac at his side, each of them wearing sunglasses despite the low lighting in the bar.

I grabbed my sister's thigh and pointed toward the stage. "Layla, look."

"What—*oh my gosh,* no freaking way."

The first verse popped up on the screen, and Beau sang first, his voice smooth like butter and that accent I'd thought he'd nearly lost surprised me by edging his words while he sang.

Then Zac took the next verse, pointing right at Layla, causing her to swoon beside me. "I think I'm going to fall out of my chair."

"Don't do that," I said with a laugh, telling myself the same thing.

Beau and Zac continued to sing the famous *Top Gun* song, and all I could think about was how sweet it must have been when his dad had done this to his mom. Did this mean what I thought it meant? Was he grand gesturing me right now? Was he telling me that this *thing* between us that we'd both been resisting was as real as his parents' love had been?

Or still was, even through loss.

When the chorus picked up, the guys shocked everyone by jumping off the stage and taking their mics with them. Layla was losing her dang mind in the chair next to me, but all I could focus on was Beau. Even though I couldn't see his eyes through his sunglasses, I could tell he was looking right at me as he sang the famous song.

They finally reached us and did a little routine that was obviously very hastily rehearsed, making us laugh before they took our hands to finish belting out the shortened version of the song.

Before I knew it, everyone at the bar was clapping and they were bowing and Layla and Zac were kissing, and it was over. Beau handed both mics to the people who were up next to sing, then turned to me with a wicked grin.

"That was unexpected," I said, raising my voice so he could hear me over the Michael Jackson song someone was singing.

He chuckled, his shoulders shaking being my only indication since I couldn't hear it. Then he leaned forward and pressed a warm kiss to my cheek. "Have fun."

I grabbed his arm before he could get away, hating that Zac had already started for the door. "That's it? You're leaving?"

"Yep. We'll talk later. But hey, call me if you need anything."

I nodded, so many words stuck in my throat as I watched him go with one more heart-stopping quirk of those beautiful lips.

When they were gone, Layla turned to me with a little shimmy in her seat. "That was probably the most romantic thing that's ever happened to me."

I took a long sip of my seltzer and nodded. "Uh, yeah. It was pretty great."

"I knew Zac turned into a big ol' softie after becoming a dad, but that was seriously next-level. And I love how Beau played along," she said, then she reached out and grabbed my arm. "Wait, shoot, sorry. Are you okay?"

"Okay?"

"Yeah. Ugh, I was so wrapped up in Zac doing that since karaoke is kind of our thing, but he totally shouldn't have asked Beau to play along. Now I'm kinda mad that he agreed to it, actually. That probably really messed with your head."

Played along. Right. Maybe that's all it was.

Beau had just played along. Because Zac and Layla

had been singing karaoke together since the first time they dated years ago, and Zac didn't know Beau and I were faking. So Zac probably suggested they do it together for both of us, and Beau probably went along with it.

No, wait. That song, though? There was no way Beau was so unfeeling that he'd sing that song to me and not intend for there to be meaning behind it, right? That would just be ... cold.

That song was for me. That gesture was for me. Zac was the one playing along, and I knew it in my soul.

Either way, Layla was right. It had messed with my head. Because Beau doing that for me didn't mean all of the things that stood between us disappeared, right?

All I knew was, I was eager for this shindig to end so I could get back to the cottage and ask him about it.

But by the time things wrapped up and we arrived back at the hotel, Beau was already asleep on the couch. We'd put the cushions out to dry all day so we wouldn't have to share a bed again tonight, and it looked like they were dry enough. He still slept at an odd angle because he was way too big for the tiny little couch, but it was better than the first night, that was for sure.

Nerves crept in as I stood there in my painted-on dress, wondering if I should wake him. I felt a little creepy, too, watching him sleep like this. Shaking my head, I headed for the bathroom to take my shower and head to bed.

It looked like our little chat would have to wait until tomorrow. Because if I was wrong about what the song meant, there was no way I'd wake him up now just to find that out. And if I was right? Well, I think we both needed a little time to figure out where we'd go from here.

22

BEAU

I woke up the next morning with more than a little pain in every single one of my joints. But after the day I'd had—after realizing I was totally and completely in love with Lyndi—there was no way I was going to risk sleeping next to her and facing all of those emotions in that ... situation.

When we talked about what was really going on between us, when I told her I loved her, I needed her to be in a position where she could take some space if she needed it. Not feel forced to share a bed with me.

So, today then. At some point, when it wouldn't steal the thunder from the bride and groom, I planned to tell her how I felt. No lies, no faking, no contracts. And most importantly, no fear. Just the real, honest-to-goodness truth.

I loved her, and I didn't plan to let her get away.

"Hey, how did you sleep?" she asked when she emerged from the bathroom in a floral dress that looked like it was made to be worn by her.

"Great, thanks," I replied once I found my voice. "The couch really wasn't all that bad once the cushions were dry. I definitely couldn't stay with you again."

I'd said it because I was leading up to telling her it was because I loved her and didn't want to put any extra pressure on the situation, but her face fell like I'd failed some kind of test I didn't know I was taking.

She sniffed. "About last night …"

"What about it?"

"Was that song … did that mean what I think it meant?"

My pulse pounded in my ears as I took in the uneasiness in her eyes. Did she not want it to mean that I loved her and wanted to be with her? Because that was absolutely what it'd meant, and I'd hoped it would have been clear as day to her.

"That depends," I said, easing into this situation like it was an ice bath, "what did you think it meant?"

She opened her mouth to reply, but then the front door opened, and Layla poked her head in. As Lyndi rushed over to the door, I let my head fall back and closed my eyes. *Nice timing, Layla.*

While they stood by the door and spoke in hushed tones, I busied myself with pulling on my suit jacket and straightening my lapels. We had to go to breakfast, so maybe now wasn't the time for this big confession, after all.

Layla slipped out again, so Lyndi made her way back over to me, looking even more conflicted than before we'd been interrupted, if that were even possible. "Listen, Beau. I think we need to break up."

I rolled my eyes, realizing I was in for quite a journey for this woman. I wouldn't trade it, because I knew once we got past all of this we'd be fire. But we had to survive all of *this* first. "*Break up?*"

"I mean, well, you know what I mean. I think we need to stage a breakup. We can do it in front of the family and make it heartbreaking enough that they'll leave me alone about dating simply because they'll know I'm not ready."

I crossed my arms over my chest and loomed over her, stepping into her space. "Oh, yeah? And what happens if they do the opposite and push you even harder so you'll get over me?"

She backed up. "Then I'll freak out and tell them to leave me alone."

I followed, not giving in. "You could do that anyway."

She backed up again, then glared at me when I took another step. "*Beau.*"

"Lyndi, we're not breaking up." I spoke slowly and clearly, so there'd be no misunderstandings this time. And yeah, I may have also *intentionally* clenched my dang jaw and made my voice sound rattled. She knew I was good at taking directions, so here I was, taking them.

Her throat pulsed as she swallowed hard. "Why not?"

"Several reasons, one of which being the fact that this day isn't about *you and me*, it's about your *cousin*. Do you really want to cause a scene on her wedding day?"

"No."

"Exactly."

"Then we'll do it—"

I shook my head with a smile. "No, we won't."

"Beau."

"What did she say to you?" I asked, jerking my chin toward the door. "Because before she came in here, it seemed like we were *finally* about to get somewhere. After last night, I figured you knew where I stood."

"You stand on shaky ground, Beau. We both do. This isn't good for either of us."

Layla popped her head into the cottage again,

causing me to bite back a curse. "Hey, guys, sorry, Grandma's asking where you are again."

"Tell her we'll be right there," Lyndi said, grabbing her purse and heading for the door.

I groaned and followed after her, taking her hand as we crossed the grass, smiling at her family as we passed them. "Lyndi—"

"Let's do it at breakfast," she whispered as we hurried toward the dining room. "It doesn't have to cause a scene, we can just talk quietly and then you can get up and leave. I'll tell Grandma later what happened. Now, come on. We need to get in there."

Then without another word, the most frustrating woman I'd ever laid eyes on shot ahead of me, slipping into the dining room before I had a chance to stop her.

Fine. We'll talk about it later, then.

During breakfast, I did my best to fake it and act the same way I had with her family yesterday. I chatted easily with her grandparents and parents, I smiled lovingly at Lyndi—meaning it—and I tried not to think about the fact that I wanted to yank her out of here and tell her how I felt so she'd stop trying to give me the signal to break up with her stubborn self.

"Beau," she purred in my ear, tone icy, yet it caused fire to flash down my neck.

"Yes, dear?"

"Stop being so nice," she ordered.

I gave her my most innocent smile. "Whatever do you mean?"

She hid her mouth behind her coffee cup so no one could read her lips. "We're about to break up and you're acting like we're madly in love."

"Sure am."

Her eyes narrowed ever so slightly as she peered at me over the rim of her cup. "Get up and leave."

"*No.*"

Thankfully, she dropped it. We finished up breakfast without any further talk on the subject, so I'd hoped I was in the clear. But then as soon as it was safe to do so, she took off so fast it made my head spin.

She really needs to stop doing that.

Even as I thought it, I shot myself down. I did this to her. It was my fault she was so wary of my motives and distrusting of everything I said. I'd made a killing selling this version of myself so I could take care of my father's debt, but I was paying for it in a different way now.

I got up to find her, but as soon as I reached the door, her mom stepped in my path. "Hey, Beau, do you have a minute?"

Smiling despite the nerves reaching all the way down to my toes, I nodded. "For you? Absolutely."

"How's everything going?"

"Great. The trip's been fun so far."

"Not the trip, Beau. With Lyndi."

I scratched the back of my neck. "Um, well, we're great, too."

"She seems a little ... *tense* this morning. But she won't talk to me. And Layla wouldn't tell me anything when I asked her. So, I'm asking you. I know my daughter, Beau. Something's not right."

I treaded carefully, wondering if this was going to be yet another one of those moments where someone we were trying to fool could see right through our act. "She'll be fine. We're just having a little disagreement, that's all."

"A disagreement? About what?" Mrs. Robinson asked, putting her hand on my arm. The look in her eye told me right away she didn't know this started as a phony arrangement. "I'm sorry, if it's none of my business, that's fine. I just knew something was wrong and was worried. I'll butt out so you two can sort through it."

Sighing, I took her hand in mine. "Mrs. Robinson, the truth is, I'm in love with your daughter. But she's either too scared to love me back, or she already does and she's too scared to tell me. But trust me when I tell you, I'll figure it out. And when I do, you'll have nothing to worry about. We'll be happy, and she'll be fine."

She looked startled by my confession, but then she softened slightly. "Why's that?"

"Because I'm not going to let her get away." With that, I ran out of the dining room, eyes scanning all the faces in the hall.

"Beau, hey. I didn't realize you were working this wedding."

I did a double take at the videographer I'd met at a few weddings in the area, instantly remembering him as one of the jerks who'd dated Lyndi for way too short of a time to have gotten to know the real her.

My jaw clenched automatically, but I shook his hand. "I'm not here working."

"Oh, you're a guest? How do you know the couple?"

"I'm here with Lyndi."

He tilted his head. "I thought you said you weren't working."

"I'm not. She's my *date*, not my *client*."

His confusion morphed into understanding, and he slowly nodded. "*Right*. I'm picking up what you're putting down. Don't worry, man. Your secret's safe with me."

"It's not—" I stopped, realizing this guy wasn't worth taking the time to defend myself to. The only person who needed to hear this stuff was Lyndi. "Never mind, I'll see you later, man."

I moved away, but not fast enough to miss the way he zipped his lips and threw away the key. Annoyance rippled through me. See? This is what happened when you built your whole life on lies. No one believed you when you were telling the truth.

I'm like the grown man who cried wolf.

On my quest to find Lyndi, I decided to stop at the men's room and wash my hands. I'd spilled a little coffee on the back of one when I'd been distracted by something Lyndi had said, and I could still faintly smell it on me.

When I came out a minute later, I heard that videographer—what was his name again? Jimmy? Johnny? *Tommy*. That was it—talking to Lyndi around the corner.

I hung back a sec, just so I knew what I'd be walking up to.

"How've you been?" Tommy asked her.

"Well, thanks. You?"

"Not bad. Listen, when Aria referred Clara to me, I have to admit I kind of thought it was fate." He let out a short laugh that made me roll my eyes.

"Oh? Why's that?"

"Well, I feel like we didn't really have much of a chance to get to know each other when we went out before, and if you're up for it, I'd love to try again."

My hands balled into fists, but I stayed out of sight. Lyndi could handle herself. She was a grown woman, and she didn't need me to step in like some white knight on a horse. Then again, that was probably exactly what a swoony book boyfriend would do. Maybe she would want that.

No.

I wasn't a cardboard cutout of a man, and she deserved to tell this creep to go away without me puffing out my chest before she got the chance.

"Tommy, that's really sweet," Lyndi said, the sympathy in her tone making me grin to myself, "but I think it would be better if we didn't."

I brought my clenched fist up and pumped the air.

"Why?" he asked, a little too abruptly. "Are you seeing someone?"

"Well, no. It's not that."

Closing my eyes, I rested my head against the wall. My fault. Not hers.

Tommy laughed, causing my head to snap up again. "I knew he was just trying to keep the secret."

"What?"

"I ran into Mr. Fake Date. He tried to tell me you were his date, not his client. Don't worry, I didn't believe him."

Seething, I held my breath for her reply.

"Right. Well, Beau aside, I think we spent enough time getting to know each other before, so I don't think we need to try again."

Done. Now Tommy could move along with a clear answer from the lady, no harm, no foul.

But then his lewd laughter hit my ears again, and rage coursed through me. Still, I waited. Maybe she'd punch him herself. She was an unorthodox heroine, right?

"Lyndi, come on. We went on a couple dates. That's hardly enough time."

"I said no, Tommy. I'm sorry."

"Lyndi," he tried again.

Eh, wrong. Enough is enough.

Looked like I was the perfect book boyfriend after all, because there was no way I'd continue to stand by and let this guy repeatedly not take *no* for an answer.

I stepped out and turned the corner, then slipped directly between this slimy jerk and my girl. "Tommy, kick rocks."

"Excuse me?" he asked, having the audacity to look confused.

"I said, get out of here. *No* means *no*."

"But you guys aren't even—"

Whatever he'd been about to say died on his lips

under the hard glare I poured over him, and he slinked away like the snake he was.

Then I rolled all of the anger right off my back as I turned to face Lyndi, sliding into a calmness of knowing that fit the real me like a glove.

Now or never.

23

LYNDI

"Thanks," I said, momentarily speechless by how hot he'd looked just now.

As usual, Beau looked like he'd just stepped off a runway. His suit was impeccably tailored, playing up his broad shoulders and slim waist. It was the color of a shark, which was fitting, I supposed. And the crisp white shirt he wore with the top buttons open just the right amount pulled it all together into the picture of a perfect summer event.

"No problem."

"I tried to handle it, but—"

"You shouldn't have had to," he cut in, grazing his knuckles over my cheek.

Shoot. This was it, wasn't it? The moment we threw it all out there only so we could both acknowledge why it would never work.

"Why didn't you go through with the breakup plan, Beau?"

His lips twitched. "Because I never agreed to it in the first place. We need to talk."

"We probably shouldn't, okay? This whole thing is going to do nothing but hurt both of us if we don't knock it off."

He reached out, placing one hand on either side of my waist to hold me gently. "I'm not leaving."

"What? Like, not leaving this spot, or ..."

"I'm not leaving South Carolina. Or, at least, I'm doing literally everything in my power to get another three years at the recruit depot."

My mind spun and I raced to keep up with the whirlwind of hope and excitement and fear. "How?"

"I'm going to put in a package for drill instructor duty and request the East Coast. It's not a guarantee, but it's something. It's better than Hawaii. Even if they put me in California—which I really hope they don't—even that would be better than putting an ocean between us."

I closed my eyes, not sure if this was amazing news or if it made me really pathetic and unsupportive, just like we'd talked about. "Beau, you can't do that for me."

"It's not only for you. I don't want to be that far from

my pops, either. It's a good move for me, and it's a good move for us."

"If it's for your dad, great. I think that's sweet. But if it would only be for me, that's not fair."

"It is, though. You know me better than, well, anyone on the planet at this point. And I know you. This is right for us. It's definitely fair."

I shook my head. "I'm sorry, but I'm freaking out. I think this whole fake date thing messed with my mind—like it's all blurring fake stuff with the real stuff and it's overwhelming."

"Lyndi—"

"No, lemme just get this out," I said quietly. "Beau, none of this is fake for me. It hasn't been since the beginning. That's the difference between us. You're so great at putting on this show for people, and you're able to act however you're supposed to act. And while I do that too, I'm also over here letting you see the real me. I can't tell if the same is true for you."

"It is."

"But you didn't *want* this. You *wanted* to protect yourself."

"I did, yeah. But it's like ... even though you try to be 'normal' around everyone else and do and say what you think you should, your brain makes sense to my brain.

You make sense to me. You get *me*, and I get *you*. It works, Lyndi."

I opened my mouth to speak, then closed it again, and his face crumbled like he was worried he messed this whole thing up. He let go of my waist and paced away for a sec, running a hand over his jaw.

Then he moved back to me and took my hands in his. "Before you curl up and die because that was the *least* romantic thing you've ever heard, and a book boyfriend would never say that, remember I know all about what you want to hear."

I chuckled, making him look a hundred times lighter. "Oh, you do, huh?"

"Yes." He stepped closer, bringing my hands flat against his chest so I could feel his heart pounding. "I know how to compliment you so you'll keep thinking about it for hours. I know how to touch you in just the right way to give you goose bumps. I know exactly what to say to you right now that would be a freaking *epic* book-boyfriend-style declaration of love. Because it's *my job,* Lyndi. And you're right, I'm good at it." He paused, hooking his knuckle under my chin and holding my gaze. "But for once in my life, I'm telling you something real. It's not a show or a game or an act. This is me, telling you, that this is *our* story and we're *it*. So, now the question is, is it good enough for you? Does it measure up to the fantasies in your head?"

The second the question was out of his mouth, I lifted onto my toes and pressed my lips to his. My entire body came alive, all the hope and fear swirled together to make a happiness in my chest that I couldn't remember ever feeling before.

His lips were petal soft as he moved them over mine, and then he took control of the kiss by cradling my face in his hands and backing me up against the wall. To kiss him forever wouldn't be long enough. If he thought those words weren't the most perfect book boyfriend words, he was dead wrong. And this kiss? There was no chance it wasn't *the kiss*.

"Did that feel real?" he asked as he pulled back slightly, his voice hoarse this time as he stared down at me with my face still in his hands.

"Yes."

"Was it gross?"

I laughed, tears springing to my eyes. "No."

He planted a quick peck on my lips and stepped back. "Good. How about the first two times?"

"Not then either."

He put his hands on his chest and sighed. "I'm so relieved."

"Hush," I said with an eye roll, stepping forward to give him a quick kiss of my own.

Then he circled his arms around me again and rested his forehead to mine. "I have something else I need to tell you."

"What?"

"I'm in love with you."

My breath caught. "For *real?*" He held up a finger between us and gave me a look, so I grabbed it and pulled it away with a laugh. "I'm in love with you, too."

As if he were unable to help himself, he lowered his mouth to mine one last time. Brief as it was, it felt like the perfect exclamation mark on our conversation.

"So, what do we do now?" I asked when he pulled back.

"Now, you go get ready for the wedding, and I'll be watching you do your thing from the crowd. And in case you have any doubts about how I'll be feeling—*for real*—just know I won't be able to take my eyes off you the whole time."

A low and pleasant hum warmed my blood. "Is that so?"

"Yep. And when you're done with bridesmaid duties, we're going to go to the reception, and we're going to dance. And hug. And hold hands. And do everything we've been doing, but this time, also *for real.*"

At this, I stepped away and shook my head, giving him a bona fide slow clap. "Now *that* was an epic book boyfriend declaration of love."

Not that the first one hadn't been.

He bowed with more than a little cheesy flair. "Fine. But I meant every word of it."

"I believe you," I promised. Those words meant more in this moment than they would have out of context. Then I turned to go into the bridal suite, but before I slipped through the door, I turned back around and gave him a wry smile. "Seriously, five stars. *So* swoony."

"Oh, you think you're funny, huh?"

I nodded with a short laugh. "A little."

He gave me one of his classic winks, knowing full well how swoony I found them to be since my body's reactions always gave me away. Then he said the only thing he could in response, given who he was. "I aim to please."

24

BEAU

"Any news about the DI package?" Lyndi asked, pursing her lips as she sat across from me at the coffee shop on Main Street.

"Not yet, but it's been less than a week. I should hear something by the end of next week, according to the monitor."

"Fingers crossed."

Fingers and toes.

But this would be fine. I'd just do what Zac said and have a long-distance thing with her if I needed to. Whether they made me go to Hawaii as planned or if I got the DI package approved but had to serve my three years in San Diego, I knew one thing for sure: I wasn't going to let her go.

We'd only been actually dating for five days, since

her cousin's wedding, but it felt like so much longer when combined with the weeks of fake-dating and the year I'd skirted around my feelings. I could picture our life together so clearly, I could taste it. And whether we had to do it thousands of miles apart or in the same town, I knew it would be great.

But there was one more thing we hadn't talked about, and that was my business. And I had two out-of-town weddings coming up tomorrow and Sunday, so we needed to bite the bullet and do it.

Mr. Fake Date would come to an end if my package got accepted, but until I left, could I keep doing this? And if I went to Hawaii, would she be okay with me doing it there? I had to tell her about the debt. She needed to know the business wasn't simply because I liked going on all these fake dates.

"So, we need to talk about tomorrow," I said, taking a sip of my coffee to soothe my desert-dry throat.

She sucked in a breath and fidgeted with the end of her ponytail. "I've been trying not to think about it."

"It makes you uncomfortable, doesn't it?"

Biting her lip, she answered me without words.

"Lyn, I do it for the money. My dad's bills ... his treatments. It's a lot. I can't afford it on my salary alone, even after factoring in his crappy insurance from his time at the factory."

She closed her eyes and looked at her lap, then when she looked up again her eyes were rimmed with red. "That makes a lot of sense. So many things make more sense."

"Yeah."

"Okay, so, listen," she said, taking my hands across the table, "I understand why you need to do it. I don't have to be comfortable with it."

I shook my head. "You do, actually. I like being the one person you don't have to make yourself uncomfortable around because you're trying to do what's expected of you."

"Well, don't forget about Layla. And my mom. She's pretty understanding."

I gave her a look to suggest that her mom might be understanding about some things, but she was also responsible for Lyndi putting herself in uncomfortable positions. Like, oh, I don't know, fake dating me in the first place? Not that I could really complain now.

She squeezed my hands and then let go, leaning back. "Beau, come on. What do you want me to say? No, I don't love the idea of you being Mr. Fake Date. But now that I know you have your dad's bills to worry about, I'm not going to be the reason that's hanging over your head."

"You'd be a valid reason."

"Either way, let's not make any rash decisions about the business right now, okay? You might have to stop anyway if you get these new orders, and I know that's going to be tough for you to let the debt keep stacking up. And if you don't get new orders, we'll talk about it then. Besides, don't you know you're not supposed to quit your job until you have a new one lined up?"

I chuckled, loving how her brain worked. "Yeah. I could come up with a different side gig idea."

"True."

"Though, I'm not really sure what else I have to offer other than my good looks," I teased.

She laughed, making the weight on my chest ease off a bit. "Stop it."

"Sorry."

"Oh, I know," she said, eyes bright. "What about shooting lessons? You could work weekends at a civilian shooting range, right?"

"Apart from the fact that I hate the idea of being on a shooting range seven days a week, it'll take me a lot longer to pay it off that way. There's a big difference in the money."

She wrinkled her nose, then she opened her mouth to speak and then closed it again. When I gave her an encouraging nod, she blew out a breath. "Have you talked to your dad about filing bankruptcy so you don't have to bear this burden?"

I shrugged. "Uh, no. That's not really something we've considered. He'd hate that."

"I bet he hates that you're killing yourself to pay down his debt."

This made me chuckle. "Lyn, to be fair, it hasn't been a hardship before now."

"Oh, brother. What am I going to do with you?"

I leaned forward, wagging my brows. "Kiss me."

She met me in the middle of the table, a scarlet blush caressing her cheeks. When her lips brushed over mine, it felt like something clicked in my brain that everything would be all right.

Until she pulled back and glared at me. "So, um, did your dates—sorry, *clients*—for this weekend pay extra for kissing?"

"Well, as you know, it's not always something that we account for in advance. Sometimes it's a spur-of-the-moment, camera in your face, kinda thing."

She rolled her eyes with a low laugh. "Oh, brother."

"Hey, I'll put a new kissing clause in the contract."

"What will it say?"

"No kissing, under any circumstances," I told her. "Even if it makes things weird in front of the people we're trying to fool."

Narrowing her eyes, she considered this. "Why would you do that?"

"Because I can't imagine kissing anyone but you?"

"Aw, swoon," she said, sarcasm dripping from her tone, though her lips were pulled up into a smile.

I grinned. "Okay, you wanna know the real reason?"

"Yes."

"Because kissing anyone else would be gross?"

The smile widened. "You're getting closer."

"Fine. Because I'm afraid you'll think kissing *me* is gross if I kiss someone else."

Poking me in the shoulder, she leaned away again. "That's the one. And it's very true. I would think that."

I stepped out of the office with way more energy than when I'd gone in. My package had been approved, and not only that, but I got my wish. Parris Island, South Carolina for another three years. It felt so good I wanted to shout it from the rooftops, but I refrained, because that would be weird.

But I couldn't wait to tell my pops. And Lyndi, too. I could call her now, but I felt like I needed to see her reaction in person. Over the last two weeks since her cousin's wedding—with all of our feelings being out in the open and not marred by fear on either side—watching her face while we talked or laughed or after we kissed had become one of my favorite pastimes.

She'd completely let her mask fall away as quickly as I'd let mine go, and every day I got to know her even better than the day before. Even through texts while we were both at work or if she was home in Bluffton while I was in the barracks over here. Which had been great to experience, since until today, I'd been low-key worrying we'd have to spend the next three years only communicating by phone. It'd been good to feel like that wouldn't be too bad after all.

But this was much better, of course.

When I stepped onto the range, Grant greeted me with a curt nod because there were recruits all around us. "Hey, how's it going?"

I beamed at him, no need to look stern in my position. "Great, actually. I just found out my package was approved."

"Nice, man," he deadpanned, ever the great actor. "When do you start school?"

"Two weeks."

"Did you get PI?"

"Yep." Which meant I'd also get to do my eleven weeks of drill instructor school here, so I wouldn't have to leave for training like I'd first thought.

His lips twitched ever-so-slightly, but once again all he did was nod. Then he stepped closer, and his friendlier voice broke through in a low tone. "Awesome, congrats. I hope our cycles can link up some day. I'd love to work with you."

"Same here, man. Hang on," I replied as he stepped back. I'd caught sight of one of my guys holding his rifle a little off his mark, so I held up a finger to Grant and stepped over to help him adjust it. "Hey, you need to loosen your grip here, and put this hand over here. Good. Okay, fire when ready."

The recruit did as I'd asked, then whooped when he saw he'd hit his target dead-on. But before I could get a word out to congratulate him, a loud boom rang out, and something wet hit my face.

Every muscle in my body went rigid as I took in the recruit's ashen complexion, all of the blood having drained from his face. It was at that moment that I noticed the crimson stain on his shoulder, and I looked down at my own chest to see if the bullet had gone through him and hit me, but I just hadn't felt it yet.

Seeing nothing there, I whirled around to see if anyone behind me had been shot, but thankfully, no. Then I turned back and caught the recruit in front of me right before he fell. As I steadied him and called for help, I looked over his shoulder that was now soaked with blood.

The recruit I'd literally just yelled at the day before for not flagging the line stood there with the same horrified expression I knew I wore, only his was edged with guilt. The smoking muzzle of his M16 still shook as he held it.

When on the range, you couldn't aim your weapon all willy-nilly. These are loaded M16s, for crying out loud. They were to be pointed down range or at the ground at all times. Turning toward your brothers who stood on our end of the line without adjusting your weapon was something that could get you banned from the range altogether. Kicked out of boot camp, even, and forced to start over.

But I'd given him another chance, and he'd done it again the very next day.

He'd done it again, and it resulted in someone getting shot.

Someone who was now passing out in my arms while I continued to scream for help, panic rising up within me and threatening to swallow me up belly-first.

All around me there was movement. Grant stripped the offender of his weapon and practically threw him to the ground with his words alone. Medics rushed over, recruits formed a tight circle around us to see if their brother was okay. And the shallow, desperate breaths that raged out of me in tight bursts as I cradled this eighteen-year-old kid in my arms.

Two hours later, I paced outside the hospital on base with so much lead in my gut I was sure it would soon tear open and fall to the ground beneath my boots. What had I done? Why hadn't I booted that recruit the first time he'd flagged the line?

Guilt and fury poured over me in tsunami-sized waves as I scrubbed my hands over my face, the smell of sweat and blood and dirt filling my nostrils. When I looked up and my vision cleared, my breath caught at the sight of Lyndi running toward me from the parking lot.

She threw herself into my arms, and I stumbled back, using all my remaining strength not to tumble backward onto the pavement. I wrapped my arms around her and breathed her in, conscious of how nasty I was compared to how clean and fresh she smelled, but unable to pull away to save her from being sullied. I needed her. I needed this like I needed air.

"How did you get on base?" I choked out, still holding her tightly against my chest.

"Layla brought me," she replied into my cammies, making no effort to move. "Is he okay?"

"He's still in surgery."

"Are *you* okay?"

"Me?"

"Yeah, you." It came out with a breathy laugh, bringing us both back to that day outside another hospital in what felt like another lifetime.

But I pushed it away, eyes focused on a random car over her head. "I'm not the one who got shot."

"I know, Beau." She pulled back, leaving me feeling empty even though she didn't let go all the way. Then she jerked her chin toward the hospital behind me. "Have you been inside?"

I tensed, then shook my head. "No, but they'll come out and get me."

"It's okay for you to sit in the waiting room with everyone else. You can handle it."

My breath snagged on something inside my chest, and I waited a beat so I could speak without breaking. "I'm better out here."

As far away as I can reasonably be, just in case I make it worse for the kid.

"Beau, look at me." When I didn't, she angled her body so she'd catch my eyes, and she reached up and gripped my dirty face. I winced and tried to pull away, but she held tighter. "Hey, I know you're freaking out. I know this is scary. But he's going to be fine."

"You don't know that," I said through my teeth.

"You didn't know that about Aria and you still told *me* that. And I believed you. So, right now, you need to believe me."

Lyndi continued to hold my face, but the longer she made me stand there and look at her, the weaker I felt. I knew the cracks would bust open soon, and I couldn't fall apart. Reaching up to take her hands, I pulled them from my face and paced away.

"I should have been paying more attention," I said, my voice breaking. "The mistake he made ... he's made it before, and I didn't kick him out for it. But I should have."

"Beau, it's not your responsibility. You can't control what other people do. Sometimes bad stuff just happens."

Exactly. I knew that better than anyone. I may have caused the crash that killed Rene by distracting my mom, but I knew I hadn't caused her cancer. Or my pops'. Sometimes bad stuff happened and there was nothing I—or anyone else—could do to stop it.

Which was why I turned back to her, my chest feeling like it was about to bust open, knowing my only option was to push her away.

But then anger replaced the concern in her eyes, and she held up a finger, stepping closer until she was right up against me again. "Don't. Don't you dare."

"What?"

"You said I get you, right?" she asked, all challenge and fire and hurricane. "Well, I do. Sometimes I feel like you can read me like I'm a freaking book, and right now I'm doing the same thing. And I know what you're thinking, and it's not happening."

I swallowed, my vision blurring. "Tell me."

"You're thinking we messed up by making this real, and you want to push me away. We didn't. And you can't."

"Lyndi."

"You will not lose me, Beau. And you will not push me away. Do you hear me? I won't let you. I'm so sorry for the things you've been through, but we're amazing. And I don't even care what happens with your drill instructor package. If you have to leave, we'll figure it out. *I* will figure it out. I'll go with you, and I can grow, and still be myself. I can—"

"It got approved," I choked out, some small glimpse of light shining through all the darkness that'd been about to break me apart.

She stilled. "What?"

With shaky hands, I bracketed her waist and dug the

pads of my fingers into her soft curves. "My drill instructor package. It's been approved. School starts in two weeks, right here at PI, then I'll stay here for three years."

Her breath exploded from her mouth and then she jumped up to press a quick kiss to my lips. "That's amazing."

I knew better than to point out how gross that must have been, but even the thought of our inside joke in the midst of all this felt soothing. "Yeah. But would you really go with me if it'd been denied?"

"Well, yes," she said with a nod. "I've been thinking about it a lot since the wedding. I've been watching Hawaii TikTok videos and reading books set there. There's even this one series set at the base there that has a bunch of Marines in it."

I frowned. "Really? Is it any good?"

"Definitely," she replied with bright, wistful eyes. I felt a tangent coming on about the tropes or story lines, but then she shook her head to wave it away. "But anyway, yeah, I've been trying to wrap my brain around the idea of leaving, and of being with you, and being without Layla. And I realized that Layla's leaving with Zac when he gets orders, and when I went away with you to visit your dad, I was really comfortable there. But looking back I think I was comfortable there because *you* were there. Which makes me think maybe I'd be comfortable with you anywhere."

I tucked her close again and let out a long sigh. "Well, that's a relief."

"Why? Did your package not really get approved?" she asked as she jerked back.

"Really? You think I'd lie?" I asked, shaking her slightly.

She grinned. "No, I guess not. Why is it a relief then?"

"Because the DI orders are only for three years, so we'll have to move eventually."

"You think we'll last that long?"

My gaze devoured her beauty, pulling it in and letting it calm the raging sea inside me. "I think we'll last forever."

"Devereux." A man's voice caused us to spring apart.

I looked toward the hospital doors and recognized my CO coming toward me with a purposeful stride. "Sir."

"He's out of surgery, and he's going to be fine," he said, putting a heavy hand on my shoulder. "His family's with him now, and they probably won't allow visitors in the ICU. You can get cleaned up, then head back to the range."

Relief washed away the remaining darkness around

my heart, and I nodded in acknowledgement. "Yes, sir. Thank you."

Lyndi and I watched until he disappeared into the hospital again, then she turned to me with eyes as wide as saucers. "Wow, right back to work? After *that*?"

"The machine has to keep moving."

"Right. Well, um, what about the guy who shot him?"

And just like that, the darkness returned. "He's already in the brig while they work out the next steps. Zac's been keeping me updated since he's military police, and I guess he's looking at an Article 134. It's a punishment, but we'll have to see what happens after the court-martial if it comes to that. It's up to the CO."

"Yikes."

"I didn't ask if I'd be in trouble, too, but I guess since he's sending me back to the range, I'm not."

Her face scrunched up in confusion. "Why would you be in trouble?"

"Because it happened on my watch."

"Weren't there other people there? It can't all fall on you."

I took a deep breath and looked around the parking lot, then shook my head. "I guess it's not. Trust me, if it all fell on me, I'd be in a cell right next to him."

"Okay. So, the kid who got hurt is going to be okay,

you're not in trouble, and the guy who did it is going to be dealt with appropriately. So, take a second and relax. It's all going to be fine, just like I said."

I knew she was being serious, but she still shook me and smiled like she needed me to smile too, so I did my best. But it felt a little flat, even to me.

She sighed. "Do you want me to get everyone together later? Maybe we can all hang at Zac and Layla's?"

"I'm okay, don't worry about me. I promise I won't sit around and mope and blame myself."

"I know you won't," she said, putting her arm around me and leading me toward the parking lot. "But I meant to celebrate your package getting approved."

"Are you going to sit in the corner and read the whole time?"

"Maybe."

"Good. Because you wouldn't be you if you didn't."

25

LYNDI

Nine weeks into Beau's eleven weeks of drill instructor school, I was finally able to see the light at the end of the tunnel for him. At first, he'd thought it was going to be like boot camp all over again. That was the perception, but he'd told me that was likely because, in the beginning, they take the Marines "back to basics" in their training.

As drill instructors, they needed to be able to do everything they wanted recruits to do—flawlessly. And a lot of things had fallen by the wayside in the years since they were in boot camp themselves. Things like calling a gunnery sergeant a gunny or, depending on their job within the Marine Corps, slacking on drill since in the fleet they rarely had to do that.

I had to admit, I was glad it wasn't like boot camp. If

it were, we'd only be able to communicate via letters. We'd be separated the entire eleven weeks while he slept in the squad bay with the other students, not being able to have any free time at all. That was what I'd geared up for.

Instead, he'd show up, do his training, and get released back to the same barracks room he'd been living in before it started. As long as he was at his report place on time with his homework done, they didn't care if he left base in the evenings or on weekends.

Though, because it was Beau and he put his all into everything he did, he rarely left base. Save a few dinners with me each week and a couple of afternoon get-togethers with our friends on the weekends, he spent his free time prepping his note cards or uniform for the next day, studying, or doing anything he could to get a day or two ahead so he'd never fall behind.

I admired watching him transition from a hard-working fleet Marine to a picture-perfect leader of Marines. As the weeks went on, he'd started to carry himself so differently. He still had great posture and the relaxed swagger that many Marines possessed, but this *new* version of him was so in control and focused. So purposeful. And yeah, so incredibly hot.

"Ah, I needed this," he said, his once smooth-like-butter voice hoarse and broken thanks to all the screaming he'd been doing. "Thanks for coming."

I grinned at him from across the picnic blanket I'd spread in the sand on Elliot's Beach on base. He had a big exam tomorrow morning, so while I wouldn't stay long, I wanted to bring him a healthy dinner and surprise him with a romantic date overlooking Broad River as it snaked in from the Atlantic.

"You're welcome," I said, popping a cherry tomato from my salad into my mouth and chewing it as we both stared out at the water. "How was your day?"

He blew out a breath and rubbed a hand over the back of his tanned neck. "Long, as usual. We talked a lot about cases of abuse, and it was pretty mind-blowing."

I held my fork in the air for a second, then lowered it to the Tupperware container in my hands. "Cases of abuse?"

"Yeah, they went over some incidents of drill instructors going off the rails and taking things too far."

"How?"

He took a swig from the sweet tea I'd brought for him, looking up as he answered. "Anything from racial slurs to physical abuse. Pushing them so hard they almost die. Ignoring injuries and making them worse. Pretty rough stuff." He let out a long breath and stared down at the salad in his own container before looking back up at me. "But they're trying to make sure it doesn't happen again by addressing it here at the school."

"That's good."

"It is. My instructor told us that what happened in the past didn't have to happen in the future, and here, we make the future. It was heavy, but it *was* good. Important."

"Definitely."

He took a bite of his salad and then chuckled slightly as he chewed. "Then things took a turn for the funny when we started talking about counseling recruits about marriage. Didn't see *that* coming."

"Why would you counsel them about marriage?"

"I guess it comes up in boot camp," he said with a shrug. "Recruits talking about getting married on boot leave and all that. Proposing when they go home to see their family so they can take their new wife with them wherever they went. I think a lot of times it's because they realize they're alone for the first time and don't wanna be. Either that or they don't want to live in the barracks and know they need to be married to skip out on that."

I gulped. "Oh, wow. They'd be so young, though, right?"

"You'd be surprised how many military marriages start at eighteen. I'm not judging, even though it was as far as Mars from my mind at the time. But I have friends who've been married since boot leave and they're still together and happy."

"Yeah, I mean, getting married early doesn't have to mean it's doomed to fail."

He squinted out at the river and shook his head. "No, but I didn't think talking about it with the recruits would be part of my job description."

"I'm surprised it would be. If they're gonna do it, that's their business, right?"

"Yes and no. A big thing they're trying to help us understand here is that these recruits are coming from all walks of life, and a lot of them didn't have a good role model or older sibling or parent to help guide them. I guess we're like the first ones they'll have."

"Huh."

"Not even kidding, we're trained to look for hygiene issues that they might have never been taught. Or things like ingrown toenails and rashes so we can tell them to get it checked out, in case they're hiding it so they won't get dropped or something. It's a lot more than teaching them what it means to be a Marine. It's basic adult stuff, too."

I imagined that as I chewed my food, then regretted it as images of Beau examining unhygienic teenage boys flashed through my mind. I shuddered and got back to the topic. "That's a lot of responsibility for you."

"It is."

I'd done some research online about drill instructor school because it made me feel closer to him to know what he was going through with this course. I could see how hard it was on him physically and mentally, so knowing the mission helped ease the sinking feeling in my gut whenever we met for dinner like this and he seemed so beaten down.

I'd read about how the school not only prepared them for the demands of drill instructor duty but also honed their skills so they'd be prepared to shape the future of the Marine Corps. It really did seem like a lot to put on their shoulders. While I knew Beau's were strong enough to handle it—given everything he'd shouldered in his family life—I also worried about him for that same reason.

Beau hadn't been able to be a big brother for very long. In fact, he barely remembered it except for the guilt he carried about his brother's death. And even though his father was now—*thankfully,* though unsurprisingly to Beau, who'd never given up hope—in remission and doing well, I wondered if the idea of being turned into a role model for so many others messed with him more than he let on.

"You doing okay with that part?" I asked, bumping him with my shoulder. "You know, the idea of being a big-brother figure to all those kids?"

"Yeah, I am," he said, looking over at me with the familiar sparkle in his eyes again. Even though I was still getting used to his painfully ragged voice, seeing he was still in there under the rougher exterior helped. Then he swallowed hard and looked away. "So uh, back to the marriage thing."

I stilled. "What about it?"

He put down his salad and angled his body toward me on the blanket in the way he did when he was preparing to study my reaction to something. "It got me thinkin'."

"Did it?"

"Yeah. I know I'm not leaving for another three years, so it's not like I'm asking this because I want you to come with me."

I cleared my throat, putting my own salad down and reaching for the end of my braid, my whole body on alert. "Asking *what*, exactly?"

"Just asking what your thoughts are on it, I guess. Marriage, that is. For logistical reasons." He winked, making my stomach do somersaults even though thoughts of an impending proposal had been quelled.

"Right. Of course."

"I was thinking about how when I'm a kill hat, I'm not going to have much free time. It'll be hard to see each other if you're living in Bluffton and I'm here."

"But I can only live on base if we're married," I said, nodding slowly.

"Yeah. And you know, since I figured I already told you I wasn't planning to let you go, I wondered if that was something you'd be open to before it had to happen when I got new orders."

Narrowing my eyes at him, I did my best to control my facial expressions beyond that. But while it used to be so easy for me to slip on my mask around him, like I could with everyone else, months of being with Beau had made it so he was almost inside the force field with me. I couldn't hide from him anymore.

Finally, I pursed my lips and gave him a pointed look. "This marriage conversation is very ... business-arrangement sounding."

A wide grin stretched over his handsome face as he pointed a finger between us. "You do know this all started with a contract pulled up on my laptop, right?"

"A contract that was pretty quickly discarded, if I remember correctly."

He sputtered out a shocked laugh. "Um, excuse me, which part was discarded? I kept up my end of the deal to a T."

"You kissed me way more than necessary at that wedding," I teased him.

"Uh, yeah, but I distinctly remember you being the first one to kiss me when no one was looking."

I sighed. "Got me there. That was a great kiss."

He leaned forward and gave me a short peck. "They're all great."

"Anyway," I said, pushing his shoulder with a laugh. "This all started as a business arrangement, but that doesn't mean this whole proposal conversation should feel like one."

At this, he laughed. "Ah, not the swoony book-boyfriend proposal of your dreams?"

"You said it was for *logistical reasons*," I deadpanned.

"Yeah, well, sometimes when it comes to military stuff that's the way it has to start. Besides, as pretty as this little picnic is, I'm not planning to spring some big epic proposal on you without knowing your thoughts on it first. Or giving you time to think about it. I know you too well."

He really did. It wasn't that I didn't like surprises or anything—though, now that I thought about it, if they interrupted my routine or ruined carefully laid plans, I guessed I wasn't a fan. But since the entire reason I hadn't wanted to fall for this man in the first place was that I was scared about him leaving and me not wanting to go with him, it made sense that he wouldn't want to propose without talking about it.

Sure, we'd made it clear to each other months ago that we were both in this for real—and *forever*. And yes, I'd told him I would have gone with him to Hawaii if he'd had to leave, which meant we'd need to be married for that to happen. But we hadn't addressed that little technicality, so from that perspective, this logistical conversation actually did make sense.

"Okay," I said, breathing through the nerves swirling around the edges of my mind, "so, you want my thoughts on the idea, but you're not asking right now?"

He reached out and took my hands, pressing a soft kiss to each set of knuckles. "Yep. And you can feel free to take your time, darlin'. I'm not going anywhere yet. And even when I do, I'm not. I won't rush you, and you'll always have me wherever I am."

Heat flooded me as he held my hands in his, rubbing the backs with his calloused thumbs. "Well, I'll think about it, then."

"Good." He leaned forward and brushed his lips over mine. Once, twice, and then a third time for good measure.

When he leaned back, I caught sight of his camouflage cover sitting on the blanket. On the inside, he'd used packing tape to attach the photo from Clara's wedding to the underside of the hat. It was a little warped from sweat and grime, but the sweetness of him carrying the keepsake photo of our first kiss with him wherever he went hit me like an arrow to the heart.

This man loved me. He loved me with his whole soul, despite all the fear he'd grown up with that he'd only wind up hurt if he let himself do that. But he did. He'd pushed through that fear in a way that made my skin tingle every time I thought about it, and while I'd sort of done the same thing on my end, he deserved for it to be all the way. He deserved the same level of commitment and certainty from me that he was offering.

I looked up and met his eyes, squaring my shoulders. "Okay, done."

"Done thinking?"

Grinning, I squeezed his hands. "Yep."

"Already?"

"*Yes*," I said with a sigh. "I think it's time for me to stop being so scared about what I'm losing in my hometown and start focusing on what I'm gaining with you. *So*, whenever you decide you want to spring some big epic proposal on me, feel free."

He smiled almost as big as he had when he'd found out about his dad's remission, then he leaned forward and pressed his forehead to mine. "Can I get that in writing?"

"Hush."

He kissed me again, his lips barely managing to close over mine thanks to the smile on his handsome face. Then he leaned back and picked up his salad again, and we ate in companionable silence.

"What do you have planned for this week?" he asked after a while.

I quirked a brow at him. "Why, you gonna propose?"

"No, ma'am. I have something in mind already, and it's not going to happen while I'm swamped with all this." He jerked his head over his shoulder in the direction of the base, then shuddered as if just the thought of going back to it tomorrow made him squirm.

"Well," I said, dropping my fork in my empty container and snapping on the lid, "I'm going to be shooting some back-to-school photos, going with Layla, Jo, and Grayson to get him fitted for his tux for Jo's wedding, and working on my videos for this week's reads."

As much as it worried me to put myself out there, I'd finally cracked and created a TikTok account for book recommendations. So far, I hadn't shown my face even once, just a collection of page flips or artful transitions showcasing groups of books.

Even though I'd gone into it thinking I was crazy for doing so, the account blew up pretty quickly. The fact that I'd been a lurker in the BookTok community for so long helped, I was sure. I always knew exactly which songs to use to make the videos trend, which filters and transitions were most engaging, and which hashtags would allow for the biggest reach.

I wasn't sure how many people looked at it like a science and how many considered it an art, but for me, it was all about patterns. I'd been studying them for ages, and now I was capitalizing on them. Not only did I receive tons of book mail every week with new books to review, but I'd even managed to get paid to do reviews, which was rare and awesome. It'd turned into a little side gig of its own, and it was all thanks to Beau for encouraging me to do it.

"What'd you read?" he asked as he finished up the last bite of his own salad before putting it away.

I gave him the list of this week's books, careful not to get carried away with what I thought about them or how well the tropes were executed. He was always so adorable when he listened to me ramble about book stuff, but I knew our time was limited since he'd have to go soon, and there was something else I wanted to run by him before we had to part ways.

"Sounds like a busy week," he said. Then he leaned

back a little and looked me over with a little half-smile. "I'm proud of you, you know."

I beamed, warmth spreading through me. "I'm proud of you, too."

"Can't believe I've only got two more weeks of this."

Ah, here was my opening. I didn't want to overstep, because sometimes I'd been known to get a little carried away. But it was Beau. He knew I did, and he seemed to love me anyway. "Speaking of your graduation, I have an idea."

His brows went up. "Oh, yeah?"

"I was thinking maybe Layla and I could road trip to New Orleans to pick up your dad? Then you and I can take him back while you're on leave and stay with him for a couple of days."

Beau's brows inched further up his forehead until they nearly reached his hairline. "You'd do that?"

"Of course. He's doing much better these days, so I'm sure he can handle the trip, right? And maybe we can even get him to come out with us and do some stuff while we're in New Orleans after."

As soon as Beau and I made our relationship official, I'd been talking with Louis more. I didn't know what it was about him that made me feel like I'd known him for years instead of months, but he felt like family. He felt like a missing piece I hadn't known I was missing.

And on more than one occasion, he'd told me he'd felt similarly for me as Beau's girlfriend, and he'd thanked me for finally coming along to bust down his son's seemingly impenetrable walls. Little did he know, Beau'd had to do some busting of his own. But we were here, and that was all that mattered.

Beau cleared his throat, then winced like it'd hurt. "That would be great. Thank you."

"It's my pleasure, really. I love your dad."

"He loves you, too," he replied, so much emotion swimming in his eyes that I had to work to keep a handle on mine. Then he chuckled and shook his head. "Every time I talk to the old man he reminds me not to mess this up."

"Well, if he thinks you could, he doesn't know you very well."

"Is that so?" he asked, poking my side.

I fought him off with a laugh. "You said it yourself. You know exactly what to do or say with me, right?"

"I do. But I don't have to keep telling you it's not an act, right?"

He'd held up a finger between us in that playfully domineering way, and I grabbed it out of the air. "No, you don't."

"Good. All right, I should probably go so I can study up for tomorrow."

We stood and he helped me gather up our picnic supplies, then carried it all while holding me tight against his side as we walked to the car. I leaned my head on his shoulder and squeezed his middle. "You'll do great. Want me to talk to your dad about the graduation and let you know what he says?"

"Yeah, thanks. If anyone can convince him to travel, it'd be you."

Louis was like me in that he wasn't a fan of leaving his creature comforts, but I had a feeling Beau was right.

He placed our picnic stuff on the back seat, then helped me into the car, stooping low to kiss me before he went to his side and got in.

I grabbed the front of his cammies and held him close. "Hey. I love you, Beau Devereux."

"And I love you."

26

BEAU

Two weeks later, just as she'd promised, Lyndi and her sister had gone to pick up Pops so he could be at my graduation from drill instructor school. Having him in the audience of that auditorium while I was given my olive-green campaign cover—worn only by drill instructors—was one of the greatest privileges of my life.

I waved at him as I jogged off the stage, winking at Lyndi as I passed her on the way to resume my seat with my fellow graduates. It was so good to see him. And not just see him but know he was doing better. Now that his cancer was in remission, I loved being able to tell him I told him so ... if only to hear him laugh. And loved that I could.

After the rest of the graduates received their

campaign covers, it was time for us to raise our right hands and recite the Drill Instructor's Creed.

I proudly stood with my class and did so, repeating each line at the top of my still-shredded voice, meaning every word. This whole drill instructor thing may have started as a way to keep me in South Carolina, but over the last eleven weeks, it'd become so much more. After surviving what was probably the hardest training I'd ever endured as a Marine, I was ready to put it all to good use. I was ready to do my part to shape the future of the Corps.

"These recruits are entrusted to my care," we shouted in unison. "I will train them to the best of my ability. I will develop them into smartly disciplined, physically fit, basically trained Marines, thoroughly indoctrinated in love of Corps and country. I will demand of them, and demonstrate by my own example, the highest standards of personal conduct, morality, and professional skill."

When we were finished, we remained standing and sang the "Marines' Hymn," as we did at the closing of pretty much every training course I'd taken in my career. It was a powerful thing, singing along to an anthem every Marine knew by heart and probably would until his or her dying day. And today, *man*, more than ever, I felt like we'd earned the right to sing it.

When it was all over and we were released, I made my way through the crowd to Lyndi and my old man. Zac, Layla, and Grayson—who I'd already started thinking of as the family I never dreamed I'd get—were right there with them.

"Hey, guys," I said as I greeted them, pulling my pops in for the first hug. "It's good to see you, thanks for coming."

"This one's hard to say no to," he said, jerking a thumb at Lyndi with a quick grin. "Not that I wanted to."

"Who would?" I replied, gathering her into my arms for a hug and a brief kiss.

I moved on to hug the others, accepting their congratulations and thanking them for coming, complete with ruffling Grayson's shaggy hair. "How was that, bud? Were you bored?"

"Sorta," he replied with a shrug. "It took forever to get through the rest of the guys after you got your hat."

I chuckled. "Yeah, them's the breaks with having a last name that starts with D."

"Mine's in the middle," he replied, then looked up at the gorgeous woman whose hand I held. "Aunt Lyndi, yours is closer to the end."

"Yeah, she'll be stuck with mine soon enough, though," I said to Gray, but I shot her a smirk. *Sooner than you think, even.*

"All right," Layla said, clapping her hands together, "everyone's going to be waiting for us at Mickey's. He was nice enough to close down the whole place for your graduation party."

I blinked at my soon-to-be sister-in-law as if I'd had nothing to do with it. "Really? I don't even know enough people to justify that."

"I pulled some strings," she said with a knowing smile. "Now, let's go."

We filed through the mess of seventy-five new drill instructors and their families as I tugged Lyndi close to my side. I know I hadn't physically left her to go through this training, but I felt different now that I'd completed it. The motivational speeches from my instructors still pumped through me, and between that dose of Marine Corps spirit and the excitement of what I was about to do, I felt a little like I did when emotions spiked after returning from deployment.

An hour and a half later, we filed through the door of Mickey's Pub in Bluffton and were immediately assaulted with cheers and shouts of congratulations.

Sure, I wouldn't have had a party this big for my graduation if it weren't for my ulterior motive. But since Lyndi had only barely caught the memo the first time, I needed a repeat performance of my grand gesture. Only this time, there'd be a very important question at the end. One I already knew the answer to, and one I knew she didn't want anyone other than her family and friends to witness. No public proposals for this girl, but I could still make it epic with only her favorite people around.

After saying hi to the few members of Lyndi's family that she was closest to—including her grandmother, to whom I was now eternally grateful—as well as Ms. Hattie and the rest of our friend group, we settled in for beers and burgers and a little bit of normalcy.

A little while later, though, I excused myself to the restroom so I could go wash my hands and try to shake off the nerves that'd surprised me by showing up halfway through my burger.

"Hey, not getting cold feet, are you?" Zac asked as he, Will, Paul, and Chase walked into the men's room.

I eyed them through the mirror as I washed my hands. "What is this, an intervention?"

"No, man. We know you got this," Will said, stepping up to pat my shoulder. "And it's almost go-time, so tell us where you want us."

"You are good, though, right? Because if you need a pep talk, I'm pretty sure Layla is dying to give you one," Zac told me with a laugh.

I dried my hands, turning toward him to lean against the counter. "Oh, yeah? Sure she's not dying to change my mind instead? It wasn't exactly the plan for me to take Lyndi out of Bluffton before you guys left."

"No way," he replied. "As soon as this whole thing became real, she got on board fast. Most of us have been expecting this for a while now."

I frowned. "The proposal?"

"Nah, just you and Lyndi in general," Paul cut in. "I'm pretty sure she's been into you since Bobby and Cassidy's wedding when you took Shelby. Which, by the way, I don't know if I ever thanked you for. Definitely lit a fire under me in that friend-zone department, Mr. Fake Date."

"Is it weird not doing it anymore?" Chase asked. "The dating app thing. Because man, I gotta tell you, I could use some cash for some family stuff right about now, so maybe I could take up your gig."

I sighed. It wasn't weird at all. Sure, I'd be making small payments to my dad's debt instead of large ones, but now that he was on the mend, he said he'd go back to work eventually and start taking some of the load.

Not only that, but the promotion I'd probably earn as a drill instructor would help, too. If need be, I'd talk to him about loans or special financing to make it work. But one thing was for sure, now that I had Lyndi, I didn't miss being a fake date in the slightest. Having something real was much better.

"If you really wanna do that, lemme know. I'll help you get set up," I told Chase. "But be prepared to give up your weekends."

He grimaced. "Man, I don't know."

I didn't have a clue about his family situation or what he needed the money for, but if it was bad enough, he'd have to get over that. Sometimes you had to do what you had to do. But right now, I had something I had to do, so we needed to wrap it up.

"All right," I said, straightening. "Here's what you're gonna do."

We huddled around like a football team gearing up for the last quarter, and I laid out my plan. Then the guys went out ahead of me, and I turned to take one more look in the mirror. I stood straighter, adjusting the collar of the dress uniform I still hadn't changed out of from graduation. Yeah, this was a good look for this. And my old man would get to watch me put him to shame.

I stepped into the hallway and waited out of sight from our table until the music started. Then I inched forward, waiting for my cue. This time, it wouldn't be me singing the *Top Gun* song for Lyndi. Paul, Will, Zac, and Chase were starting off the song, and I grinned as I heard the whoops and hollers from the crowd.

Reaching into the pocket of my uniform pants, I

wrapped my hand around the small box and pulled it out, opening it to make sure the ring hadn't miraculously disappeared. There it was. A cushion cut diamond sat in the center with smaller ones in a halo around it and lining the top of the band. Yellow gold, as was trendy when my pops had bought it for my mom.

As soon as Lyndi had told me her plan for bringing him to my graduation, the idea had taken root. If he could bring this ring with him, I could propose with him there, with his blessing, and with this ring. It couldn't be more perfect.

When I heard the song gearing up for my moment, I snapped the lid closed and took a deep breath. Then I strode out of the hallway and into the main room of the bar, smiling wide as my eyes met her teary ones. I held her gaze as I moved closer, timing it just right so I could drop to one knee in front of her right when the music swelled. The guys weren't great singers, but it didn't seem to matter as they provided the painfully cheesy and totally *right* backdrop for this moment.

"Lyndi Robinson," I said, grateful that the music wasn't so loud that I'd have to shout, "this ring was my mother's."

I opened the box to reveal the sparkling diamond, then paused while she gasped, her eyes flitting to my old man in the seat next to her. He brought up a hand and patted her shoulder with misty eyes, giving her an encouraging nod.

"I never thought I'd find a love like theirs," I went on, "or that I'd want one. But with you, I never stood a chance."

She made a strangled noise and fought to keep her composure, and I swallowed past the lump in my own throat, trying not to get choked up myself. Everyone around us was reacting in their own ways and I could feel the excited energy buzzing around us. But I kept my eyes trained on Lyndi's while I popped the question, unwilling to be distracted.

"Will you marry me?" I asked, holding the ring higher from my position on bended knee.

She nodded and slipped off the stool, so I stood and pulled her into my arms, crushing my lips to hers. Cheers rang out around us, but I still heard her whispered, "yes" over and over against my lips.

When I pulled back, I plucked the ring from the box, then handed the empty container to my pops with a grateful smile. He winked in return, closing his fist around it, and bringing it to his chest.

Lyndi's hand shook as I slid the ring onto her finger. It was the perfect fit, just as I'd somehow known it would be. Then she threw her arms around me and hugged me tightly as the instrumental music enveloped us in nostalgia. The guys had stopped singing at some point, but the song didn't really need their help.

"You know," she said as she looked up at me, apparently not ready to break our private moment to face the others quite yet, "this song doesn't really work as a love song."

"Tell that to Tom Cruise," I shot back with a wink.

"Or me," my pops added from behind her, making us both laugh.

She wrinkled her nose and turned in my arms so we were facing the table of our friends now. "It's about rekindling a lost love, though."

Layla stood from her seat and came over, taking Lyndi's hand. "I know it's hard for you not to read too much into words, sis, but you gotta just go with this one. I'm so happy for you. *Both* of you."

Lyndi laughed and pulled her sister in for a hug. Then we made the rounds, getting congratulated by everyone else, her grandmother being the most excited of all. Ms. Hattie was the last one to come over, a sly smile on her face.

"Well, looks like you've officially caused another wedding at Starlight to happen," Lyndi told her with playfully narrowed eyes.

Our town florist waved a hand. "Oh, all I do is give little nudges. You would have found your way to each other eventually. All I do is make sure it doesn't take you too long."

I wrapped my arm tighter around my girl, tugging her against my side. "We're grateful either way."

And as shouts of agreement and a toast to Ms. Hattie's meddling sang out around us, I pulled Lyndi into my arms for another heart-stopping kiss.

EPILOGUE
CHASE

"Thanks for the ride tonight," I said, holding the door for Zoe as we slipped out of Mickey's Pub. My old Jeep was in the shop, so she'd offered to let me borrow her car, but of course I'd insisted she tag along. "And for coming. It was cool to have you there."

"No problem," she replied. "That was really sweet what your friend did. That proposal was amazing."

"It was."

"But I have to say, don't quit your day job. You're a pretty terrible singer," she teased.

"I'll try to remember that," I replied with a laugh. Then I glanced over my shoulder at the bar, sighing as I shook my head. "Speaking of jobs, I still can't believe Beau's hanging up the fake dating app. He made a *killing* taking women to weddings. Doesn't get much better than that."

And I'd kill for that kind of money right now with everything on my plate. If I were him, I wouldn't be so ready to give it up. But as close as Zoe and I were, I still hadn't told her about my folks and what they were going through. And I didn't want to go there right now. It was too big. Too frustrating. Not even venting would help.

Zoe sighed. "I think it's weird. But then again, the weddings in my family are always a little nuts, so maybe it'd be different if it wasn't a *Greek* wedding every time."

Zoe Katsaros was one hundred percent Greek, fluent in the language, and complete with the family that hit most major stereotypes about Greeks if you heard her tell it. But she hadn't wanted to join the family business running a restaurant like she'd been expected to. Instead, she'd joined the Marines, and was one of the toughest chicks I'd ever met in my entire life. *The* toughest, actually.

But looking at her now, you might not guess it. Not with how her soft brown hair fell in luscious curls around her shoulders. Or with her petite frame covered by a lace dress that looked painted on, wearing heels that would have me staring at my ceiling all night, no doubt. The woman looked like fire —but not in a scary way. In that enticing way that

The Fake Date

made you want to light a match just so you could watch it burn.

I shook my head to clear it. I couldn't have thoughts like that about Zoe. She was all those things, but she was also my best friend in my shop. I had the guys here at Mickey's tonight, for sure. They were my brothers—in every sense of the word that mattered, and I knew they'd have my back if I ever needed it. I was closest to Will since he'd been my mentor when I'd needed it most and had brought me into his friend group without a moment's hesitation.

But Zoe? This friendship was different. We'd worked side by side through our first deployment together. It was the first time either one of us had been that far away from our families for that long. Hers was right up the road in North Carolina, but mine was all the way in Hawaii, where I'd been born and raised after my tourist mom fell in love with a local fisherman.

Zoe and I had gotten close on a level that I'd never had before, and since I'd known from the beginning that she was destined to marry "a nice Greek man" and that most definitely wasn't me, that closeness never morphed into anything beyond friendship.

Which was fine. With everything going on back home, I liked having someone I could talk to. Zoe was a great listener, and since she had her own family stuff to work through, she could also relate and help me navigate it from the perspective of someone who felt the same way I did: family was everything.

Or, at least, that was how I told myself I felt. Maybe being around her made me feel like it was true.

So, there was absolutely no part of me that wanted a fling with Zoe Katsaros if she was only going to leave me so she could do what her family wanted and marry some guy named Nick. Or Christos. Or the actual guy her dad had already picked out for her—*Thanos*. Chef at their family restaurant and an all-around really nice guy. And I knew because I'd met him when I went there with her after our deployment.

Meeting Thanos and the rest of her family on that trip taught me two things. One, I was lucky to have a friend like Zoe, and two, I was plenty good enough to be her friend, but her family would never, *ever* accept me as more than that.

You'll see more of Lyndi and Beau's happily ever after as the series continues! Check out the next book about Chase and Zoe! In this marriage of convenience story, how will Chase solve his family's money problems, and how does Zoe fit into it?

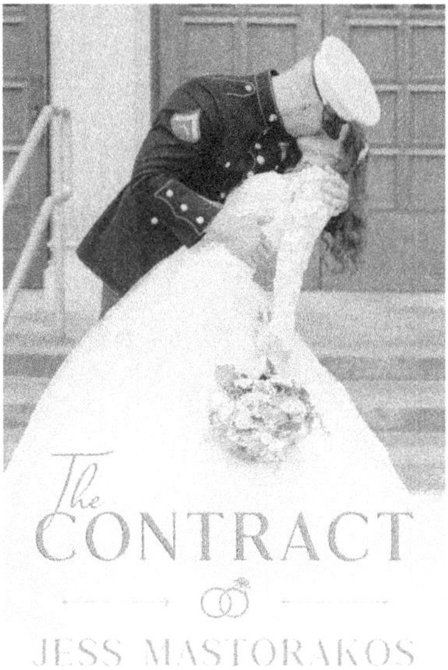
The
CONTRACT
JESS MASTORAKOS

ALSO BY JESS MASTORAKOS

THE SAN DIEGO MARINES SERIES

Forever with You (Vince & Sara)

Back to You (Spencer & Ellie)

Away from You (Matt & Olivia)

Christmas with You (Cooper & Angie)

Believing in You (Jake & Ivy)

Memories of You (Brooks & Cat)

Home with You (Owen & Rachel)

Adored by You (Noah & Paige)

Related Standalone

Trusting in You (Eric & Lucy)

THE KAILUA MARINES SERIES

Treasured in Turtle Bay (Roman & Molly)

Promises at Pyramid Rock (Mac & Ana)

Stranded at the Sandbar (Tyler & Kate)

Romance on the Reef (PJ & Maggie)

Heartbeats in Honolulu (Hunter & Nora)

Christmas in Kailua (Logan & Tess)

THE BRIDES OF BEAUFORT SERIES

The Proposal (Paul & Shelby)

The Planner (Will & Aria)

The Bridesmaid (Zac & Layla)

The Fake Date (Beau & Lyndi)

The Contract (Chase & Zoe)

The Runaway (Nate & Nikki)

Related Standalone

The Beginning (Thatcher & Hattie)

THE FIRST COMES LOVE SERIES

A Match for the Marine (Dex & Amy)

A Blind Date for the Marine (Mateo & Claire)

A Princess for the Marine (Huck & Zara)

A Royal Christmas for the Marine (Theo & Maya)

CHRISTMAS IN SNOW HILL

A Movie Star for Christmas (Nick & Holly)

Christmas with the Boy Next Door (Jack & Robin)

SIGN UP FOR JESS'S SWEET ROMANCE SQUAD

Jess MASTORAKOS
sweet & swoony military romance

Sign up for my newsletter at http://jessmastorakos.com/forever-with-you to get the free ebook version of Forever with You: A San Diego Marines Novella. You'll also get bonus content, sweet romance book recommendations, and never miss a new release!

- instagram.com/author_jessmastorakos
- bookbub.com/authors/jess-mastorakos
- goodreads.com/author_jessmastorakos

ABOUT THE AUTHOR

Jess Mastorakos writes sweet military romance books that feature heroes with heart and the strong women they love. She is a proud Marine wife and mama of four. She loves her coffee in a glitter tumbler and planning with an erasable pen.

- instagram.com/author_jessmastorakos
- bookbub.com/authors/jess-mastorakos
- goodreads.com/author_jessmastorakos

CPSIA information can be obtained
at www.ICGtesting.com
Printed in the USA
LVHW102152270722
724601LV00022B/326